Special Envoy

Special Envoy

A Spy Novel

JEAN ECHENOZ

Translated from the French
by Sam Taylor

THE NEW PRESS

25 YEARS

NEW YORK
LONDON

© 2016 by Les Éditions de Minuit, 7, rue Bernard-Palissy, 75006 Paris
English translation © 2017 Sam Taylor

Originally published in France as *Envoyée spéciale*, Les Éditions de Minuit, Paris, 2016

Published in the United States by The New Press, New York, 2017
Distributed by Perseus Distribution

ISBN 978-1-62097-312-7 (hc)
ISBN 978-1-62097-313-4 (e-book)

CIP data is available

The New Press publishes books that promote and enrich public discussion and
understanding of the issues vital to our democracy and to a more equitable world. These
books are made possible by the enthusiasm of our readers; the support of a committed
group of donors, large and small; the collaboration of our many partners in the
independent media and the not-for-profit sector; booksellers, who often hand-sell New
Press books; librarians; and above all by our authors.

www.thenewpress.com

Composition by dix!
This book was set in Centaur MT

Printed in the United States of America

2 4 6 8 10 9 7 5 3 1

Special Envoy

I

1

I WANT A WOMAN, the general declared. A woman is what I need, you see.

In that case, you're not the only one. Paul Objat smiled. Spare me your infantile humor, retorted the general, stiffening. This is no joking matter. Show a little decorum, for God's sake. Objat's smile vanished: I beg your pardon, General. Very well, now, let's move on, said the officer. We must give this some thought.

It was close to noon. The two men proceeded to give it some thought, seated on either side of a green metal writing desk, an old regulation coffered model belonging to the general. The top of this desk was occupied only by an unlit lamp, a box of Panter Tango cigarillos, an empty ashtray, and a very worn-looking desk blotter that looked as if it had absorbed and then concluded a number of cases since, let's say, the Ben Barka affair in 1965. The green writing desk was situated at the back of an austere room with one window overlooking a paved barracks courtyard. In addition to the desk, there were two tubular chairs upholstered with fake leather, three filing cabinets, and a shelf bearing the weight of a cumbersome, grime-encrusted computer. All of this was rather old-looking and the general's chair did not seem especially comfortable: its armrests were rusted, its first-generation polyurethane padding clearly visible—falling out in clumps, in fact—through the cracks in the corners.

The bells of the nearby church, Notre-Dame-des-Otages, tolled twelve times. The general picked up a cigarillo, examined it, massaged it, sniffed it, then put it back in its case. A woman, he repeated quietly, as if to himself. A woman, he said again, raising his voice, but not just any woman. Certainly not one of those interns that one finds everywhere. Someone with no connection to the networks, if you see what I mean? Not entirely, Objat felt obligated to admit. Well, you know, someone innocent, the general explained. Someone who has no idea what is going on, who will do whatever we tell her, who won't ask questions. And pretty, too, if possible.

That's quite a list of requirements, Objat pointed out. It won't be easy to find one like that. I realize that, the general nodded. He opened his Panter Tango box again, stared affectionately at the cigarillos, and then delicately closed the lid, while Paul Objat's gaze wandered over the room's walls, which had not been repainted in years and large portions of which were decorated with various documents: photographs (some more blurred than others) of people, things, and places, many of them connected by arrows drawn in marker pen, index cards clipped to abstruse diagrams, press cuttings, lists of names, maps crisscrossed with threads held in place by multicolored pins. An official portrait of the president of the republic. Nothing personal: no pictures of family, no postcards sent by vacationing colleagues, no van Gogh reproductions or any nonsense like that.

Putting aside all notions of professional discretion and national security, let us first specify the identity of the superior officer. General Bourgeaud, sixty-eight years old, a former member of the Action Service—devoted to the planning and implementation of secret operations—specialized in the infiltration and exfiltration of sensitive persons for intelligence purposes. Sharp-faced, cold-eyed . . . but let's not go into too many details just now: we'll return to his appearance a little later. Given his age, his superiors have gradually lightened his responsibilities in recent years. In consideration of his faithful service, however, they have allowed him to retain the use of his office, and of his orderly. He is still on full pay but no longer has an official vehicle. Unwilling to be thrown onto the scrap heap completely, Bourgeaud continues to organize a few operations on the sly. To keep his hand in. To keep himself busy. And to keep his country safe, of course.

Facing him, likewise dressed in civilian clothes, Paul Objat is rather a handsome man, half the general's age. He is soft-spoken, with a calm gaze, and his lips are constantly curled in an almost imperceptible smile that might be reassuring or disturbing, depending on the situation, a little bit like the actor Billy Bob Thornton's smile. I might have an idea, said Objat. Good, develop it then, the general encouraged him, before going into more detail about his project.

The most important thing, you see, will be to put her through a sort of purge once we've found her. Take her completely off the grid for a while before the operation begins. A kind of isolation therapy, if you like. The personality changes in cases like that. I'm not saying the character is destroyed, but it creates more suitable reactions; it leaves the subject more ductile.

What do you mean by ductile? Objat asked. I don't know that adjective. Well, let's say tractable, obedient, flexible, malleable. You get my drift? Yes, said Objat, I think I do. In fact, I think I may have several ideas regarding that.

No need to go overboard either, the general made clear, having given the matter some more thought. When I talk about this purifying treatment, which strikes me as necessary, it might not be a bad idea to begin by provoking a mild state of shock. And don't hesitate to scare her a little bit, if need be. No violence, though, of course. That goes without saying, General, Objat smiled once again. In fact, I think my idea is beginning to take shape. Given the outline of your plan, it might even be a very good idea. Yes, I think I know someone who could be the perfect fit. The right profile, available . . . She might prove to be quite ductile, as you put it. With the right preparation, it could work. Pretty, is she? the general asked. Not bad at all, Objat reassured him.

Do you know her well? Not really, said Objat. I met her once at a dinner party and found her interesting. The main thing is that she doesn't know me. Of course, agreed the general, that's fundamental. This is a delicate operation, with a unique scenario. I agree, Objat said, but aren't you getting a little hungry? I've heard about a pretty good restaurant, not far from here, next to the Jourdain metro station. We wouldn't even have to change trains. Well, it's true that I don't have the car anymore, the general mused, but . . . well, yes, all right. Let's go by metro, then.

After the general took a cigarillo from the box and slipped it into his breast pocket, the two men put on their raincoats—slate gray for one, pearl gray for the other—despite the fact that not a single drop of rain was falling on the Boulevard Mortier, where they proceeded to walk, in the twentieth arrondissement of Paris. As they made their way toward the Porte des Lilas station, about a quarter of a mile from the barracks, General Bourgeaud congratulated Paul Objat without looking at him, in a grumbling, almost severe voice that did not go with his words. I knew I could count on you, Objat. You often have the right kind of ideas. You've served me damned well, and I . . . well, I like you, Objat. Knowing his superior officer as he did, Objat could not help being rather startled by this declaration.

At the restaurant, they had a pig's ear salad followed by beef cheek stew. So, that woman? the general asked. I'll get started on it this afternoon, Objat promised. I need to do some research and make a few phone calls. But the more I think about it, the more I think this will work. Even better than you can possibly imagine. I won't have any trouble finding her—I know more or less where she lives.

Whereabouts is she? inquired Bourgeaud distractedly while tearing off a piece of ear. She's in the sixteenth arrondissement, replied Objat, near Chaillot. Nice area, the general noted. Very peaceful . . . but slightly sad, isn't it? Well, that's what people say, anyway. For myself, I've never left my little first-floor apartment near the Observatoire; I've always liked it there. What about you, Objat? Whereabouts do you live? Well, to tell the truth, General, Objat answered evasively, it's a little bit complicated at the moment. Let's just say that I'm between places.

2

Trocadéro. On the top floor of an art deco building designed by Henri Sauvage, this 690 sq ft dual-aspect apartment is ideally situated. Designed as an artist's studio (16 ft high ceilings), south-facing, this rare and calm property enjoys an unrestricted view of the Palais de Chaillot and the Passy Cemetery.
Elevator, cellar, parking available.
Price: upon request.

IT'S THE PRICE that's the problem, the real estate agent said. You're asking way too much. I know, Constance replied, but I'm not in a rush to get rid of it. It's just a guide price, to see if I can sell it for that much. The agent, whose name was Philippe Dieulangard, shrugged, then sat down in front of his computer. As he made this movement, a powerful scent of Hugo Boss aftershave balm spurted from his person and Constance's nostrils retracted. Dieulangard added a few details to the listing (layout of the rooms, built-in kitchen, separate toilets, etc.) before formatting the document and printing it out, stamped with the adjective EXCEPTIONAL in oxblood gothic capital letters. Once he'd arranged it among the other ads in the agency's window, he and Constance went outside to see how it looked.

It would be better with a photograph, Dieulangard pointed out to her. A picture's worth a thousand words, as they say. When she reminded him that she was not keen on the idea, he shrugged again, this time with just one shoulder, said good-bye to her, then left her standing outside the agency's window, where Constance diligently read all the other ads for houses and apartments to buy or to rent, imagining for each one another possible life, other fates, other loves, other sorrows. She wondered how she would change her appearance in accordance with this or that dwelling, as if at a casting session: wardrobe, hairstyle, makeup. While daydreaming in front of the window, she quickly reviewed her reflection's appearance: after a jump cut to her Burberry 308 pink azalea lipstick and a quick glance at her Chanel 599 Provocation nail varnish, she mussed up her bangs a little, powdered the sides of her nose, then took a step back: establishing shot of Constance in the window of Dieulangard Immobilier, with a backdrop of light traffic on the one-way Rue Greuze.

Tight blue blouse, skinny charcoal pants, flat shoes, haircut à la Louise Brooks and curves à la Michèle Mercier—which might not seem a particularly good match, but actually goes very well together. Thirty-four years old, not very active and not highly qualified—she barely passed her basic legal studies diploma—married to a man who's successful, or was at least, but her life with this man is far from successful: in material terms, they're fine, but in matrimonial terms, not so much. Vague desires for a divorce, vague intentions to work things out, bust-ups followed by compromises . . . it changes from day to day. And so she divides her existence between their conjugal home (albeit less and less often) and the apartment that she has just put up for sale, while she waits to see what will happen. With this brief biography out of the way, Constance turned her back on her reflection and moved away from the agency. From Rue Greuze, it was a six- to eight-minute walk, via Passy Cemetery, to her rare and calm property.

As she moved homeward, she did not notice two other movements following her in parallel: a man, about fifty yards away, and a small van, about a hundred yards away. The man was dressed in very clean and almost abnormally well-ironed overalls, and what looked like a toolbox was hanging from a shoulder strap. Behind him, the utility vehicle had only one front door and window on each side, with the rest of the bodywork being covered by a logo for a repair company. As Constance stopped outside the cemetery's monumental entrance, the man and the van immediately came to a halt. Then, as she had nothing to do (a frequent occurrence), and encouraged by the early spring weather, the idea came to her that she might go for a walk in the cemetery. As soon as she disappeared between the gravestones, the van and the man, respectively, parked and lit a cigarette on either side of the entrance.

Passy is easily the most chic cemetery in Paris. With its relatively small size, it is unmatched in the proportion of rich, famous dead people it offers per square foot, particularly in the field of arts and literature. It was also built on an overhang, allowing the people lying there to remain above the level of the living. The atmosphere is hushed amid the carefully tended gravestones; the stone paths are cleaned with tweezers; there is an innate distinction to the clothing and bearing of the widows and heirs who walk under the chestnut trees and magnolias armed with watering cans to refresh their dead. And even the living are treated with a touching concern for their well-being: this is the only necropolis in the city with a heated waiting room.

It is a little-known fact that in Passy Cemetery, far from our century and the spotlights, the residents regularly put on a star-studded end-of-year show: Fernandel, François Périer, Jean Servais, with Réjane and Pearl White in the female roles. The quality of the work is guaranteed by the talents of other deceased locals: script by Tristan Bernard and Henri Bernstein, based on an idea by Octave Mirbeau; dialogue by Jean Giraudoux; sets by Robert Mallet-Stevens; costumes by Jean Patou; music by Claude Debussy. The stage curtain is by Édouard Manet, and the play is directed by Jean-Louis Barrault. The script is published by Arthème Fayard. Spectators are few.

So Constance went for a walk around the cemetery. This was in April, a late morning in April, and a number of buds were starting to open around the headstones, notably on the locust shrubs. The pansies, marigolds, and daffodils looked in fine form, although there also remained quite a few withered, wilted, rotting flowers on the graves, not yet removed by the factotums.

When she emerged from this graveyard, the man in overalls walked up to her, looking worried, holding a piece of paper that he seemed to be trying to decipher. Constance instantly judged him very good-looking and was more than willing to offer him any help he might need. The man said he was looking for Rue Pétrarque, and of course Constance knew exactly where Rue Pétrarque was. For a start, as she told him, it was only a few streets from here. Furthermore, ten years before this, she had spent two whole months there sleeping with a certain Fred, without ever leaving the building, or the bed for that matter, without ever opening the shutters of that two-room first-floor apartment overlooking a courtyard.

But Constance did not mention that episode to the man. She just said it was nearby and that she could even show him the way, and the man thanked her, flashing her a smile that was welcoming, complicit, innocent but also cunning, amused, a little sad. A strange guy, but very pleasant, thought Constance, who instantly had the feeling that he liked her too, that the timing was perfect, and that whatever it was that was happening was really getting off to a pretty good start. So they walked up Rue du Commandant-Schloesing together until they came to the corner of Rue Pétrarque. This is a very quiet junction and as they reached it they exchanged a few words about the burgeoning spring, while the repair van slowly moved past them. Since there are also plenty of parking spaces on that street, the van driver did not have any difficulty finding somewhere to stop.

As they drew level with this vehicle, the man in overalls paused and said, Hang on a minute, I wanted to show you something that might interest you, and Constance appeared perfectly willing to be interested. He slid the strap of his toolbox off his shoulder, opened the box, and, still smiling, took out a drill. Look at this, he told her, it's a really nice one. It's amazing, this drill, it's what we do best. Compact, light, efficient, absolutely silent. Not bad, huh?

As Constance politely nodded, someone grabbed her elbow. She turned around: it was a guy who'd just come out of the van's passenger-side door and who was now gently holding her arm. He was just as smiley as the man in overalls, but considerably less handsome: tall, bony, scrawny neck, ostrich-like face. You see, the man in overalls went on, it's ideally adapted to delicate, precise, repetitive work. It's a screw gun too, you know. Look, I'll show you. And Constance became aware then that a third man, presumably the van driver, was holding her other arm. He, too, was smiling and not especially attractive: squat, sturdy, red-cheeked, with a face like a sea cow. There was nothing immediately reassuring about this setup, admittedly, but the three men looked so friendly, considerate, attentive: out of a silly kind of mimicry, Constance smiled back at them.

So, said the man in overalls, I'm going to turn it on; watch, and Constance did indeed watch, in total silence, as the drill bit started quickly spinning around while one of the men, without letting go of Constance's arm, used his other hand to lift the van's tailgate. Then, when the man in overalls moved the sharp end of the drill toward her lower jaw, like a dentist who doesn't bother asking you to first open your mouth, she stopped smiling. Ostrich and Sea Cow now had a firm grip on her arms.

All of this happened without witnesses because, although it is close to the main roads, allowing a quick getaway, the corner of Rue Pétrarque and Rue Commandant-Schloesing is also largely free of traffic, ideal for discreetly dealing with a problem. Constance blinked furiously. But obviously I'm not going to do anything like that, the man in overalls reassured her. I just wanted to show you. Anyway, I'm going to leave you in peace now, he announced, indicating the vehicle's open tailgate, if you wouldn't mind. And as Constance was turning toward the vehicle, she saw that its inside—separated from the front seat by a metal wall—was occupied by a comfortable-looking armchair whose feet and armrests had the unusual additional features of polypropylene straps with plastic buckles. An elegant black hood was casually folded on the seat back.

Constance hesitated, as any of us would, but—noting that the drill was still spinning—she decided she would rather get in the back of the van than submit, without anesthesia, to an undefined maxillofacial procedure. While Ostrich, as jovial and reassuring as a real dental nurse, secured her firmly in the armchair, she spotted Sea Cow in brief discussion with the other man, who put away his drill before walking off toward Trocadéro without turning back, apparently having fulfilled his task. Before they closed the tailgate on her, Constance watched him go, regretting the turn their encounter had taken. It was a shame, because he really was a very handsome guy, in his neatly ironed overalls. A real shame. Poor Constance: she just can't stop herself thinking this kind of thing. But, as we have gathered by now, she does not enjoy a satisfying love life.

3

AND NOW, IF it's okay with you, we are going to take a look at Constance's husband. This man is currently in the Paris metro, somewhere on Line 2, which crosses the city from west to east, and his name is Lou Tausk. Sounds like a pseudonym, doesn't it? But let's not dwell on that for the moment; we'll return to the matter in good time.

So Lou Tausk, with his bag on his knees, is sitting in the first car of a train that links Porte Dauphine to Nation, transporting him every morning from his home (Villiers station) to his studio (Couronnes station), and vice versa in the evenings. It's practical, it's direct, and there's no need for him to check the name of the station at each stop—no need to look up from his newspaper or his smartphone each time the train slows—because a recorded female voice repeats it twice. When the voice announces Couronnes, Tausk stands up. When the voice repeats Couronnes, Tausk heads for the nearest car door, opposite the platform exit, from where forty-seven steps, divided into three unequal flights, take him up to Boulevard de Belleville.

Not so long ago—and even now, sometimes—this boulevard featured a sort of sparse, unregulated market where, with their goods laid out on the sidewalk, poor people sold all kinds of poor third-hand objects to other poor people: juicers and ice cream makers in broken blister packs; sets of chipped teacups; packs of yogurt that were discreet about their expiration date; toasters without plugs; blenders unconcerned with niceties such as warranties; piles of ancient TV guides with no illusions about their future; old toys; mismatched gloves; worn-out clothes; and many other things that we could go on enumerating.

But first, alerted by local residents who saw this as a nuisance and ended up complaining about it, the forces of law and order cleaned up the area, dispersing these amateur merchants toward the city gates to the north and east of Paris. And what came after that, we would quickly get tired of enumerating.

Around the Couronnes metro station, small streets and alleys pour like tributaries from the northeast into the main stream of the boulevard: Passage de Pékin, Rue du Sénégal, Rue de Pali-Kao. Tausk takes the last of these after walking past a few Chinese stores (furtive effluvia of monosodium glutamate), Tunisian restaurants (subtle fragrances of *ras el hanout*), two convenience stores, and an electronic discount store, Tout à €1 waging a fierce price war with Tout Mini €. Modest and ugly buildings with poorly rendered façades—crumbling brick or Paris stone—are demolished for reasons of age, hygiene, and speculation, before being replaced by others, no less ugly but more lucrative, until the cycle starts over again.

As Tausk is about to walk up the street to his recording studio, what should he hear bursting from some scaffolding, lustily sung by a demolition worker in his fluorescent vest, but the cheerful melody to "Vamos a la Playa," an old global hit that Tausk has not heard since 1983. For the rest of the day, that tune will itch inside his head like a mosquito bite.

Shoulder numbed by his shoulder bag, cerebral cortex invaded by "Vamos a la Playa," Tausk arrives at the studio, a vast subterranean space with no fenestration except for a single basement window, which, left open, lets in a bit of air and sound from Rue de Pali-Kao. The name of this street commemorates a victory by Anglo-French troops during the Second Opium War, and on its sidewalks, not so long ago, you could still buy diverse products derived from that opium, cut to varying degrees with lactose or caffeine or ibuprofen or plaster or strychnine or detergent or other, even worse products that we could, once again, enumerate. But first, alerted by local residents who saw this as a nuisance and ended up complaining about it, etcetera. And what came after that, etcetera.

Two-thirds of the studio is occupied by musical equipment—a dozen keyboards, synthesizers, drum machines, and sound effect makers, all laid out on trestle tables; three computers of decreasing size on the desk—while the remaining third has been arranged to resemble a living room: chairs, couch, coffee table, rows of shelving bowed under the weight of vinyl records, magnetic tapes, and various boxes. On the wall are two illegible trophies, a gold disc in a Plexiglas frame, and a signed photograph of the composer Lalo Schifrin. There is also a small kitchen area where Lou Tausk, after turning on the lamps and the main computer, makes himself an orange juice and a pot of tea, proceeding in an unchanging parallel order as he knows that the time it takes to squeeze two oranges is equal to the time it takes for the water to boil and then that rinsing the juicer equates to the time needed for the tea to brew.

Once this is done, Tausk sits in front of the main computer and studies the file containing his work in progress. He tries to improve it, but only a few minutes pass before this undertaking strikes him as futile. His attempts at composition proving fruitless, he opens an old emergency file containing old ideas—fragments of melodies, experiments in dissonance, potential chord sequences—that he has kept up his sleeve for just such an occasion as this. He strives to adopt these leftovers to his current project, but again, very little time passes before he gives up.

Because while he is, as already indicated, generally successful in his career, it has to be admitted that he is currently stuck in a rut and has been for some time now. In a sign of his helplessness, he types up the first two bars of "Vamos a la Playa" before giving himself time to think, puts his computer to sleep, examines his fingernails. Then he notices the small pile of junk mail and letters that the building's caretaker (who has the keys to the studio) leaves on his table every day.

These documents concern a singles club, an offer of a credit balance transfer, the manifesto of a united far left / far right coalition, and a proposal to substitute your crappy old bathtub—stained, impractical, poorly adapted to your needs and soon to your age—for a high-performance, custom-made, poly-relaxing, chrome multijet hydromassage machine. Tausk studies this one for a bit longer because, well, why not, before scrunching it up like the others and tossing it in the trash can: a full trash can is the sign of an active man. The only real mail is a large beige envelope with an elastic band around it, with a smaller white envelope attached to it by a paper clip.

Tausk must feel some instinctive mistrust of these envelopes because he doesn't open either of them, postponing the act of reading their contents the way we sometimes postpone reading bank statements. He puts the two envelopes in his bag to be dealt with later, although he does remove the elastic band and the paper clip first. Looking pensive, he stretches the elastic until it snaps, then unbends the paper clip and attempts to twist it into the shape of a human figure. The snapped elastic band, which he has thrown onto his desk, lands in the shape of an ampersand; a quick flick and it is briefly transformed into an *at* symbol, before ending up as a treble clef.

Lou Tausk might have interpreted this musical sign as an encouragement to start work again, but he then receives three telephone calls. The first two are similar in tone to the junk mail he received: a lady with an Asian accent offers to sell him French doors and Tausk says no; then a second lady with an Alsatian accent wants to know if he is interested in God and Tausk says no to her too. But the third time the phone rings, it is Franck Pélestor, announcing that he will be there in five minutes.

I'm pretty glad to see you, aren't I? says Pélestor when he arrives. What do you think? This sort of ambiguous phrasing, pronounced in a muffled voice and delivered with a sorry smile, is typical of Franck Pélestor, a slumped, stooping man whose dark eyes tend to stare down at his feet and the floor beneath them, his gaze rarely venturing any higher than the feet of his fellow humans. In all seasons, his clothes are strapped tight and buttoned up: sweater, jacket, coat, scarf, zip-up fur boots. Let the sun blaze down, let the rest of humanity waltz around in T-shirts: Pélestor is always dressed in the same shades of gray. His skin is slightly gray too, as is his daily mood. He's probably afraid of catching a cold; in fact, he probably already has a cold since he regularly extracts the same flat, stiff, compact Kleenex from his pocket—the much-used tissue shaped like a pumice stone or a sliver of soap—from which he manages to unpeel a translucent fragment that he can touch to his nose.

Up to now (although it is not particularly recent), the partnership of Franck Pélestor and Lou Tausk has brought them success. There have been songs co-written by Tausk-Pélestor and sung by the likes of Gloria Stella, Coco Schmidt, and others, which have done pretty well. "Nuisance" and "Dent de Sagesse" were genuine hits, but, while "Excessif"—that's the gold disc in the Plexiglas frame—was a global sensation, to which we will return later, the reception granted to the productions that followed it has been increasingly reserved. "N'est-il Pas" sold poorly; then "Te Voici, Me Voilà!"—despite being more accessible—didn't even make the shortlist for the Eurovision Song Contest. So that is where they are, seeking to bounce back and struggling.

I may as well tell you right away, I haven't written anything, Pélestor warns his partner, if that's any reassurance, and Tausk makes a grimace indicating that he hasn't either. I did have a beginning, Pélestor adds, but you're not going to like it. Never mind, let's hear it, Tausk encourages him. It's not ready, Pélestor sniffs, I need to rework it. Well, tell me when it is, sighs Tausk, handing him a fresh Kleenex. No, thanks, says Pélestor, I've got mine. So where are we going to eat lunch? They settle on their usual Chinese restaurant, on Rue d'Eupatoria.

Like most such establishments, the Pensive Mandarin features a large aquarium whose auspicious placement, intended to bring luck to the business, was carefully chosen by a feng shui master. While they eat lunch, Tausk explains to Pélestor that their production of songs—which they have been doing in the same way for fifteen years—is no longer working, that they can't go on this way, that they need to change direction. And this direction, it seems to him, he says, turning over a pork rib, should be toward a more total kind of work. Oh yeah? says Pélestor, what do you mean by total? Let me explain, says Tausk.

He pauses before replying as he watches the movements of the dozen carp in the aquarium: pastel-colored, almost translucent, a few of them appearing to suffer from some kind of skin disease. They are moving at a distance from an intimidatingly large adult carp that seems to possess all the power: the little ones around it do their best to keep out of its way. A sort of opera, Tausk finally continues, an oratorio if you will. A kind of concept album—you remember concept albums. Based around one woman's voice, you see. First you have to find it, though, your voice, Pélestor objects. I know, says Tausk, I don't know, I'm looking for it. Maybe you could look too.

So they look, without speaking anymore, and the waiters come and go around the aquarium, and then, as they are about to leave, they bump into the restaurant owner. That is one fat fish, Tausk says, just for something to say. Oh yeah, agrees the owner, he's the real boss; the others are scared of him. And what's his name? Tausk asks, feigning interest. He doesn't have a name, the owner smiles seriously. Oh right, says Tausk, surprised. So how come? Because he doesn't have any ears, the owner patiently explains. He can't hear, so we can't call him. So there's really no point in him having a name, you see. It's very simple—no ears, no name. Oh yeah, says Tausk, of course, I understand. Naturally.

Pélestor goes home. Without any reason to stop by the studio again, Tausk catches the metro at Couronnes and, ten stations later, after the voice utters the name of Villiers, he, too, makes it to his home on Rue Claude-Pouillet. He finds himself without any plans, with nothing much to do, idle. Though barely begun, the afternoon is already taking on the form of a ball that he will have to keep dribbling forward, hour after hour, until it's time to have a drink, then eat dinner (halftime), before the start of the evening (second half). And he can't think of anything that will accelerate this game except picking up his shirts from the dry cleaner on Rue Legendre and a pretty nice pair of green pants from the tailor on Rue Gounod, who is adjusting them for him after he bought them in a clearance sale last week. (Who can resist a clearance sale?) It's not much, admittedly, but it could kill quite a bit of time if he proceeds methodically. Then maybe a little walk around the park in the late afternoon to put off his first drink of the day.

But first Lou Tausk leaves his bag in the entrance hall, goes into the living room, takes off his jacket, and empties his pockets, and then, back in the entrance hall, picks up his bag and takes it into the living room to empty that too. And so it is that he finds himself holding the large envelope and the small envelope that he received at the studio earlier. He is not happy to see them again, he is slow to look for the paper knife, and he is visibly reluctant to open them. And then we understand his suspicious attitude toward the letters that morning. The little one contains a small photograph of Constance, the large one a demand for money.

Constance looks surprised in the photograph: her smile is incongruous, her left eye half-closed. The sum of money demanded by the letter is also incongruous. It is a very large figure, an exorbitant amount. We won't specify the number of euros, but the startled look on Tausk's face when he reads it gives us an idea of its size. There is something childlike about the handwritten note that makes this demand. Peppered with vague threats, the block lettering is obviously the work of a right-hander using his left hand or vice versa, designed to look rough and unsophisticated. After a brief pause to get over the shock, Tausk decides to skip directly to his first drink of the day. "Vamos a la Playa" . . .

4

THE PHOTOGRAPH OF CONSTANCE was taken just after she was injected with propofol, in the back of the repair van, after it had been parked in an underground parking garage on Avenue Foch. The lowering of the left eyelid before the subject loses consciousness is a well-known side effect of this common, short-acting anesthetic, another effect being said subject's rapid recovery of consciousness. So, conscious again, and cautiously opening that left eyelid—closely followed by the right eyelid—Constance was able to see the place where she was being kept: namely, a long, narrow space, maybe one hundred square feet in total.

The furniture in the room consisted of the bed where she lay, a chest of drawers, and a chair pushed in front of a corner shelf fixed to the wall, all of it made of high-gloss MDF boards. It looked like a cheap hotel room, except that there was no letterhead notepaper in the drawer and no list of rules stuck to the inside of the door. And that door—Constance checked as soon as she got up—was locked from the outside. The floor was marbled linoleum, the walls covered with beige woodchip wallpaper. Pinned to the wall was a violently colored poster of a horse on a beach at dusk, rearing up in the spurting foam, and near that was a metal support for a television, of the kind you also see in hospital rooms, but without a television. There was a shower cubicle in one corner. The absence of a toilet might have made Constance hope for a brief stay, but her capacities for anticipatory reasoning were still too slow to make that leap. The room had no distinguishing features, no detail that might have enabled her to identify the nature of the building, the name of the city, or even on which continent it was located.

She was able to see all of this thanks to a spindle-shaped wall lamp near the bed, which constituted the only light source. The room did contain a window, but it was hidden by a shut blind, its slats so tightly wedged together that not even the faintest hint of light, artificial or otherwise, filtered through. The long crank handle that would have enabled her to open this blind had been removed.

Approaching the window anyway, Constance had no idea what she was doing here, nor why nor how, nor even the idea of wondering about any of this. The weight of the situation was enough to squash any curiosity she might have had about its motives, its terms and conditions, or any fears she might have had regarding the future. The same was true for the past: her memories ended with her visit to Philippe Dieulangard's real estate agency. After that, nothing; even the walk in Passy Cemetery had been expelled from her memory. When, by chance, her gaze alighted on a red dot fringed with pink about one-third of the way up her left forearm, she remembered the injection she'd been given, but only as an isolated event, purely physical and without any context. Then the present slipped away from her like the past when, her gaze sliding down her forearm, Constance noted that her wrist was bare: they had taken her watch.

At the foot of the bed, she saw her handbag and quickly checked its contents. At first sight, nothing was missing: passport, wallet with money inside, house keys, cell phone. The latter, however, with its battery and SIM card removed, was no use to her whatsoever, not that she'd even thought of calling anyone, but at least she would have known what time it was. She had to think about doing her makeup before she realized that her cosmetics bag—containing nail varnish, lipstick, powder, compact mirror—wasn't there either: confiscated, apparently.

So there was no way of figuring out where or when she was, nor how long her artificial sleep had lasted: not long, perhaps, as the imprint of her watch strap was still visible, its side seams embedded in her skin. Then a sudden desire to go back to sleep took hold of her, illogically since she had just woken up, but as this setting offered no entertainment or any alternative to sleep, she didn't see what else she could do. And it was as she lay down that she finally noticed an important phenomenon that, fully occupied as she had been with what she was experiencing in the moment, she hadn't perceived when she opened her eyes: the noise. The huge noise. The massive, constant background noise.

Despite the shut window and the lowered blind, a ceaseless and close-sounding engine roar filled the room, making all the furniture vibrate. To judge from the volume and tone of that engine noise, it had to be produced by heavy-goods vehicles, probably a very large quantity of eighteen-wheelers in fact, the nuances of the sounds indicating an incessant succession of vehicles crossing, passing, changing speed, and double-clutching, on a highway situated just below the window and which, given the volume of the noise, must be at least four lanes wide, if not six. This phenomenon did constitute a clue, at least: wherever she might be in the world, Constance had not been removed from all civilization.

It may seem surprising that it took her so long to become aware of such a din, and indeed she was surprised by it. But perhaps it was because the sheer immensity of the volume had become, in a way, the perfect inverse of silence, to the point where the two were exactly equivalent. Perhaps. In any case, while the roar of heavy traffic on that truck-filled highway hadn't troubled her chemical lethargy, it was going to be an entirely different matter to fall asleep normally with it in the background. After switching off the lamp, after tossing and turning fruitlessly on the bed, after trying to block her ears with the edges of the pillow, she turned the lamp back on and the poster of the horse on the beach suddenly brought back a memory.

A childhood memory: a vacation house by the ocean, very close to the beach, nighttime, rocked peacefully to sleep by the sound of waves, their regular ebb and flow, waves being born and growing louder as others wear themselves out, collapse, and stretch out over the sand with a hiss, reduced to foam. When the ocean was rough, it roared and howled just as loudly as a highway full of trucks, but not only did the backwash not prevent Constance from falling asleep; it acted like a narcotic on her. There was nothing to stop her, now, from imagining those eighteen-wheelers as equally hypnotic waves, just as long as she could filter out their squealing brakes, their screaming revs, and above all the fact that the sea does not honk its horn.

It was amid this racket that Constance distinctly heard a fine metallic sound from the other side of the door: the sound of a key turning in a lock.

5

LOU TAUSK DID NOT INFORM the police. First of all because of those threats, even if they struck him as puerile, and then also because he had his reasons. He decided it was better not to rush into anything, to take his time to consider the matter and go to Neuilly to see Hubert, not the most enjoyable of tasks. Seeing Hubert, and being in Neuilly, was no fun at all, but it had to be done: the next morning, he took the metro again. The usual line, with its system of automatic announcements, but this time in the opposite direction.

And so it is a pleasant young woman's voice—she might not be a bad choice for his concept album, in fact—that, before each stop, proceeds to name the station, not once but twice. The first announcement comes when the train is about to reach the station: the register is that of an alert, its sense almost interrogative, pronounced in an ascending melodic curve: attention, we're arriving. Then, once the passenger's attention has been caught and the station reached, its name is pronounced again, this time in the imperative mode of an official statement, the inflection descending and conclusive, confirming arrival: that's it, we're here.

There is no variation in the way that the station names are pronounced, though, beyond these two modes, interrogative and conclusive. If they chose to, they could individualize it, according to the person or the place that it evokes: there might be a dramatic pronunciation for Stalingrad, for example, a Flemish accent for Anvers, a devout voice for La Chapelle, or Cornelian for Rome. But no, nothing personal; everyone is treated the same way. The succession of these two tones, rising and falling, also sounds as if the voice were introducing two people during a social function, which most of the time is completely pointless: there is no reason to engineer a meeting between Pigalle and Jaurès. Unless one was to introduce a woman named Blanche to another woman named Blanche, or Alexandre Dumas père to Alexandre Dumas fils. But anyway . . .

So Tausk took Line 2 as far as Étoile, where he caught a Line 1 train toward Neuilly. Not a very complicated change, but he was already in a bad mood before he had to walk through the corridors, and then the escalators were out of order, and it began to get on his nerves. He sat in the only available place: a folding seat next to a young mother dandling a baby on her knee. The child appeared serene at first sight, but Tausk regarded it warily. When it started to scream, as he'd feared it would, Tausk grew even more tense, though the mother stuck a pacifier in its mouth.

On Line 1, the names of the stations are also announced automatically, but the girl who has lent her voice to the system lacks the gentleness and thoughtfulness of the Line 2 girl: first, she pronounces the station name with indifference—she really sounds like she couldn't care less—and then, when the train enters that station, she repeats it in an annoyed voice: if you haven't understood, I'll remind you, but it's really your fault. It is much, much less considerate. Not only that, but Tausk's car contains a mandolin player doing awful things to *canzone napoletana*, which ratchets up his exasperation a notch. Whenever he's in a bad mood in the metro, the musicians who pass from car to car with their steel guitars or bandoneons, their bagpipes or rondadors, the string quintets or Central European choirs who set up camp in the entrances of corridors in the stations themselves, these people always make him want to shoot randomly into the crowd.

When he got to Neuilly, Tausk opened his cell phone and called the caretaker of the building on Rue de Pali-Kao, to check whether he'd received any more mail. Hang on, said the caretaker hurriedly, standing in the building's entrance hall and holding a thick wad of envelopes tied up by the mailman. I'm distributing the mail now. Hang on, I'll look. And behind him, a huge man suddenly appeared, bald or with a shaved head, dressed in a baggy gray suit that made him look even more huge, pushing open the door to the street.

There's hardly anything, the caretaker said, just a letter from your insurance company and some kind of bill, gas or something. However, as the gray suit turned around, we noticed that his face had a very distinguishing feature: a long reddish birthmark on his forehead, an angioma in the exact shape of New Guinea, down to the smallest capes, isthmuses, and gulfs. All right, said Tausk, walking toward Hubert's office, well, let me know if you get anything else.

The mansion that houses Hubert's offices—located on the first floor—is also his principal residence. As for Hubert himself, he is not only Tausk's legal adviser but his younger half brother too. Hubert's full name is Georges-Hubert Coste and, as they have the same father, Tausk's real name is Louis-Charles Coste. But as there was a risk, when Tausk decided to enter the world of showbiz, that this name would not fit the bill, literally and metaphorically, he decided to adopt—as already suggested—a stage name: Lou Tausk. Lou because of Louis, Tausk because of the psychoanalyst Victor Tausk

(1879–1919), and because he liked the way it sounded. Out of respect for his decision, we will continue referring to him this way.

So, back to Hubert's mansion, which has a garden behind it and a courtyard in front of it, where the gravel crunches with pleasure under the tires of the expensive vehicles owned by a clientele who come to consult Hubert on points of fiscal, business, and corporate law. Barely has Lou Tausk set foot in the entrance hall, decorated by a large Tancrède Synave oil painting, before Hubert comes out to welcome him. He is not dressed remotely like a classic lawyer: lime-green polo shirt, slightly faded under the armpits, flared jeans, tasseled loafers. Hubert's client list is so rich and varied that he gets away with this carefully scruffy style. In this way, he is able to put the bigwigs at ease when he meets them at the golf course or the tennis courts or the squash club, but he also doesn't scare away the anonymous Toms, Dicks, and Harrys, magnetized by his reputation but reassured to see such an eminent lawyer dressed so simply, taking care of their humble interests. In this way, Hubert gains the fascinated respect of the Tom, Dick, or Harry, making him fully aware of the honor that is being done him, until the day when Hubert's secretary announces to said dumbstruck Tom, Dick, or Harry the total amount, including VAT, of his fee.

His teeth immaculate, his thick hair gelled backward, embellished with one unruly comma—a recalcitrant lock of hair that he throws back with a flick of his head as he moves lithely toward Tausk—Hubert takes his half brother in his arms and hugs him, because they're family. Tausk submits to this with bad grace, though he tries not to let this show on his face. There is no way to get out of it, even though it means a hard clash of cheekbones (Hubert's are very prominent): a somewhat painful experience for Tausk, but it's done now. Hubert Coste is taller than Lou Tausk, slimmer, more cheerful, more tanned, more muscular, more everything-that-can-be-imagined, and let's not even mention his extremely pretty bitch of a wife or his nasty little wonderful children. Physically, he is perfect, while Tausk—each of them taking after his mother—is rather less so.

Maybe that is why Hubert, each time he sees his half brother, makes a remark intended to express his consideration and affection. This morning, for example, holding Tausk by the shoulders and stepping back to take a good look at him, Hubert says with concern: You look a little red, don't you? Tausk immediately panics and fearfully touches one of his cheeks. Oh, do I? Well, you've got some color anyway, says Hubert, that's good. I guess you've been sunbathing. I don't think so, Tausk replies evasively. Well, yes, I did actually, he lies. Last week, that must be it. That's good, reiterates Hubert, brushing a real or imaginary bit of dust from his half brother's sleeve, you need to get some fresh air now and then. And what brings you here today?

They moved into his office, and Tausk explained the situation. The abduction of Constance, the ransom demand, the disturbing photograph, the traditional threats, what can you do? In all honesty, it's such a banal situation, the kind of thing you see every day, that we are all a little embarrassed: Tausk by the humiliation of having to ask his half brother for help, Hubert by the fact that Tausk is yet again bothering him without offering a dime in return, and me by this completely unoriginal plotline.

But as always Hubert knew just how to smooth away all the rough edges, avoid all the pitfalls, remove all the obstacles. Seems like rather a shabby operation, he observed, a bunch of amateurs, I would guess. You shouldn't pay them a cent, trust me. Don't react, let them come, wait for things to deteriorate. They'll blink first. Either that or you should go see the cops and let them deal with it. I'd prefer not to bring in the cops, Tausk sighed. How come? Hubert asked, suddenly interested. Nah, it's nothing, said Tausk, it's just that it always causes trouble, getting the cops involved. All right, Hubert concluded, getting to his feet, well, keep me in the loop.

During his trip back on the metro, Lou Tausk spent a long time mulling over this affair; then—to distract himself—he tried to think about something else. He would have liked to look through the window at the landscape, but as this was an underground train, nothing was visible through the windows except his own reflection, and we've already written enough about that. He could examine the other passengers, of course, but on the metro it is not a good idea to stare at people too much. With women it might be taken the wrong way, while with men it might be taken the wrong way too. And that only leaves children: the good thing about children is that you can look at them as much as you like; you can even look them in the eyes and smile at them without any fear of reprisals. Well, you'd think.

Because in reality, beneath their mask of indifference and candor, they are watching you, taking notes, digging into your private life, identifying you in every last detail thanks to their superpowers, adding you to their files, writing your name on their list, and one day or another, when they're adults, or even before that, as soon as they're old enough to settle their scores, you will enter a whole new world of pain.

6

WHILE IT IS NOT ENTIRELY FALSE to say that getting the cops involved can cause trouble, they also have their good sides. But Tausk remembers a certain case and he would not like to see the police's memory of its details refreshed.

He recalls—this is going back about thirty years, when he was still named Louis-Charles Coste—identifying with a radical, independent, far left ideology; he recalls spouting confused councilist convictions and attempting to compose an equally radical and confused kind of music, which he imagined was in tune with those convictions. He had just bought his first Farfisa keyboard and had joined forces with a novice drummer named Clément Pognel, a fairly nice if somewhat bland boy who had strawberry-blond hair and no distinguishing features except for a W-shaped scar on his cheek. Pognel was totally devoted to Louis-Charles, who criticized the drummer's too schematically binary—and therefore reactionary—use of his instrument. Such was Louis-Charles's hold over Pognel that the balance of power between them bordered on serfdom, but both of them—each in his own way—enjoyed the authoritarian nature of this relationship. Musically and politically, it was Louis-Charles who had the ideas, while Clément Pognel attempted to follow them unquestioningly.

A time came when—despite the contempt Louis-Charles felt for the whole notion of a cultural market and for culture in general— the progress in his compositions gave him the idea of recording them and producing an album. Given the intractability of his beliefs, it was not conceivable to audition for anyone, to send demo tapes of his work to those reviled major record labels, or to independent labels, which were all sellouts in the capital. So this meant self-producing the album, which required a budget that Louis-Charles Coste did not possess. Pognel blindly offered all his savings, but they were nowhere near sufficient and they quickly vanished once Louis-Charles had, unhesitatingly, accepted them. Soon after this he hatched the plan— in accordance with his ideals—of taking the money from where it resided: a bank, where we will go, my dear Clément, and steal the contents. It shouldn't be too complicated, people do that kind of thing all the time, as any intelligent scan of the news would attest.

So now they had to prepare. There, too, it was Louis-Charles who came up with a plan and Pognel who unflinchingly adhered to it. First they spent quite a lot of time at the movie theater, studying scenes of armed robbery. Next they sought to procure two guns, not the easiest of tasks when you do not know anyone. They found only one that worked, a PAMAS G1 pistol stolen by persons unknown from a gendarme and bought, for a pretty hefty price, by another person unknown. The only other weapon that presented itself was an impressive Borchardt C-93, but this was a collector's item, neutralized by welding the trigger in place and consequently incapable of propelling any kind of projectile. For want of a better alternative, they would have to rely solely on its dissuasive appearance. Pognel would be in charge of the Borchardt. Now they just had to choose the bank they intended to rob, and they agreed on a discreet branch, not too many customers, located on the short and compact Avenue de Bouvines, near Place de la Nation. However, as they had planned to park a car outside this establishment in order to flee as quickly as possible once the operation was complete, they had to patiently wait for more than a week before a parking space became available.

On the day in question, they put on gloves. Entering the bank, Pognel immediately covered his head with a balaclava, while Louis-Charles thought it very smart to hide his identity behind a mask of a politician's face: Georges Marchais, the incumbent secretary-general of the French Communist Party. Once they had burst into the building, drawing inspiration from the numerous movies they had analyzed, they unfortunately made two failed attempts before they were finally able to attract the attention of the staff and the few customers who were there. Even though their voices were hardly assured, even though they handled their weapons clumsily, the employees obeyed their orders and the customers lay on the floor. As Pognel headed toward the cashier's desk (banks were less secure thirty years ago) and handed the cashier a gym bag, the employees followed the orders even more willingly because they had immediately noted the carelessness of the robbers' method, its flagrant lack of maturity: they knew that everything was in place to deal with such a slack operation.

So, while the cashier obediently placed wad after wad of cash into the bag under Pognel's wide, staring eyes, two security guards came out of nowhere and tried to apprehend Louis-Charles, who resisted them. As he did so, his mask slipped, and now his eyes were no longer level with the holes in Marchais's face. Blindly, he pressed the trigger of his pistol. A bullet lodged in the gallbladder of one of the guards, who collapsed. But when Louis-Charles attempted to use his weapon again, he discovered that he was out of bullets. Luckily for him, the first gunshot had caused widespread panic, and amid the screaming, fleeing crowd he spotted his chance to escape. He tore off his mask, tossed the pistol, and ran frantically out of the bank and away down the street, leaving the car parked in Avenue de Bouvines. He didn't know how to drive; Clément Pognel was the one with the license.

And Pognel, put out by the turn events had taken, finding himself alone and knowing perfectly well that his gun was harmless, did not even try to threaten anyone with it but simply let it hang from one hand as he took off his balaclava. I surrender, he didn't have time to stammer idiotically, because the staff and customers immediately overcame their fear and joined the security guard in overpowering the bank robber, tearing his useless weapon from his hand before beating him to a pulp—except for one selfless soul who, reluctantly extricating himself from the carnage, sacrificed his pleasure in favor of calling the police. After that, the case followed the normal course of events and Pognel took the rap. Even though he didn't fire the shot himself and even though the gallbladder is not a vital organ, the act was considered attempted homicide, which, combined with armed robbery, saw him sentenced to ten years in prison.

During the interrogations that followed the robbery, Pognel maintained a polite silence: he did not say a word about the preparation of the crime and firmly refused to name his accomplice. Maybe he thought himself solely to blame for the robbery's failure and decided to sacrifice himself to protect Louis-Charles, whom he had never ceased to admire. Louis-Charles never once visited Pognel during his incarceration. And, after he had been released, Pognel did not attempt to get in touch with his former partner. It is not impossible that

Clément Pognel ended up holding a grudge against Louis-Charles Coste for letting him take all the blame and then abandoning him. Even if the statute of limitations may apply to this case—something Louis-Charles has never attempted to find out—the fact remains that it was he who inspired the crime, he who shot the security guard. The whole thing is still a sensitive issue and overall it seems preferable not to get the police or the courts involved. In any case, now living as Lou Tausk, Louis-Charles Coste has no idea of Clément Pognel's current situation. He doesn't know—nor does he want to know—where he is, what he's going through, or even if he's still alive.

We, however, always better informed than anyone else, know perfectly well where Pognel is. We had no trouble locating him: at this very moment, he is walking next to a woman on the median strip of Boulevard de Charonne, heading toward Place de la Nation, not far from the bank where, thirty years earlier, he committed his criminal offense. As they approach the Avron metro station, the woman signals imperiously and Pognel follows her across the road to a supermarket. He is not a very tall man, not exactly ugly but not especially handsome either. He has a sparse red mustache through which his upper lip is visible, even though he seems to have deliberately avoided shaving his nose hair in an attempt to give the mustache more volume. He wears thick-lensed glasses, a canvas jacket, a cheap pair of jeans, and dirty yellow and brown sneakers. On his head is a gray cap emblazoned with the word DIAZEPAM in beige; the W-shaped scar on his cheekbone, seen through the cap's transparent brown plastic visor, does not look quite so obvious. You can tell that he has a slight limp.

He is grocery shopping in the company of this woman, who, apparently the dominant one, brusquely points at food items on the shelves, which Clément Pognel unquestioningly grabs and places in the cart that he is pushing. About forty years old, the woman is dark-haired, plump, and robust, her hair cut very short, eyebrows and nostrils pierced, an amateurish tattoo (which she must have done herself) vaguely resembling a dog on her forearm, tight black top and pants, fat thighs, large breasts, aggressive voice, belligerent expression.

Clément Pognel can't have known her very long—perhaps he's just met her—because, between the transfer of two cans from shelf to cart, she asks him what his name is and he replies. His voice is soft and immature, making him seem younger than the woman, whereas the truth is that he must be six or seven years older. And why do you limp like that? she asks in a harsh voice. It's from when I was in prison, he says.

He remembers how, thirty years ago, when he first entered prison, he had been beaten up after he took exception to the idea of becoming a sexual servant: his knee was broken against a washstand to give him a clear understanding of the ambient culture. Everything went more smoothly once he had made his orifices available to a protector, then to several protectors, then to an indeterminate number of these protectors' clients, who hired Clément Pognel by the half hour. And as he gave full satisfaction to all, they wanted to keep him, to guarantee his services for as long as possible, so that each time the possibility of his early release for good behavior came up, they created all sorts of trouble for him. In that way, Pognel served his full term and his protectors and their clients were able to eke maximum enjoyment from him.

The fortysomething woman, far from appearing shocked by this etiological account of his limp, actually seems to take pleasure in it. She gazes lustfully at Clément Pognel and he, in return, manages a wretched little smile. We can imagine, given their developing relationship and the satisfaction they apparently hope to glean from it, that the woman must have a penchant for dominance and submission, and that Pognel—who enjoyed his submissive relationship with Louis-Charles—must have developed this taste during his spell in prison.

And apart from that, she asks him, what do you do? Pognel replies that he is a shelf stacker in a discount electrical goods store named Titan-Guss, in Villeneuve-Saint-Georges. That's handy, says the woman, my microwave's just died. Is it still under warranty? Pognel asks. I'm not sure, she says; I'd be surprised. They've got some pretty good offers on microwaves, he informs her, at the store where I work. I'm not talking about buying one, she makes clear to him, I'm talking about you stealing one for me. And as this sounds more like an order than a mere suggestion, Pognel says that he will see what he can do.

And what about you? he asks. What about me? the woman replies aggressively. Well, what's your name? Pognel asks. Marie-Odile, replies the woman. That's a pretty name, Pognel ventures. Yeah, agrees Marie-Odile, it's okay.

7

WHEN THE DOOR OPENED to reveal the three men from the corner of Rue Pétrarque, Constance closed her eyes, the memories of that moment suddenly rushing back en masse. It would have taken her five seconds to organize those memories in order, but she didn't have that long. One of the three leaned over her bed, saying to her in a gentle, almost affectionate voice that he was sorry he had woken her. When she opened her eyes, she recognized the handsome man who, standing in the street in overalls, had introduced her to his drill. Now dressed differently, he stroked her forehead with two fingers and said his name was Victor.

Behind this Victor, Constance could see the two others who had taken her into the utility vehicle. They stood back at a slight distance and smiled, waving to her in a friendly, relieved way, as if they were watching her recover consciousness after an operation in the hospital. I can see that everything's fine, Victor declared; then, turning around and raising his voice—since the volume of the trucks' roar outside the window had suddenly increased—he confirmed that everything was fine to the others, whose smiles grew wider. They moved closer to Constance's bed and Victor introduced them: the ostrich was Jean-Pierre, the sea cow Christian. Jean-Pierre and Christian were not dressed the same way as they had been the other day either; they were now wearing jackets and pants, the kind you see all the time, with Jean-Pierre in an open-neck shirt and Christian in a diamond-pattern tie.

The fact that they were not attempting to cover their faces or distort their voices, that they were using their first names—even if they turned out to be false—and acting in an affable, considerate way, all of this was on the face of it reassuring, even if the idea that it might not be—I've seen their faces, so maybe they'll kill me—did cross Constance's mind briefly, before she pushed the thought away. I brought you a cup of coffee, Victor announced. We're all going to have coffee together. They drank it; it wasn't bad; they commented on this; then Victor said that they'd better get started. Jean-Pierre and Christian turned back toward the door, went out onto a sort of landing, then began transporting what sounded like a very heavy object. Constance heard them giving brief instructions, the kind of practical advice you'd expect from men accustomed to such work. Watch out on the left, it won't get through. No, a bit higher. There. Now lift. Their voices were calm. They proceeded patiently and methodically, like piano movers. She almost expected to see Victor holding a delivery slip.

The heavy object consisted of a very bulky box that sounded simultaneously clunky and hollow. It was a trunk the size of a human being, a bit like a coffin, and Victor must have seen Constance's face tense up because he reassured her in a kind voice, advising her not to worry as he handed her a plastic tumbler decorated with little red and yellow dancing flowers and asked her to swallow the contents. She obeyed—the drink tasted of sage and verbena, synthetic but not too bad—and she quickly felt more relaxed. Holding her under the arms and by the ankles, Jean-Pierre and Christian laid her gently inside the box, arranging her bag next to her. Victor smiled at her again, stroked her cheek, and asked her how she felt. Constance wanted to say fine, but as the drink was rapidly taking effect, all she managed to utter was f.

Then, after Victor had fitted the lid in place above her, everything went black. Constance kept her eyes open and a dribble of spit hung from her open mouth, but she still felt fine; in fact, she was feeling better and better. When she realized that the lid, once in place, was now being nailed shut, it was less agreeable, though still not really frightening, even if the sound of the hammer gave her a headache and even if each nail seemed to barely miss her body.

Constance still had enough presence of mind to worry that she might suffocate inside this box, but her new friends must have thought about that too because they had brought along a drill—the same one as the other day, presumably—and they used it to pierce holes in the wood just above her face (she had to close her mouth and eyes so she didn't get sawdust in them) so she could breathe. She sensed the box being lifted and then carried, without hearing any groans or grunts of effort from the bearers. The only sounds: the narrow echoes of a corridor; the vibration of an elevator; the cavernous resonance of a garage; the thuds of the box being loaded into a trunk; the roar of a diesel engine; and then she fell asleep.

The next time she woke, she was lying on an adjustable canvas sun lounger. The rubber straps that held the canvas to the metal tubing were eaten away, hollowed out, worn almost completely through. Her bag lay at the foot of the sun lounger, and beyond it Constance gradually distinguished a soot-filled fireplace containing mismatched firedogs, a yellowed sink with oxidized utensils, and an ancient butane gas stove whose pipes were not connected to anything. Aslant on the walls were two or three flaking frames containing faded chromos featuring scenes from the 1970 war and a sticky opal glass globe hung over a table scattered with the leftovers of a meal on which—the only sign of life—a congregation of flies were busy feeding, a two-thirds majority of them large greenbottles. Probably the product of decades of absence or negligence, covered with layers of coagulated, melded, coalesced goo and dust, this entire scene was barely visible in a half-light that excluded all notions of color. Turning around on her sun lounger, Constance also noticed a set of shelves behind her, robust enough to hold—lined up in order—the ten volumes of the Quillet encyclopedia. But there were no other works that might—like a phone directory or a local guidebook—have given some indication which region, which country, she was in.

In terms of luminosity, some daylight was coming through a half-open French door, which did not seem a good sign to Constance. The fact that they had not bothered to lock her in, that she was apparently free to move around as she wished; these things suggested that any attempt to escape would be futile. The glass panes of the French doors were encrusted with the shit and cobwebs of dynasties of bugs and spiders, from before the latter devoured the former, but through the opening Constance was able to glimpse some undergrowth by the side of a meadow. The grass in the meadow was tall, but a slightly beaten path led through it to a sort of clearing converted into a terrace, filled with some lawn chairs and loungers and a tray of glasses on a table shaded by a lime tree.

In terms of sonority, there wasn't much to report: insect buzz and birdsong, interspersed with moments of silence that helped to create an overall impression of rural peace and quiet. This calm was suddenly disturbed by the distant howl of an animal, a powerful, harrowing cry that affected Constance like a splash of acid, a razor slash, or an antipersonnel mine. She had no idea what kind of beast—onager or glyptodont—could have emitted it. And, as if making their entrance onstage, Victor and his co-workers appeared at that moment on the doorstep.

They had changed their clothes since the last time she saw them. Given that they were now in the countryside, apparently in good weather, they had opted for a more relaxed weekend-type look. Christian had exchanged his shirt and tie for a pair of baby-pink jogging pants and a shapeless sweatshirt that made him look plumper, while Jean-Pierre had gone for cigarette jeans and a Lacoste shirt. Victor, the only one to retain his business clothes, asked Constance in his suave voice if she would prefer tea or coffee, but the only response she gave was to shake her head.

Okay, said Victor, as you like. We'll be eating lunch pretty soon anyway. We've been shopping; there's plenty to eat. Do you like *merguez*? We could even eat outside—we can open an umbrella—but I think we're short of bread. Jean-Pierre and Christian will go and get us some bread, won't you, Jean-Pierre? I don't have my wallet, Jean-Pierre objected, while Christian pointed out the absence of pockets in his jogging pants. Ah, me neither, Victor said, tapping his empty jacket pocket. It's stupid, I know, but I forgot it. I'm sorry, he said to Constance, I feel bad asking you, but do you happen to have a bit of cash you could lend us? Not much, just enough to buy two or three baguettes. Looking away, Constance rummaged around in her handbag and pulled a €5 note from her wallet. Thank you so much, Victor said apologetically. I'll pay you back, of course. Don't forget to remind me.

While they were busy preparing lunch, Constance's eyes drifted toward the terrace in the meadow. There, an extremely fat man had just sat down on a striped deck chair, while next to him a slender, pale, frail-looking woman perched on the edge of a plastic folding chair and gazed at him devotedly. As the canvas of the deck chair groaned beneath his weight, the fat man leaned back and Constance noticed a dark stain on his forehead—unless it was just the shadow of the lime tree. She watched as he took a folded piece of paper from one of his pockets, then a cell phone from another pocket; he typed a number into the phone, then handed it and the piece of paper to the young woman. After a moment's hesitation, she appeared to read the contents of that document out over the phone. When she gave the phone back to the man, Constance was too far away to hear her tell him that she had not been able to get ahold of the person she was calling, that it was an answering machine, that the person would therefore hear the message when he returned, and that that should be fine, shouldn't it?

8

THE RINGING OF HIS PHONE, in the living room where he left it, does not disturb Tausk's sleep. After waking up late, he opens the windows of his bedroom to air it—one of the main disadvantages of sleep, apart from the crazy amount of time it wastes, is that nothing smells very good afterward—then cautiously tries to remember his dreams and is relieved to discover that he can't. And thank goodness for that, eh, because there's nothing duller than an account of someone's dream. Even if they might initially appear funny, inventive, or prophetic, their Hollywood-style pretensions are illusory and their plots never hold up to scrutiny. Shooting one would cost a fortune in casting, extras, set construction, transportation, and equipment rental (even if it's true that, these days, special effects make it possible to do many things at a fraction of the cost), and all this for what would undoubtedly be a tiny audience, with no return on the investment. A bad idea all around. In fact, on numerous levels, dreams are a scam.

In the living room, Tausk sees a red dot flashing on his phone. Date and origin of the missed call: one hour ago, number hidden. There is a message, though, which he listens to, frowning, then again, and then another six times, and soon he isn't frowning anymore. He puts the phone down and opens a window in the living room, creating a draft with the window in his bedroom that makes the door slam shut. After a brief trip to his office to grab a Pall Mall cigarette (whatever happened to Pall Mall, by the way? Apart from Tausk, it's a long time since we've seen anyone smoking one of those), he goes back to the living room and leans on the windowsill, smoking his cigarette, apparently deep in thought, without noticing that a bright morning sun is shining down on the almost deserted Rue Claude-Pouillet: not many people walking past, not many cars parked there. He tosses the butt of his Pall Mall out of the window and—bull's-eye!—it lands dead in the center of the O in LIVRAISONS, painted on the pavement below. Not that Tausk notices this either. He picks up his phone again and calls Hubert.

He is not exactly thrilled to call his half brother and has no desire at all to take the metro to Neuilly yet again, but this is a case of force majeure: Hubert or not, the content of the message demands prompt recourse to a lawyer. So it is a wonderful surprise to hear Hubert say: Perfect timing—I have to see a client near where you live, so I'll drop by this afternoon. Seeing Hubert at home can be worse than going to see him in Neuilly, but at least it means one less metro journey. While he waits, Tausk paces around his apartment in his bathrobe. His only scheduled appointment for the day is a work meeting with Franck Pélestor around four o'clock. He goes to the bathroom to wash up and, in the mirror, notices that his hair is sticking up behind his ears and on the back of his neck, that he looks like he is receding around his temples, and that a lock of hair is drooping down into his eye as if it had suddenly grown much longer during the night. So he has to act, if only to take his mind off things.

Another phone call, and he has an appointment at the hairdresser's in an hour. Tausk is looking forward to seeing his usual hairdresser—a very pretty girl, very lively and very chatty, not to mention very curvy—but when he gets there the salon manager informs him that she is on maternity leave, which vexes Tausk for at least two reasons. The manager points out her replacement, and Tausk feels a shiver run down his spine: her head is shaved almost to the scalp, she's tattooed like a jailbird, she has two rings in her eyebrow and another in her nose, and her face and mannerisms are harsh, with not even the hint of a welcoming smile. Fearful of a collateral scissor cut, Tausk does not dare to specify the kind of haircut he wants, so, without a word, the girl starts cutting it any old how. During this operation, in an attempt to soften her up, Tausk asks what it's of, that tattoo on her forearm, and she replies soberly that it's her dog. Oh really, what kind of dog? he asks, and what's his name? But this technique of using animals to forge a connection with people, which he seems very fond of, proves as fruitless now as it did with the owner of the Pensive Mandarin.

Around four o'clock, the conversation with Pélestor isn't much better, with his musical partner as somber and silent as usual. The good weather has not incited him to undo a single button on his coat nor to loosen the knot of his scarf. Preoccupied by the phone call and still upset by his haircut, Tausk is in no mood to work either, so the two of them sit there saying nothing for a long while before Pélestor suggests in his wily manner, We could go for a drink, don't you think? Or maybe you don't feel like it.

The bar is reasonably lively, with people coming in and going out, walking away before disappearing. All these people going away, says Pélestor, it's terrible . . . We don't even know where they're going. Pélestor ends up going away too, dragging his misery with him, without having made any progress whatsoever on—or even having mentioned—the concept-album project, and Hubert turns up later that afternoon. He is much better dressed than he was the other day: a ruinously expensive lawyer wearing a ruinously expensive suit, visiting his superwealthy clients. His tie and pocket-handkerchief match the shade of his shirt, and he wears appropriate English shoes. What on earth have you done to your hair? he exclaims immediately. Never mind that, Tausk says, almost annoyed, and hands him the phone: I want you to listen to this.

She's got a nice voice anyway, the girl, is Hubert's first reaction. I like that kind of delicate, slightly fragile voice. Girls with that kind of voice are often called Cécile, Estelle, Lucile, if you see what I mean. Really? says Tausk. Let me hear it again. And it's true: the voice on the phone is gentle, fresh, not especially assured, almost soothing, in contrast to the words it is enunciating: a final demand, brutal and threatening. At the present moment, it is the content of this message, rather than its form, that interests Tausk. All right, he says, and what do I do?

Nothing at all, Hubert says. You let it happen. They'll calm down in the end. But, Tausk objects, these are pretty serious threats, aren't they? I already told you, Hubert reminded him, that's just part of what they do, the threats. How else are they supposed to proceed? You could even consider them a confession of weakness. It's the classic first stage. After that, we'll see. Then, stepping back: Your pants are funny—where did you find them? Why? Tausk asks defensively, don't you like them? Oh yes, I do, Hubert says. Of course I do. I like them a lot. Well, I mean, they're kind of green, very green in fact, but I understand. Or I imagine that's the idea, anyway.

9

SO HERE WE ARE AGAIN in the French département named Creuse. Second to last in the national population density rankings, Creuse includes vast swathes of unoccupied land, particularly in the south. Here, moorland alternates with high plateaus, forests, and peat bogs. There's no one here, and nothing to eat for anyone who is here, except mushrooms in the fall. But this isn't the fall and we're wary of mushrooms, which—as is also true of berries—only survivalists and extreme nature lovers know how to choose correctly. In the forests, apart from a few wild animals—emotionless wolves, oversensitive stags, haughty wild boar—who are also looking for something to eat—you, in certain cases—it is even rarer to come across a human being, as the region is depopulating before your very eyes. And the fewer people there are, as we know, the more forest there is.

Such a wild and isolated environment is ideal for the illegal confinement of a person in an open space. This person, if the location of her confinement is well chosen, need hardly be guarded at all; in fact, you could leave her alone without bothering too much about surveillance. If the idea of escape enters her head, she will—without someone to guide her—end up dying of solitude, fear, despair, or hunger. So it can save you quite a lot of money in security.

In Creuse, then, it is not uncommon to have to go several dozen miles to procure food. Hence the necessity of a car to make the trip between the place where Constance is being illegally confined and the nearest town. Jean-Pierre is, at this moment, behind the wheel of this car, while Christian sits beside him admiring the landscape. It is a simple, discreet vehicle: a gray Renault Scénic. Seeing these forests, this shade, those hills, says Christian, I have a feeling for beauty again. Raw nature, clear air, hardly any pollution . . . It almost makes me want to live here. We could live here together, don't you think? We could grow our own vegetables, rear chickens. We don't know anything about those things, Jean-Pierre pointed out. We'd learn, Christian enthused. It can't be that complicated. And anyway, we know about guns, so we'd probably be fine for the hunting. And then there's fishing and all that stuff—this place is full of rivers, I saw them on the map. We could grow beards too. You're just saying that because the weather's good, Jean-Pierre objected. The climate is harsh here in winter, very cold and wet. It's extremely tough. Doesn't matter, argued Christian. Have you read Thoreau? He couldn't care less about climate, Thoreau; it's part of the whole thing. He lives his life and that's all. He's happy, Thoreau. Let's talk about this later, said Jean-Pierre. We've arrived.

Indeed, little by little, after a long time of seeing nobody on these winding byways and back roads, a few portents of civilization had appeared: rows of crops, pastureland, even the odd warehouse. One time, they saw—back turned to the road, standing in the middle of a field of protein peas—a farmer in a cap, pissing. There he was, holding his member in both hands, eyes fixed on his plot of land as he attempted to estimate how much it would fetch after the notary's fees. In the distance, on more wide-open land, they noted the presence of a wind farm: slowly beating the pure air, the tall machines gave a hint of movement to the landscape. Did you see the wind turbines? Christian asked. Did you see how they turned? Counterclockwise! Funny, eh? Yes, Jean-Pierre replied.

The beginnings of a village named Châtelus-le-Marcheix soon appeared. Two or three prefabs, a gas station, a traffic circle followed by a church, a café / newspaper store, and a convenience store. They had no problem finding a bakery. So I shouldn't get anything, Christian asked, apart from bread? Maybe some wine? We've got what we need, Jean-Pierre reminded him, and besides you know we have to take it easy when we're on duty. And I know you're a nice guy, but please make sure you're discreet with the storekeepers. Oh, give me a break, Christian said, irritated, I know my job.

Inside the bakery, having sculpted his face into an impassive mask, Christian soberly pointed with his index finger to a pyramid of French sticks behind the checkout and then, still without uttering a word, used his thumb and his middle finger, on either side of said index finger, to communicate the figure 3. The employee handed him his baguettes wrapped in a brown paper packet with a transparent plastic window, bearing the name and address of the bakery. Christian paid with Constance's money, then left the store without saying anything. No hello, no good-bye, grumbled the baker after he had gone, not even a simple thank-you. And people complain about youngsters.

Everything go okay? Jean-Pierre asked when Christian had climbed back in the car and slammed the door shut. Fine, said Christian. The woman behind the counter wasn't bad-looking. Have we got time for a drink? Jean-Pierre shrugged without responding and they drove back to the farm. Christian sulked for a while, then took one of the baguettes from the packet, broke a piece off the end, and bit into it. And give me that packet, Jean-Pierre ordered. It's got the address on it and they said she mustn't know where she is. Christian blew into the packet like a balloon, then popped it. Jean-Pierre jumped. Christian snickered. God, you're a dick sometimes, Jean-Pierre said.

The farm, nearly twenty miles from Châtelus-le-Marcheix, was flanked by a pretty big barn. You could park three vehicles in it side by side, with nothing to indicate that it was inhabited. Located at the end of a twisting path, invisible from the road, it was surrounded by tightly planted broadleaf trees, their foliage partly covering the house's roof, a camouflage that made it difficult to spot even in a helicopter. As Constance had observed, a short beaten path separated the building from a lime tree. A fast-growing tree, 130 feet tall, two hundred years old, and with a life-span of close to a thousand: under the vast, spreading branches of this lime tree, they could meet up in privacy, and in an atmosphere of calm ensured by the antispasmodic qualities of its sapwood.

It was in the shade of this tree that Victor, having made a kir in a mustard glass decorated with a peeling decal of *Space Pirate Captain Harlock*, sat next to the table while he waited for his subordinates to return. After they joined him, we heard the growl of an engine, signaling the arrival of new characters. A navy-blue Audi A3 Ambition appeared, containing a mature man accompanied by a young woman.

The mature man is the same one we saw earlier with the wine-stain birthmark in the shape of New Guinea on his forehead, first on Rue de Pali-Kao, and then here, more recently. He looked preoccupied, a tough man whose sour mood was deepening a vertical wrinkle that ran through his birthmark, like the border that—on maps of the island, in a dotted line as is customary—separates the eastern Indonesian provinces from Papua New Guinea itself.

With regard to the young woman who is accompanying the New Guinea man—very fine if nicely styled blond hair (though perhaps a little sparse, running the risk that her scalp will, in the long term, one day become visible), not very tall or muscular, somewhat chlorotic and very quiet, quick to blush—we can also say that she responds (albeit rarely, given that hardly anyone ever speaks to her) to the name of Lucile. So Hubert, it has to be said, does not lack discernment. She is dressed in an inexpensive but fairly stylish beige suit, and her handbag consists of an oblong zip-up case redolent of a manicure kit. Her colorless eyes rarely stray from the tall, bulky, big-boned New Guinea man, whom she seems to regard as if he is on a pedestal.

So what's new, the New Guinea man inquired anxiously, the wrinkle on his forehead deepening a little more. Not much, Victor replied with a grimace that produced furrows in his own forehead, arrowing diagonally from his eyebrows, a phenomenon known to aestheticians as pillow wrinkles. Behind them, Jean-Pierre went to fetch a seat for the newcomer, a large camping-style folding chair more solid than the others, while Lucile remained standing until someone noticed her presence and Jean-Pierre went to find her a stool. We've still got the girl, said Victor, making a gesture with his thumb over his shoulder. She's over there. She's doing fine, but the husband doesn't seem to be reacting; that's the problem. He doesn't respond to anything. We wrote to him, we called him, we gave signs . . . nothing. Maybe he doesn't understand your signs, the New Guinea man suggested. Maybe he thinks she left of her own accord or that she's arranged all this to get money out of him. Or maybe he just doesn't care that much about this girl. Deep down, you know.

After checking on the level of the liquids so that he could refill glasses as needed, Jean-Pierre brought over several slices of *saucisson* on a board while Christian, having set the table, cut one of the baguettes into slices. It looked as if they were about to eat lunch under the soothing shade of the lime tree: a Sunday afternoon kind of atmosphere, maybe even an Easter Sunday. We could have a barbecue, Christian suggested. I saw an old one in the barn. It's nicer when it's grilled, *merguez*, don't you think? *Merguez* again? Jean-Pierre reacted. And what about the smoke? You can see it from far away, smoke. I thought you knew your job. Drop it, Jean-Pierre, said Victor. A barbecue, yeah, that's a good idea, Christian.

This group, under this tree, around this table, does not give the impression of a conclave of dangerous gangsters. These characters seem likable, urbane, calm, in spite of a few linguistic lapses. They are capable of showing determination, however, as is demonstrated a little while later when they enter into a more serious discussion. They appear increasingly annoyed by Tausk's attitude, by his lack of reaction to the messages they have sent him; as they eat the spicy sausages, they become indignant that he has not flown to the aid of his wife, and they exhort one another to find solutions that will make him bend to their will. Unable to find any solutions, they blame first themselves and then one another. The tension mounts, all the way up to the cheese course, the discussion growing more heated.

Let's all calm down, the New Guinea man proposes. What can we do? he wonders, scratching his head northeast of the wine stain—in other words, in relation to New Guinea, somewhere near the Bismarck Archipelago. Let's think logically, he continues. How can we pressure this guy? There is one solution. Experience has shown that, in general, it works. What solution? Victor asks, curious. Well, how can I explain this? The New Guinea man hesitates. We, uh, send him a sample, if you see what I mean. Ah, yeah, says Victor, I get it. I'm not sure I do, admits Christian. I fear I see what you're getting at, Jean-Pierre worries. Yes, Victor confirms, we'll have to send a bit of the girl to her husband. That'll give him food for thought. We'll have control over him then. That's what Lessertisseur means.

And so now we know that the New Guinea man is, in fact, called Lessertisseur. It is not without regret that we will abandon our original designation—we liked calling him that—but we must respect people's identities. And anyway, it's true that Lessertisseur's physique does not resemble the characteristics of the people from that far-off region; there is nothing Indonesian or Papuan about him; he seems more likely to come from Sarthe or Moselle, Charente-Maritime or Cher, somewhere like that.

What? Christian exclaimed. You mean cutting off her fingertip? I think that's disgusting. Well, I refuse to be part of this. We'll have to see, Jean-Pierre declared. Victor wiped his lips with a paper towel. Listen carefully, said Lessertisseur, I'm not suggesting anything savage. I'm not saying you should cut off a hand, for example. Nor am I saying you should remove an ear, an eye, or any other precious attribute. I'm just wondering if our approach might benefit from putting a little more pressure on the guy by sending him a very small fragment of the girl. But really, I'm talking about a tiny little bit of her, you understand?

It's been done before, Christian pointed out. Personally, I've seen a thousand things like that in the newspapers, and it never ends well. And it hurts, you know; it'll hurt her a lot. Let's not exaggerate, Jean-Pierre intervened. Let me finish, Christian snapped. We'd be causing her huge personal damage too. That's the kind of thing that wrecks a person's life. No, seriously, Lessertisseur reassured him, it wouldn't be a major handicap. The very end of a pinkie finger, for example, you can live perfectly well without that. It doesn't stop you living a normal existence; just look at the compensation figures in an insurance policy.

From that perspective, he isn't wrong. Any intern at Lloyd's would be able to confirm that in terms of anatomo-physiological deficiency, the excision of a phalanx of a little finger represents barely a 0.8 percent infirmity. You could even, suggested Lessertisseur, go a little further with that finger, knowing that three phalanges—in other words, the entirety of the digit—are not worth more than 2 percent, or, to put it another way, they are equal to one single phalanx of an index finger. Whereas a thumb phalanx is counted as 10 percent, two as 15 percent, and an entire hand is 55 percent. And on and on he went, the percentages rising as less and less remained of the body, all the way to a state of stupor or coma, which is worth 100.

But it really hurts, Christian insisted while Jean-Pierre picked up the dirty plates. It's painful. Not at all, Lessertisseur said evenly. I'm sure you still have a bit of propofol left; that should do the trick. As for the, uh, surgical material, we have it here, he went on, pointing to the manicure kit that was lying on the knees of Lucile, who was staring with even deeper devotion at Lessertisseur. But let's not get ahead of ourselves; it was only a suggestion. A possible scenario. A hypothesis. In any case, he pointed out, we can't make a decision of that order without first submitting it to the silent partner. Let me remind you that we are mere subcontractors—project managers, if you will—and we must first seek our client's advice. After that, we can always come to an arrangement, he concluded, turning toward Lucile. I'll go to see the silent partner as soon as possible. What time is it? Ah yes, that's unfortunate, it's a little late; we are only able to reach him in the mornings. And what about the girl, in fact? Christian asked anxiously. She must be hungry. And we've eaten all the *merguez*. I think we bought some ham, too, Jean-Pierre remembered, and there's plenty of cheese left. I'll go and fix her something to eat.

And I have to get going, said Victor, rising to his feet. Things to do. So, he said to Jean-Pierre and Christian, I'm leaving you alone with the girl but I don't want anything to happen with her, you understand? No messing around with that girl. What? exclaimed Christian. Of course not! You know us. Exactly, said Victor, I do know you.

After his departure, Jean-Pierre prepares Constance's lunch. He puts the ham and cheese on a plate. He pours some wine in a Pyrex glass. He adds two slices of bread, the saltshaker, and a paper towel, then he heads over to the farm. Constance does not look up at him when he opens the door. She has moved her chair over to the French doors to read. Having decided that she may as well start at the beginning, she is still on the first volume of the Quillet encyclopedia (*A–Class*). She is currently reading the entry for *argent*.

10

WHILE WE'RE ON THE SUBJECT of money, let's see how Lou Tausk is doing.

From what we know of him, his material situation might seem comfortable, but no more than that. We might even be surprised that strangers are inciting him to pay a ransom, the amount of which we imagine as being very high, even exorbitant. This apparent disproportion, however, ceases to exist if we go into detail on certain facts concerning his life and work.

Tausk's career was marked, about fifteen years ago, by a rare musical and commercial event. He is one of those lucky few to have composed, even if only once in their life, a hit song. And when I say a hit, I mean an enormous hit, the royalties for which will allow you a wealthy existence, without ever having to lift a finger again, for the rest of your life, you and at least two generations of your assignees. I am talking about a global, cosmic, universal hit, bought and frenetically danced to by the inhabitants of the entire earth, from Yemenites to Laplanders. A hit that, fifteen years later, is engraved in their memory to the point of being genetically transmitted to their children, their grandchildren, and so on. A hit that was awarded some fifty gold discs—of which there remains, framed for posterity, only the single example that we glimpsed in the studio the other day. Lou Tausk is not the first person to have experienced this, of course; there have been others, albeit not many. Take Patrick Hernandez, for example, who did nothing at all with his life except "Born to Be Alive"—written in ten minutes, recorded in two days, initially rejected by every record label in France before becoming an intercontinental success whose royalties enabled its author to take it easy for the rest of his life. Tausk could, like Mr. Hernandez—who is, as I write, still wisely taking it easy—sleep peacefully forever on his gold. Because, just like Mr. Hernandez, after blowing a large portion of the massive windfall that landed on him back then, as young men will, he invested the rest in shares, risk-free bonds, and property— including the pied-à-terre in Trocadéro that he gave to Constance— and he still receives a pretty good sum in royalties, a steady cash flow pouring down on him every God-given day from his old hit: each week, his checking account is blessed with the equivalent of what a middle manager would consider a good monthly wage.

So Tausk is not far from being rich, particularly as his later singles ("Dent de Sagesse," "N'est-il pas," "Te Voici, Me Voilà!," and a few others), while they never sold anything like as well as that first hit, did bring him some money, even if he had to share the royalties with his partner, Franck Pélestor—a chronic melancholic after paying his dues as a lyricist in the pop industry. But for Tausk's megahit, entitled "Excessif," it was he and he alone who reaped the rewards. It was a success in France first of all, and then the foreign adaptations—"Desmesurado," "Senza Limiti," "Perda Total," "Too Too Too," "Reiner Wahnsinn," "Abnormaal," "Taşkin," "беспредел," "هذا مبالغ," "το παράκανες," or "הגזמת," among others, and restricting ourselves to those that are still available—sold like hot cakes in Europe and the three Americas before really taking off in the Far East, where, not content with having occupied the number one spot in China ("太邪乎") and Japan ("過激"), the song became a massive bestseller in South Korea, followed by even greater success in North Korea—albeit this time under the counter and only in the highest spheres of power ("너무 해").

And Tausk did indeed create "Excessif" on his own: composed it, wrote it, produced it. The vocal line was sung, in a rush and completely by chance, by Constance, who had just entered his life, who had never sung anything in hers, and who recorded it in a single afternoon under the first pseudonym—So Thalasso—that came to Tausk's mind. And then: triumph, against all expectations, first in its original version and then in numerous cover versions—Gloria Stella, Boz Scaggs, Coco Schmidt, and many others. And the profit from all of this: a magnificent hoard coveted by everyone. That might have been enough, but no: Tausk wants more. Tausk is not content to stick with what he has. Aware that the world has forgotten him a little bit, that his glory is dog-eared, that the people in his agent's office no longer greet him the way they used to, Tausk wants to create a new global hit, more adapted to today's tastes, in order to earn another fortune, naturally, but above all to win the world's admiration once again.

Having made clear this point, let's join him in bed as we did the other morning, just as he's waking up. He has opened his eyes, but this morning, instead of getting out of bed right away, he picks up his tablet from his nightstand, clicks on a newspaper website, scrolls down through politics, economics, and sports, and heads straight for the crime section, in which he finds nothing about Constance. Then, just to see, he types his own name into a search engine. It's true that he hasn't done this for a long time: there's no reason, after all, why anyone should be talking about him, but you never know, maybe this or that new star might have mentioned his influence on them. But no, there's nothing. He gets out of bed.

Black screen 1: The opening of a white door prompts the incandescence of a bulb, casting a stark light on the interior of a stainless steel, four-door, 535-liter fridge-freezer with multiple compartments, a minibar, and a water and ice dispenser. This appliance contains lots of food, behind which, between two racks, we see Tausk, his hair mussed up, in a Missoni bathrobe. He looks like he's in a bad mood. He hesitates, then decides not to bother. The door closes.

Black screen 2: Twenty minutes later, the opening of a sliding panel triggers a fiber-optic system that softly lights a walk-in closet. In the foreground: a collection of shirts and suits arranged in chromatic order, through which we again see Tausk, his hair combed now, wearing boxer shorts. Same thing happens: he hesitates, then decides not to bother. These clothes don't really suit him anymore anyway, most of them dating from the golden age of "Excessif," when he was constantly appearing on television. He makes do with a pair of jeans, a long-sleeved T-shirt, an old, worn Arnys jacket, and even more worn pair of Fratelli Rossetti loafers. The panel closes.

From the office in his apartment—a comfortable place, but we're not going to kill ourselves describing it in detail*—Tausk phones Pélestor since he has to start somewhere. He has a few tunes in reserve, all of them at a standstill, but as he has no desire to go to the

---

*VILLIERS. On the fifth floor of a cut-stone building, a superb 6-room apartment, 2,023 sq ft, consisting of an entrance hall, a very large living room, a dining room, an American kitchen, four bedrooms, a bathroom, a shower room, two WCs, and a cellar. Calm and light-filled. Five minutes from Parc Monceau. Price: upon request.

studio, it might be a good idea to deal with the lyrics before starting on the sound. Franck, would it bother you to come to my place instead? Silence, then a drawn-out sigh. It wouldn't take you much longer to get here, Tausk argues. You can come on the metro without changing trains. It's not that it's far to go, Pélestor points out, but morally it's a long way. And the metro, you know . . . I'll order you a taxi if you want, Tausk says. Another sigh and then Pélestor says, All right, I'll drop by.

He actually arrives pretty quickly. Still wearing his coat like a suit of armor, he looks like he's having a bad day. Admittedly he looks like that more or less every day. That was fast, remarks Tausk. Yeah, says his partner, but the taxi driver was a pain. And it's too hot: I don't have enough air, or any ideas. Conciliatory, Tausk suggests they go and work somewhere else for a while, mentioning his two second homes—one near Honfleur, the other near Hendaye, both close to the beach—which he rarely visits. We can take a break for a few days, it's nice and cool down there, and then we can get started. What do you think? It's kind of you, Pélestor acknowledges, but I think that's the sort of place I like hearing about more than I actually like going there myself.

So they're not off to a good start. They are sitting in the office, facing each other. Neither says a word. It goes on for a while like this; then the conversation goes around and around in circles without any result, before getting bogged down, and at last the lyricist checks his watch and says, I'd better get going. Tausk tries not to look too relieved. So I'll see you at the studio tomorrow morning? Of course, says Pélestor. As Tausk has not paid for his return taxi trip, Pélestor walks to the Rome metro station. Let's follow him. He stares at his feet as he walks, as usual, and sees some of the things that surround them, and all of it depresses him. A lost playing card, for example, behind the news kiosk on Place Prosper-Goubaux. It doesn't look like much at first sight, a stray card, but all the same it ruins the career and future prospects of fifty-one others, who are mourning it or maybe cursing it, and who are no longer any use to anyone, finding themselves out of work because of that one card. The fate of those other cards saddens Pélestor.

Next, the legs of a passing woman. It's easy to forget that women's legs are also useful for helping them move forward: we hold them so dear as art objects that we tend to neglect that functional aspect. Uncovered and inelegant, the legs that Pélestor sees not far from his own feet force him to pose an important question: if ugly legs serve no other purpose than walking, then why expose them? This thought depresses him, but worse than that, the guilty knowledge of having had it distresses him, oppresses him exceedingly, and to subdue this feeling he reaches into his pocket for a new pack of anti-anxiety capsules. He starts to open them, but.

But on that subject, Pélestor would like us to explain why, when he opens a new box of medication, it is always from the wrong side: the one with the package insert folded around the pills, tablets, or capsules, forming a barrier to their extrication, so that Pélestor has to close the box every single time and open the other side, where the pills, tablets, or capsules are easy to reach. This phenomenon seems inevitable, in the same way that a dropped piece of toast always lands on the buttered side, as if influenced by a curse that pursues him even after the initial opening of the box: each time he needs the same box in the future, it is always the insert side that he chooses, invariably, over and over again. One solution would be to get rid of that damn insert, particularly as Pélestor knows it by heart anyway so it's completely pointless, but, well, you never know.

In any case, he does not have a glass of water to hand to help him swallow the pills, so he postpones that operation and goes down the stairs to the Rome metro station, which is a large rectangular parallelepiped, the only nonvaulted station on the underground network. The train that arrives is full, so Pélestor has to stand, which is trying, but, because of the microbes, germs, viruses, and other bacteria, it is out of the question for him to hold himself upright by grabbing onto any of the available handles or bars. It takes an effort to keep his balance: Pélestor dances on the spot, without any particular method, hopping from foot to foot until the train stops at Barbès-Rochechouart and a seat becomes available: an individual folding seat, ideal in theory. But as it is out of the question to occupy a seat that has been warmed by anonymous buttocks, Pélestor has to wait for it to return to its normal temperature. And then, finally seated, increasingly oppressed, he reaches for the capsules in his pocket: he'll just have to manage without the water. Using his tongue and his cheeks, Pélestor tries to accumulate enough saliva in his mouth to wash the medicine down; it takes him several goes before he has the necessary volume. But in the meantime the capsule has melted against his palate and it tastes disgusting. Life really is totally shit.

11

AFTER THE LYRICIST'S DEPARTURE, Tausk went back to his office. Several things seemed to have left him impatient. Constance's disappearance, Pélestor's depression, the deadline for his tax returns, the weather, his cleaning lady's vacation, the international political situation, and decisions to make, which he was still, always, putting off. Drumming his fingers on his desktop, as you do when you're impatient, he had the impression that his fingernails, based purely on the sound they made, were too long. Finally he made a decision, with immediate effect: taking a pair of nail-clippers from the drawer, he began to shorten his nails, a useful pastime that can take you quite a while if you really apply yourself.

Too short. So much so that, for the hours that followed, his fingertips felt suddenly fragile, as defenseless as a newborn, their tender flesh touching the open air and breathing it, an uncomfortable sensation, like the moment when a plaster cast is removed. This postoperative effect never lasts long: soon you stop thinking about it, and in the days that follow you are happy with your short, clean nails, freed of those corners where dust and grime can insinuate themselves. You wait to cut them again, knowing that the entire cycle of nail regrowth, for the fingers, lasts three months. For the toes, you can count a good nine months because they spend their existence in the dark so they are slower to grow.

Having done this, Tausk leaves his office and opens a window in the living room. A huge fly with a glistening blue thorax enters the room and flies warily around it a few times; it must find the apartment to its taste because it then flutters from room to room, lingering like a bailiff on each piece of furniture, each painting hung on the wall, without any apparent intention of leaving, then going through to the library, which, buzzing, it inventories, volume by volume, until Tausk turns on the television: an American series; medium shot of a busty blond actress in a Californian apartment? Yeah, why not. Distracted by this new spectacle, the fly lands on the actress's left breast and Tausk, using animal magnetism, evacuates the dipteran from the screen.

The actress is explaining that it's you, Burt, who got Bob to poison Shirley with the aim of disinheriting Howard, with Nancy's help, and getting your hands on Malcolm's legacy, just so you can marry Barbara. Whom you don't love. And Walter? Have you thought about Walter's future? (With this being a very long reply and the actress having to reread the script on set to remind herself of her lines, the tirade is interrupted on two occasions with cutaways to Burt, who, in fact, does not look particularly confident.) You're a monster, Burt, diagnoses the actress, and you'll get just what you deserve. And at the moment when she takes a stubby Smith & Wesson from her Prada purse, the doorbell of the apartment rings—not the Californian apartment, but ours. My God, it never stops, does it?

Over the intercom, the concierge informs Tausk that a parcel has arrived for him: I can bring it up, if you're there now? Of course, says Tausk as a gunshot explodes in the living room. When the concierge has delivered the parcel, Tausk turns off the television, leaving the fly to get by on its own, and goes off to find some scissors while continuing to examine the package: a standard French post office parcel, delivered without signature or any indication of the sender's name. A gray-printed line gives the date and place of the package's origin: day before yesterday, Agen Carnot post office. Tausk, who does not know Agen or anyone in Agen, weighs the parcel in his hands. Very light, the size of a pack of playing cards or cigarettes. It could be a lighter, a knickknack, a pair of cuff links, or a USB key.

In fact, it is a box of matches with the matches removed and, in their place, a slender cylindrical object wrapped in a cloth held in place by a Band-Aid. Unwrapped on the work surface of the kitchen, this object looks to us very much like a finger. A real human finger: Tausk recoils, sickened, turns away, and feels slightly dizzy. But let's not overdramatize the situation. It's not an entire finger, just the tip of one. Anatomy is not Lou Tausk's strong point but, glancing at his own hand to compare it, he estimates that it is probably the tip of a pinkie finger, extended and protected by one varnished nail. It's hard to say whether it's from a right or left hand: nothing looks quite so similar to the first phalanx of a little finger as the first phalanx of another little finger.

The only clue is the nail, and God knows there are almost infinite varieties of fingernails: mandarin nails, clawlike or spiraling; porn-star nails, white painted and square cut; newborn nails, as fragile as eyelids; mechanics' nails, charcoal gray and short; old people's nails, thick, hard, ribbed like corrugated iron; Tausk's freshly clipped nails, and so on and so forth. But this one is instantly identifiable because of its Chanel 599 Provocation varnish, which was always Constance's favorite color. Tausk pauses, short of breath, and slowly approaches the phalanx, examining it more and more closely before finally picking it up: it seems to have been cleanly cut but cauterized in haste, a somewhat casual modus operandi, the way you might treat any old Baron Empain.

The large, gleaming fly returns at that moment. Having carried out its bailiff's duties, methodically explored the apartment like a surveyor, a real estate agent, and then an antiquarian bookseller, it now proposes to visit the American kitchen. It is common knowledge and self-evident, after all, that flies love kitchens. As for Tausk, reflecting on what he should do with this finger, he puts it on the countertop, between the open dishwasher and the refrigerator. Seeing the fly reappear, he opens a window in the kitchen, folds a newspaper in four, and shakes it about to chase away the insect, which seems unfazed but bumps into the closed windows for form's sake while avoiding the open one, then nose-dives toward the countertop, naturally attracted by this piece of fresh meat.

No, absolutely not. Tausk absolutely refuses to let this fly land on that pinkie—you don't joke around with this kind of thing—so he has to act and he does act: just as the dipteran, changing course, takes a walk along the edge of the dishwasher then goes inside, thinking that it will just have a quick look around to complete its inspection of the premises before taking care of the finger, Tausk instantly slams the dishwasher door shut and presses firmly on the economy setting, to seal the fly's fate at a more reasonable cost.

So now what? Well, first of all, put the phalanx in the freezer. Next, take advice. And in terms of advice, I can see only Hubert. Which means another trip to Neuilly. Too distressed to take the metro, Tausk calls for a taxi, whose African driver, having typed Hubert's address into his GPS, returns to a conversation in his native language on the telephone grafted to his ear. Though barely more knowledgeable about linguistics than he is about anatomy, struggling to distinguish Fula from Lingala, Tausk nevertheless wonders whether

"Excessif" was adapted into one or two or—why not—maybe even more of those two thousand documented African idioms. Not impossible. He'll have to check the archives. And the accounts.

When he reached Hubert's mansion, he was announced by Hubert's assistant, whose body Tausk discreetly admired from behind as she walked into her boss's office: nice legs, nice neck, nice ass. He looked at his reflection in the entrance hall mirror as he waited—that hairdresser really did overdo it; he'll have to go back to the salon to get it fixed—and then Hubert arrived, this time dressed midway between professional and relaxed, his tie loosened, blue jacket and pants artfully mismatched. I'd better tell you right away, he warned Tausk as he followed him into his office, I'm really snowed under. I can give you five minutes, but that's all. Then, glancing at him sideways: You're looking a bit pale, aren't you?

Never mind that, said Tausk, before briefly outlining the story of the phalanx. Hubert frowned with one eyebrow: This case is starting to get on my nerves. Are you sure it's her finger? Tausk advanced as evidence the presence, on this fingernail, of varnish number 599, but Hubert seemed unconvinced: Sure, but anyone could knock up a nail varnish. They're going to continue, Tausk predicted. Next time I'll receive an eye. No, no, Hubert soothed him, they won't go that far. But this is getting more serious; are you sure you couldn't pay? When I say pay, I mean pay a little bit, not necessarily the whole ransom. Just to see. No, you don't understand, Tausk sighed, she's already cost me so much.

The lawyer shot him a brief reproving glance—as do we all, for that matter, not having imagined, before now, this unpleasant aspect of his personality—then he went on: Listen, I don't have a second to spare right now, but my assistant can deal with this case perfectly well. She's putting together a dossier—she's good at that—and afterward I'll take care of it. Make an appointment with her. You'll see, she's very good. They were back in the entrance hall now: Nadine, allow me to introduce you to my half brother. Louis Coste, Nadine Alcover. It was true, the assistant did look very good, and from the front this time: nice eyes, nice hands, nice breasts. Well, said Hubert, I'll leave you to sort things out, and let's keep in touch. I'll call you, you call me, we'll call each other. He headed back to his office then, turning for an instant toward Tausk: In fact, you have a little white thing in your eye, there. No, just there, in the corner of the left eye. You should take it out.

12

CLÉMENT POGNEL HAD BEEN SHARING his life with Marie-Odile Zwang for more than a month now, and nothing was going as we might have expected. One of them appearing to us an abulic wreck, the other an implacable harpy, it was hard to imagine any other common existence for the two of them than a basic S&M lifestyle: a daily diet of insults and bruises, black eyes and smashed teeth, a bowl of Pedigree for lunch and a dash of Clorox in the coffee.

But not at all. Seriously. Right away, their relationship was tender and full of mutual respect. They lived in the one-bedroom apartment near the Gambetta metro station that Marie-Odile rented from a public housing agency. Located on the fourth floor, the apartment was not very big, but it was calm and well-lit, the living room overlooking the quiet, one-way street Rue de la Chine and the Tenon hospital, the bedroom with a view of a courtyard lined with old artists' studios, planted with sweet gums and lilacs. The furniture was very plain and simple, picked up from wherever, but none of it was truly ugly. It was really not bad at all.

It was fine for two, and even for three if you counted the dog whose tattoo Marie-Odile wore on her forearm, born from a beagle mother and an unknown father, named Biscuit, with whom Pognel immediately got along. Biscuit took after his mother's breed: small build, well-proportioned, affectionate character, docile temperament, no health problems . . . basically all the traits that make that type of dog the ideal pet, as well as the perfect guinea pig for laboratories.

The harmony of their cohabitation was aided by the fact that they both worked only in the mornings. Pognel took Biscuit downstairs for a piss after Marie-Odile had fed them both; then they had another coffee and the two of them walked arm in arm to Place Gambetta, where they entered the metro station. As she had to continue her journey all the way to République, near where the hairdressing salon was located, they kissed tenderly at Père Lachaise, where Pognel changed for Nation. His journey, as he described it to Marie-Odile, was on the long side: the suburban train RER A with a change at the Gare de Lyon–Banlieue, RER D to Villeneuve-Saint-Georges, then another ten-minute walk to Titan-Guss, the superdiscount electrical goods store, wholesale and retail. It was long, but that was how it was; he had to do it and he did do it. Clément Pognel explained that he had obtained that job as a shelf stacker as part of a reintegration program after serving his sentence; he was initially hired for a trial period and then given a permanent contract. About his life before prison—as with the causes of his detention—Pognel, who was not very chatty anyway, never really went into details with Marie-Odile Zwang. She accepted this, returning to the subject discreetly at times, but never insisting. So, yes, everything was going very well indeed.

Around one thirty, Pognel returned to Rue de la Chine, where Marie-Odile, who got back before him, had already cooked lunch, a task made much easier as he had, in Villeneuve-Saint-Georges—in accordance with her desire—found her a new combination convection microwave. Contrary to her initial suggestion, Pognel assured her, he had not swiped it from the back room. As he was on staff at

Titan-Guss, he was entitled to a discount on the discount, so that even an oven such as this—which Marie-Odile planned to use to make all sorts of gratins—had not, he implied, cost him very much money.

During lunch, while Pognel never found anything to say about his working day, Marie-Odile was positively loquacious regarding her mornings at the hairdressing salon. And so, by chance, she happened to tell him about having cut the hair, that morning, of a new client whose photograph, she felt sure, she had seen in the celebrity gossip pages of a magazine. Or maybe on TV, probably a variety show hosted by Michel Drucker, she wasn't sure, it was such a long time ago. A pop star of some kind, anyway, she was almost certain of that. She described him in enough detail for Pognel to be able to identify—or at least be reminded of—Lou Tausk's appearance, before he became known under that ridiculous pseudonym. Faced with this description, Pognel might have blushed—let's skip the list of other possible reactions—but no, he sat there impassively and went back to eating his gratin.

After lunch, Marie-Odile warmed up—thanks be to the microwave—the morning's coffee. They relaxed a little bit, they exchanged a few words, they smiled at each other, sometimes they kissed each other on the neck, under the ear, and so on. Do you feel happy here? inquired Marie-Odile with emotion. Oh yeah, definitely, said Pognel. Where did you live, before? she still asked him, from time to time. Pognel always answered evasively. As she had often asked about his pre-prison life, the question recurring regularly during their first weeks together, Pognel had ended up inventing a classic abandoned kid's childhood: social workers, specialized institutions, high school dropout, homeless shelters, crappy temporary jobs, then the spell behind bars, followed at last by a stable situation at Titan-Guss. Marie-Odile, moved by this unhappy childhood, soon resigned herself to not touching on this question anymore, out of respect for her boyfriend's feelings. Likewise, on days when she wasn't working at the salon, she obeyed Pognel's order that she not come to pick him up after his shift in Villeneuve-Saint-Georges.

In the afternoons, three metro stations from Gambetta, they often went to the nearest swimming pool, in Tourelles, which was right next to the vast and very well-guarded offices of the DGSE, located at 141 Boulevard Mortier, home to the French external security services, though this has nothing to do, for the moment, with what concerns us. They had gone swimming together from the first days of their shared life, and that was where Pognel discovered, on Marie-Odile Zwang's shoulder blade, another tattoo that he had not seen (because the lights were off) during their first nights together. It was a polychrome image whose original bright colors had faded—red gone pinkish, green and blue turned gray—diluted in what becomes of the skin with age. (*"Visit the skin! Its wrinkles, its bulges, its varicosities, its rosaceas! An unforgettable experience!"*) It was no longer easy to tell whether the subject of this tattoo was a classic mermaid, a customized dolphin, or something else entirely, but without doubt it was the work of a qualified tattoo artist—the profile of Biscuit, on Marie-Odile's forearm, giving an indication of what an amateur tattoo looked like.

Mermaid or dolphin, this image had faded to the point of appearing almost abstract, vaguely resembling an old label on an old, baggy shirt that no longer suits you and that you never wear anymore, or an old sticker on the back window of a used car, a vanished brand of lubricant or anti-theft system. But its presence allowed Pognel to imagine that Marie-Odile must have had fun in her younger days, given that the vogue for tattooing behind the shoulder—taking into account her age—dated from an era when girls who did it tended to be on the brazen side. Anyway, the idea came to Pognel that, back then, Marie-Odile must have been what some call a *bonne vivante*, others a high-spirited girl, and still others, less distinguished than us, a dirty little slut.

They spent their afternoons reading the newspaper, doing the crosswords, taking a nap, or playing video games. When it got dark, Pognel took Biscuit downstairs to piss again. They ate dinner together and then they would sometimes go out to see a movie at the Gambetta multiplex or—without ever arguing over the choice of what to watch—stay at home to see a film on TV, unless they chose to watch one on the computer, with Biscuit snoring loudly at their feet. As for their nights of love, they were fantastic. There too, against all expectations, Marie-Odile proved herself capable of playing various roles in bed: protective mother figure, innocent little girl, imaginative whore. Clément Pognel, whose only experience of sex prior to this was the services he provided—in a passive role—while in prison, felt a little apprehensive to begin with. But he managed to face up to this new situation and to take care of his responsibilities: and he did very well, surprisingly. As a lover, Pognel was highly active, thorough, attentive, and eager to accomplish his task: extremely virile, in short. So yes, everything was going just swimmingly for the moment.

13

AS FOR CONSTANCE . . . well, things weren't too bad for her either. Who would have thought she would get used to this reclusive existence to the point where she no longer thought of it that way? It's true that she was very well treated: she was looked after as well as she would have been at a luxury spa, vacation resort, artists' residence, or nursing home.

That particular late morning, as they always did when the weather allowed—which it did more and more often with the approach of summer—Jean-Pierre and Christian had arranged a sun lounger for her under the lime tree, with some light reading arranged on a coffee table: women's magazines, movie magazines, magazines full of puzzles and brainteasers, with some randomly bought bestsellers that might distract her from the Quillet. They went all the way to Bénévent-l'Abbaye to fetch them, as there was no newspaper store in Châtelus-le-Marcheix. Since Victor had given strict instructions that Constance must not be allowed to read any publication—be it daily, weekly, or monthly—featuring news, particularly crime stories, it was up to Jean-Pierre to read and censor anything in *Elle*, *Cosmopolitan*, and *Grazia* that might contravene these rules, before passing the magazines on to Constance. Over time, in these magazines, she would read articles on summer fashion and advice on tanning, makeup, and looking elegant on the beach, before awaiting the fall trends in August and September. At this time of day, the coffee table was also loaded with pre-lunch snacks—cold drinks and bowls containing pistachios, almonds, and peanuts—prepared by Christian. No, she couldn't complain about the way she was being treated.

Christian and Jean-Pierre were the ones she saw most of the time. Lessertisseur dropped by occasionally, sometimes with Lucile, sometimes not, to ensure that the logistics were taken care of. As for Victor, who seemed to be a sort of technical adviser, he appeared much more rarely, to Constance's disappointment. So it's true that there were not many distractions—no radio or television, and obviously no Internet connection—but, as her life before this had mostly been spent in a city, she found it quite pleasant to discover a more rural area, with its flora and fauna, about which she knew nothing at all. Just as she still knew nothing about where exactly she was.

A few major clues did exist in this regard, but they were contradictory. Over the fireplace hung a colorful relief map of the Mayenne département, suggesting that this was where they were, but near the dresser was a wall thermometer advertising a butcher's store located in the center of a neighboring village with a name unknown to Constance. These clues were the work of the sophisticated Lessertisseur, intended to further disorientate his hostage—the village of Saint-Affrique, site of the aforementioned butcher's, was a good four hundred miles from the département of Mayenne—but they had no effect on Constance, whose grasp of geography was hardly any better than her knowledge of natural history.

Anyway, wherever they were, the farm must have been occupied just before being taken over by her kidnappers. Various floral and faunistic clues attested to this. In terms of flora, other than the distant views of grassy fields and trees, where Constance couldn't venture, her study was confined to a nearby patch of well-known flowers—zinnias, cosmos, anemones, all of them now untended—whose blossoming she followed with interest, looking after them and discovering other species that she couldn't name or even differentiate, as her knowledge of flowers up to this point had generally been restricted to conical clusters wrapped in transparent plastic.

In terms of fauna, out by the barn a condescending rooster ruled over six twitchy hens, not far from three rabbits, which lived, more relaxed than the chickens, in the skeleton of an old piano. You sometimes find pianos where you least expect them. This one—a worm-eaten upright, its varnish eroded, without a manufacturer's name, standing in the entrance of the barn—was used primarily as shelving for various empty recipients that had once contained agricultural products. Constance, having lifted its lid—with a sticky noise like a dry mouth opening—found a keyboard with almost all its teeth remaining, albeit very yellowed, the sharps and flats decayed. There was no way to get a sound out of it: the cords must have been recycled for gardening, its soundboard used for kindling, and wire fencing wrapped around its metal frame and its feet to transform it into a hutch.

As for the less domesticated animals, at least one of them showed a bit of life. As the sun grew low, after an afternoon of reading and gardening, Constance would return to her sun lounger under the lime tree and an evening bird would regularly serenade her. To judge from the sound, it might have been an improved prototype of a merle. Whatever bird it was, it sat at the top of this tree in all weathers, singing its heart out, repeating ad libitum a melody that seemed more human than avian: tonal and composed of fourteen clearly articulated, well-balanced notes, it could have been the chorus of a pop song that—with the addition of a few appropriate, easy-to-write couplets—would have enabled the pseudo-merle to make a fortune. Maybe it repeated itself like this because it hoped to catch the ear of a passing impresario, agent, or producer who, sensing a hit, would climb straight up the lime tree and grab a feather from the bird's back to make it sign a contract in its own blood.

But after initially admiring the bird for its melodic invention, Constance ended up finding the constant reiteration of this same tune boring, annoying, and finally exasperating. Soon she was cursing the song's composer, devaluing his work, and regarding him merely as an inept disciple of the minimalist school, a poor man's La Monte Young or Charlemagne Palestine. This bird apart, Constance could also inspect the comings and goings of polychromatic butterflies, sometimes fluttering around on their own but more often in couples. There were a prodigious number of butterflies in the area that summer, far more than usual, despite the fact that you never saw a single elephant.

This last line might seem incongruous to you: after all, why should you see elephants in Creuse? Well, you're right. The only reason we mention it is because, according to the work of Dr. L. Elizabeth L. Rasmussen, the females of *Elephas maximus* use—as all animal species do—a certain combination of molecules when rutting becomes conceivable or even desirable. Such a chemical signal allows the female elephants to inform the male elephants that they are at their sexual peak, madly in love, wildly horny, and ready to mate whenever they like. In her studies, L. Elizabeth L. Rasmussen successfully proved that this molecular gathering—this pheromone, in other words, technically designated as (Z)-7-dodecen-1-yl acetate—is exactly the same in an elephant as it is in more than a hundred species of butterflies.

We thought it would be good if this little-known zoological phenomenon were brought to the attention of the wider public. Naturally, said public has the right to object that such a piece of information seems purely digressive, a mere didactic amusement, permitting us to bring the chapter to a smooth ending without any connection to our actual story. To this objection, which is of course admissible, we would like to respond as we did earlier: for the moment.

14

FOLLOWING HUBERT'S INSTRUCTIONS, Tausk made an appointment with Nadine Alcover, who turned up at his apartment around five o'clock in the afternoon. She was a pretty girl, as we have already established, with shoulder-length brown hair, a look that—like any other look, for that matter—can be appealing. Before her arrival, Tausk put on some Mahler at low volume, partly to give an elegant atmosphere, but above all to express the fact that, while his own songs might be shallow and poppy, he was open to serious, moving, dark works too, let's say, Kathleen Ferrier in the *Kindertotenlieder*.

Nice place you've got here, Hubert's assistant said as she sat down, and it's a peaceful neighborhood too. Ah yes, agreed Tausk eagerly, such silence, such peace, you can't imagine. Some tea? I'll make it. Be with you in a second, he shouted from his American kitchen and, back in the living room, he put the tray on the coffee table, where he saw his dossier already open. This is the documentation on your case, said Nadine Alcover, with an initial summary written by Maître Coste. It's not much, but it's a start. Yeah, muttered Tausk, flicking through the documents, but there's nothing here about the finger, is there? Do you want to see it, the finger? No, thank you, Nadine Alcover replied very quickly, turning her eyes away, not for the moment.

I understand, said Tausk, I understand. But if you change your mind, it's in the freezer. So, anyway. Let's take a look.

But it was then that everything went wrong, initially in that domain of calm and silence mentioned by Lou Tausk when Hubert's assistant arrived: from a nearby apartment, the whir of a drill started up. And yes, I know that is a lot of drills in a relatively short time in the same story, but what can I do? That's just how it is. Beginning quietly, the whir became a whine that quickly grew loud enough to compromise a serene examination of the dossier. At first, they acted as if they couldn't hear the drill, before raising their voices and frowning, repeating or asking the other to repeat what had been said, and in that way the hushed atmosphere that Tausk had wanted was completely ruined.

In normal circumstances, you need to use a drill only once to hang up a painting, twice to fix a curtain rod, three or four times for a bathroom mirror, and not more than a dozen times for a set of shelves. And in all these cases, they are only temporary operations, brief monotone drones that last no longer than twenty seconds . . . an everyday nuisance, annoying for the neighbors but generally pretty brief: you roll your eyes and then it's over. But this was different. Its rumble—so powerful that you might have suspected it of coming not from an ordinary drill but from some kind of genetically manipulated machine tool: the illicit progeny of a jackhammer and a bulldozer with chromosomes from a power jigsaw—became an increasingly loud roar that, far from content to emit a single note, kept modulating as it swelled, yowling like a cat or trumpeting like an elephant depending on its angle of attack, perhaps, or the depth, resistance, or density of the material it was drilling through.

This machine soon showed such modal inventiveness that, to begin with, it didn't hesitate to hum the first notes of the hymn "À

Toi la Gloire, Ô Ressuscité"—albeit without, as is traditional, following it with the line "À toi la victoire, pour l'eternité"—morphing furtively into the chorus to "Standing on the Corner" before going wild in a tribute to the variations improvised by Jimi Hendrix in his famous version of "The Star-Spangled Banner," as performed on Monday, August 18, 1969, at about eight in the morning.

They looked at each other, embarrassed and then apologetic, with half smiles of perplexity. As it was clearly impossible to examine the dossier now, they decided to be patient and wait for the noise to end. It's very nicely decorated, your apartment, shouted Nadine Alcover, just to shout something. I could give you a tour if you like, yelled Tausk, getting to his feet. Follow me. And he showed the assistant into all the rooms in the apartment, where, despite everything, the machine tool seemed to follow them or even precede them, its howl growing ever fiercer. When, despairingly, Tausk suggested they go out to the balcony—so they could admire the view at a lower volume—the machine went into overdrive, perhaps because its operator had opened all the windows to get rid of the dust clouds. And then, suddenly, it went quiet. They exhaled. You can see how calm it is, observed Tausk. Normally, I mean. Let's go back inside. They did, and it was as if the sky had clouded over. It's getting a bit dark; I'm going to turn on a lamp, he announced, walking over to the lamp in question.

But apparently the drill's operator had only taken a brief pause, enough time to go for a piss or make some coffee or both. Whatever he did, it seemed to have re-energized him, because when it started up again, his power tool was even louder than before, if that's possible, first sounding like high-pitched flatulence and then opening its new recital with an audacious variation on the first movement of *The Rite of Spring*.

The noise's unexpected resurgence made Tausk jump as he was leaning over the lamp, and he must have pressed too hard on the switch because it emitted a flash of light, accompanied by a dull crack and followed by a brief puff of smoke, and then the power went out throughout the entire apartment, silencing Kathleen Ferrier, whom we'd hardly heard at all amid this racket, though she had provided a discreet background presence.

Tausk's visible discouragement, his extreme helplessness—because he knows nothing about electricity and cannot do anything with his ten fingers except, in an emergency, on a keyboard—were so obvious that Nadine Alcover couldn't help noticing. A little disconcerted, but far less distraught than her host, she tried to calm him down by assuring him that it was probably nothing, that there was no reason to get upset, it must have just short-circuited. Or it could be the fuses. While indicating that she wasn't especially good with her hands either, she thought she might be able to fix it because it would probably be very simple. But first, where was the fuse box? And second, did Tausk have a flashlight?

After Tausk took a moment to recall where those two things might be, Nadine Alcover got up on a chair to inspect the fuse box. Already Tausk felt slightly better: there was nothing more comforting than a woman who was happy to take care of this type of thing. On top of the chair, Hubert's assistant put on her glasses and, raising her voice (because of the altitude and the continuing din of the machine tool), diagnosed in professional-sounding tones that she could see what was wrong, and it wasn't anything to worry about, but did he happen to have a screwdriver handy? Tausk knew that he didn't have much in the way of tools in the apartment, but he felt sure there had to be something like that, in a box somewhere with a tape measure, a roll of duct tape, and a box cutter. He went off to look for them, then remembered that he had a box containing six screwdrivers arranged by size, still in their packaging. He found it. Things were looking up.

But unfortunately, they soon looked down again, because those screwdrivers were all either slightly too big or slightly too small for the screw, each one passing the buck while blaming its neighbor and laughing behind its hand, as if they were all conspiring to appear incompetent. We need hardly remind you that it is not a good idea to buy screwdrivers in a group, as they are often a bad influence on one another. As for the machine tool, it wasn't showing any signs of flagging, now launching into a rendition of the "Galgenlied" from Schoenberg's *Pierrot Lunaire*.

Still perched on her chair, Nadine Alcover did manage to finish the job, despite having to ask Tausk several times to keep the flashlight beam aimed at the fuse box. The operation took no more than five minutes, enough time for Tausk to observe that the assistant was left-handed, deft but left-handed, and also to take a good look at her legs and what they led up to—hence the deviations of the flashlight beam. They are always a little disconcerting, left-handed people: we imagine them having a special interior life, hidden discord, inner torments, a very private suffering. All of this is almost certainly unfounded, but it can make them seem quite touching. For instance, it is difficult to imagine a left-handed torturer, even if there are probably lots of them.

And so, in the space of less than a second, all the lights in the apartment came back on and Kathleen Ferrier started singing again, at least as far as you could tell under the thunder of the machine tool, which was clearly being used for a very big job. Once Nadine Alcover had come down from the chair, they spontaneously agreed to have a drink, to celebrate the successful conclusion of the operation. Tausk suggested champagne, so they had a glass of bubbly each, and then another.

In any case, it wasn't possible to calmly study Constance's dossier as they had intended, because the conditions of quiet and comfort were still missing. All the same, though, there was no need to go their separate ways just yet; what they had been through together had brought them closer. So, we may as well finish off this bottle, don't you think? said Tausk. Nadine Alcover had enthusiastically agreed, and Tausk had smiled at her as he poured it, batting his eyelids and spilling some of the champagne. Nadine Alcover smiled in the same teasing spirit and soon they had done everything they needed to end up in Lou Tausk's bed together.

Nadine Alcover really was left-handed, but, contrary to perceived wisdom, she was also very good with her hands. In any case, we know that the sexual organs are ambidextrous, and there lies one of their advantages: right-handers and left-handers can, with the same ingenuity, stimulate any genitalia that come to hand. So anyway, everything went very well, for a very long time, several times over. And, from the point of view of the neighbors, the machine tool at least had the advantage of covering up the vigorous expressions of satisfaction emitted by Nadine Alcover.

She left Tausk's apartment that evening, just in time for a meeting with a female friend in one of those chic, quiet bars—leather, copper, varnished wood—where you sit on a high stool, legs crossed, looking around out of the corners of your eyes. Nadine Alcover was expecting to find her friend on one of those stools, in front of her first Alexander, already being chatted up by some old flame. But she was wrong: in fact, her friend had taken refuge at the very back of the room, facing the wall, at a discreet table with only a club soda, and it took Nadine Alcover a while to find her. Physically, the two women are complete opposites: while Hubert's assistant is all smiles, luxuriantly thick hair and generous curves, her friend is reserved, skinny, with dull, thin blond hair. On top of that, she did not look very well: slumped shoulders, waxy complexion, miserable expression.

She managed a feeble half smile when she saw Nadine Alcover, who ordered a gin fizz, and then the two women talked about various things, some trivial, some not: clothes, work, men, but all of this on a general level, without any anecdotes or particular confidences. So, Nadine Alcover did not mention her afternoon with Tausk, and her friend didn't mention what she'd been up to either. But listen, said Nadine Alcover, you look kind of pale, are you sure you're okay? I'm fine, her friend replied. A bit tired at the moment but I'm okay. And what's that, Lucile? Nadine Alcover frowned, pointing to a large bandage around the other woman's left pinkie. What happened to your finger? Oh, said Lucile, that's nothing really, just a little domestic accident.

Ah, exclaimed Nadine Alcover, no one realizes how important domestic accidents are! Did you know it's the third biggest cause of death, after cancer and heart disease? Can you imagine how many people must die in France every year from domestic accidents? More than twenty thousand! You had a lucky escape, if you think about it.

II

15

IT'S BEEN A LONG TIME since we saw General Bourgeaud, hasn't it? It was right at the beginning of our story, when he was organizing this operation with Paul Objat, while caressing cigarillos in his office.

That office hasn't changed much since the last time we saw it. There is another box of Panters (a different type) within the general's reach, near the empty ashtray, but the same arrows and pictures are still taped or pinned to the wall, albeit enriched with some recent additions: two-day-old press cuttings, not-yet-dog-eared Post-its, new photographs, and various other signs that the case is progressing. The only notable change: the computer has been hooked up to some new wires and electronic gizmos.

The general hasn't changed much either. If he hadn't been a general, it's hard to imagine what he would have done with his life, given his bearing, his physique, and his facial appearance. Short, sturdy, neat, crew-cut hair, facial paralysis (more or less deliberate): he is the perfect incarnation of the archetype of a general, as played by Erich von Stroheim. Even if we have seen or even known butchers, foreign exchange brokers, Franciscan monks, or high school principals who looked very much like him, and even if Erich von Stroheim also played other roles: butler, telepath, English teacher,

Beethoven . . . But let's not digress too much, because Bourgeaud is growing impatient.

The bells of Notre-Dame-des-Otages tolled three times quite a while ago, and the vexed general has just slammed shut the lid of his Panter Sprint box when finally there is a knock at the door. Enter, the general bluntly commands, and once again we see Paul Objat as he steps into the office: it's been a while since we saw him too, we think; at least, that's the impression we have. You're late, Objat, the general noted, glancing at his watch rather than his visitor. Enter. Sit down. What news?

It's coming along, Paul Objat replied. It's brewing, if I may put it that way. And will it need to brew for much longer? the general asked, concerned. I'm not sure, said Objat. It's like with cookery, don't you think? You have to check on it from time to time, brown it, deglaze it, add the right spices at the right moment, you know how it is. Not at all, said the general. Of course you do, said Objat, it's simple, I can make you understand. Take an eggplant curry, for example. Absolutely not, said the general impatiently, let's get back to the facts. Let me remind you that it's out of the question for this affair to be traced back to us. I'm counting on you to have put together something solid. A girl who just vanishes like that, it has to be justified.

All taken care of, General, Objat reassured him. Everything is in place. It took me a while to hand out the roles. It's not easy, casting something like this. You have to tweak it to get it right, but I think it's all sorted now. Everyone is playing his part. They have no idea what they're doing, but they're all doing what I planned. Perfect, sighed the general, good to hear, good to hear. That reminds me of the title of a novel by Balzac, he confided, *Les Comédiens sans le savoir*, I don't know if you know it. Ah, no, not at all, said Objat, I've never read it. Well, neither have I, obviously, exclaimed the general, but the title is very good, don't you think?

Paul Objat flashed his handsome smile at the general, who, satisfied with this reply, took a Panter from the box, examined it, then pulled himself together again: Good, and in terms of a deadline, could we hazard a guess at a date? As I said, Objat responded, the subject is not yet fully ripe, but the process is well on its way. It'll take a while longer before the girl is à point. Because here, unlike in the kitchen, if I may return to that analogy, the cooking time is variable. It's a question of terrain.

It mustn't drag on for too long, though, grumbled Bourgeaud. I have contacts in many places who are growing impatient. I understand perfectly, Objat acknowledged, but I would say that the subject should be operational within two or three months. That is very, very long, two or three months. The general exhaled, consulting his watch again. But all right, if you're sure about this. I'll see you again in two weeks. Now, please excuse me but I have things to do. Fall out.

Paul Objat left the office, went downstairs, walked through the barracks courtyard, showed his badge to the guard, and found himself back on the sidewalk. He lifted the collar of his raincoat and buttoned it up to the top. The sky above Boulevard Mortier was clouding over.

16

ELEVEN IN THE MORNING, Rue du Faubourg-Saint-Denis: in his kitchen, wearing a bathrobe and rubber gloves, Lessertisseur washes the dishes while listening to the radio, before taking a shower, shampooing his bald pate, and putting foundation over his New Guinea birthmark.

Lessertisseur piles a good week's worth of dirty plates and dishes into the sink, in order of decreasing diameter. Various contours—dry splinters and frozen sludges—are stuck to the surfaces of these plates. The telephone rings every five minutes, distracting Lessertisseur from the radio. Each time, the caller ID shows Lucile's number, but he does not pick up: Lucile has played her role, and that's all for now. She needs to stop bothering him. He keeps having to turn up the volume on the radio, which is not very practical—the glove slips off the knob—but he is determined to listen to this program until the end, when the presenter concludes: We have been talking today to Marie-José Sureau, whose book *Palimpsest of Shadow* is published by Éditions du Frein.

Later, washed, shaved, made up, and dressed, Lessertisseur types a number into the phone that he must know by heart, having been ordered not to write it down anywhere. Using a classic code, he lets it ring twice before hanging up, lets it ring twice more, hangs up, calls again, and waits for it to be answered—and after eight rings, a voice responds. It is the voice of the silent partner. What? asks the harsh voice. We're not making progress, Lessertisseur complains. The target isn't reacting. I've told you a hundred times, the silent partner says angrily, only to call me if you're making progress. I know, says Lessertisseur, but we're really not making progress at all. It just seems to be dragging on forever. It's stagnating, you see. Silence from the silent partner. I was thinking, says Lessertisseur. Go on, the silent partner condescends. Well, it's just my point of view, coughs Lessertisseur. But that point of view is as follows.

Bearing in mind that it's been going on for months now, that the project is not advancing, and that Tausk—No names on the phone, grunts the silent partner—is not reacting to any stimulation, Lessertisseur suggests they start another project. Without increasing his own commission, he offers to make his staff—presumably Jean-Pierre and Christian—available for another, more profitable operation. There are lots of vulnerable rich people on the market. We could get ten times more out of them than out of Tausk. Especially as he's really not budging, that guy Tausk. I said no names, the silent partner sighs, exasperated. And we are not going to change the target. I have my reasons. All right, says Lessertisseur resignedly, it was just a suggestion. And don't breathe a word of this to anyone, obviously, adds the silent partner. I never tell anyone anything, claims Lessertisseur. Compared to me, the grave is positively chatty.

Lessertisseur hangs up, then dials Jean-Pierre's number. Everything's fine, answers Jean-Pierre. We have the situation in hand. The young lady is very calm. And Victor? asks Lessertisseur anxiously. Does he still drop by occasionally? Victor is unreachable, complains Jean-Pierre. We haven't seen him for quite a while. All right, let me speak to Christian, says Lessertisseur. Christian, listen to me, he warns Christian in similar terms to the warning Victor already gave to Christian. I know you, Christian. I'm aware of your qualities, but I'm also aware of your weak points. So behave properly with this lady, you understand? I'm counting on you. I mean it, I'm really counting on you. Okay, grumbles Christian evasively into the phone, while with his other hand he flicks through the handbook for a DVD player.

To pass the time—the life of a hostage taker leaves quite a bit of leisure time—Jean-Pierre and Christian have brought this DVD player with them, along with about twenty cases containing, on the one hand, American crime series that sometimes include kidnapping scenes, which they obviously identify with very enthusiastically, and on the other hand, works in a genre that involves very little dialogue, presided over by flimsily dressed and impressively endowed creatures with names such as Jewel De Nyle, Chloé Dior, and Karma Rosenberg, or even Bolivia Samsonite.

That day's movie stars Miss Samsonite, who accomplishes everything an artist accustomed to such roles can accomplish: in other words, always the same thing, in varying degrees of excellence. But Bolivia Samsonite accomplishes all these things very well indeed, and, watching her, Jean-Pierre and Christian both find themselves admiring her as much as they envy her partners. Christian gets very hard while he watches, Jean-Pierre slightly less so.

Don't you think she looks a bit like the girl? Christian eventually asks. What girl? mutters Jean-Pierre. The one we're guarding, specifies Christian. You're right, acknowledges Jean-Pierre. Maybe she does the same kind of thing, daydreams Christian. Maybe, Jean-Pierre nods. We should find out, insinuates Christian. Then, without any further comments, they watch the movie until its happy ending.

After which, to kill time, they play a game of dice. An hour later, Christian wins.

What if we tried? he starts to daydream again. Tried what? asks Jean-Pierre. Well, the girl, you know, if we tried our luck? We could try, couldn't we? I don't know, muses Jean-Pierre. Not all three at the same time, he qualifies, at least not right away. I agree completely, says Christian. You're right, we should take things gradually. So, to start with, it's either you or me. How do we decide? No idea, declares Jean-Pierre. We could play dice for it, Christian smiles slyly. That's kind of shocking, protests Jean-Pierre. Nothing ventured, nothing gained, Christian reminds him, taking the dice from his pocket. Another game? If you want, sighs Jean-Pierre. Christian wins again and says triumphantly: It's me! I get to screw the idiot's wife.

As it is also getting chilly in Creuse that day, Constance has not gone out to her sun lounger under the lime tree, preferring to stay in her room, which has been summarily moved upstairs, above the shared living room. It has to be said that she really quite likes it here, peacefully reading on her bed, shunning the bestsellers bought by her guards in order to devote herself to the Quillet encyclopedia. She is currently in the middle of volume *F–K*. You might think she is advancing very quickly. You might also suspect her of skipping quite a few entries.

Constance puts the book down and gets up to make a cup of tea. Opening the window, she sees some picturesque fog enveloping and enshrouding the landscape, including the lime tree, like a special effect intended to conceal while revealing all the outlines. Then she lies on her back with her legs up and knees bent, the encyclopedia resting heavily on her thighs, turning the pages with her right hand, holding her cup in her left, her pinkie finger pointing outward and—as we have surmised by now—perfectly unharmed.

Constance is leafing through the book when Christian knocks at the door, opens without awaiting a response, and enters like a conqueror, absolutely cocksure, before immediately making some rather heavy-handed advances—I'll spare you the details—on the young woman. Although she obviously understands the nature and aim of these advances, Constance prefers to ignore them while smiling faintly—the indulgent smile of a distracted mother, a nun interrupted while praying, a social worker well versed in children acting out. Christian, who is not as dumb as we might think, very quickly realizes the futility of his actions, which, lacking in patience and subtlety, are doomed to failure. Blaming himself for his inadequate strategy, he forces himself to put on a brave face.

Now, you remember that we mentioned the unusually large number of butterflies in Creuse this summer? Well, one of them just entered through the window. Triangular in shape and enormous in wingspan, swooping and gliding around the room, it is a splendid specimen of an Old World swallowtail with straw-colored wings edged with scarlet and cobalt markings, decorated with fringes and dark stripes. While it floats, quivering, toward the bed where Constance lies, eyes wide as she watches it in silence, Christian can contain himself no longer. Probably jealous of the admiration she seems to feel for this new arrival, and wanting to justify his own presence by his concern for the young woman's comfort, he starts waving his hand at the swallowtail to shoo it away, as if it were a mere pest. But as the swallowtail haughtily ignores him, Christian grabs hold of the butterfly and crushes its body in the hollow of his palm, tearing its vast wings to pieces with a faint, fabric-like rustle. There you go, he says proudly, it won't bother you anymore. Get out, Constance says angrily. Fuck off.

She starts to tremble. It's the first time since she was captured, but it's over quickly. When it's over, Constance heads toward the window. Just as she is about to close it, a helix of fog enters the room. It, too, dissipates pretty quickly, dissolving almost instantly above the oil radiator.

17

ON THURSDAY MORNING, Lou Tausk is at his apartment on Rue Claude-Pouillet, detained there by maintenance work. He hasn't been back to the studio on Rue de Pali-Kao in quite some time. As Pélestor is going through an even darker tunnel than usual, the two men have postponed their partnership until the lyricist's mood has stabilized. The maintenance work consists in checking the electrical circuit: the outage the other day led Tausk to call up a handyman he often uses who goes by the name of Hyacinth.

Though his day job is a driver on the Paris metro, Hyacinth is indeed very handy when it comes to working around the house, and he is also pretty quick and not very expensive. A likable, extremely attractive man, he is faithful to the origins of his name, the Hyacinth having driven the entire Greek pantheon alphabetically mad with love, from Apollo to Zephyr. So, a bit like him, only preferring girls, Hyacinth could indeed seduce practically anyone he wanted: he was always flanked by an attractive woman in his driver's cab, never the same one, and their presence never disturbing the smooth running of the network. As he is busy, for the moment, reorganizing the fuse box in Tausk's home before leaving for his next shift on Line 2, the telephone rings. It's Nadine Alcover, who asks Tausk if he'd like to have lunch with her. Okay, says Tausk, and maybe we can do something afterward? Yes, promises Nadine Alcover.

Excited by this prospect, Tausk goes to the bathroom to inspect himself. Staring into the mirror, he pushes back his hair, then calls the hairdressing salon: a slot open in an hour . . . Good, I'll take it, he says. On the off chance, he tries to get hold of Pélestor, and—after it rings six times without response—leaves a basic message on his voice mail: Hope you're feeling better, call me back when you get a chance, etcetera. There is a very good reason why Pélestor does not answer his cell phone: because it is, at that moment, lost under an unmade bed, surrounded by crumbs, fruit peelings, abundant dust bunnies, ancient tissues, and stray pills and capsules with their crumpled package inserts, while Pélestor himself, dressed in pajamas, is avoiding his reflection in the bathroom mirror as he sorts into categories (anxiolytics and antidepressants, narcotics and other sedatives) his opulent collection of psychotropic drugs.

And so, leaving Hyacinth to his fuses—and agreeing that they will meet up later—Tausk goes out to get his hair cut. He is assigned the same woman he saw the other day—pierced, tattooed, rugged and muscular, cold-eyed and unsmiling—but this time opts to keep his mouth shut and wait for it to be over. After a robust hair wash, however, once he is in the chair, immobilized under a towel, half-strangled by the string of the apron, blinded by an interrogation-style spotlight, he hears: Don't I know you from somewhere? The hairdresser stares at him while she rubs her hands. Well, yeah, says Tausk warily, I came here last month. No, it's not that, she replies, dismissing this possibility with a sinister swish of scissors, I'm sure I've seen your face somewhere else. Tensed in his seat, frowning at the scissor blades, Tausk says, Oh? Well, I guess it's possible. Could I have seen you in a magazine? the hairdresser suggests, choosing a razor. Uh, says Tausk, growing even tenser, I suppose you could have. I even wonder if I've seen you on TV, she insists. Maybe, acknowledges Tausk, sweating profusely now, but if so it was a long, long time ago. The hairdresser is silent for a moment as the clippers attack his temples; then she offers a hypothesis. You wouldn't be a pop star by any chance, would you?

And that is how Tausk comes, quickly and unexpectedly, to get on friendly terms with this hairdresser, who, having identified her client, completely changes in terms of her behavior and attitude. Not only does she easily remember the artist's name; she recalls some of his hits (Ah, "Excessif," of course, she says, clearly moved, how many times have I danced to that . . .), even the less successful "Dent de Sagesse," which, she admits, made her cry more than once. She seems keen to prolong their time together almost indefinitely, and Tausk has to step in to avoid finding himself with a shaved head. He leaves a magisterial tip and dashes off.

Having finished her shift, the hairdresser dreamily swept up the scattered locks of hair before going home, where she was preparing lunch and listening to the radio—it was Georges Aspern this time, who had just played "Oublions" by Bradoc & Bradoc—when she heard a key turn in the lock and Clément Pognel walked into the room: Did you have a good morning, my darling?

Just the usual, replied Pognel, how about you? Oh, pretty normal too, she answered. Ah, except I saw that guy again. That guy? Pognel repeated. The one whose hair I cut the other day, Marie-Odile elaborated. I told you about him. Well, he came back. I thought he reminded me of someone, and I was right. He's a pop star, can you believe it? I'm sure you've heard some of his stuff. Really? said Pognel, stiffening. What does he look like? How can I put this? Marie-Odile wondered. And what's his name? insisted Pognel.

———

On Thursday afternoon, after carefully categorizing his medications, Pélestor arranged them in order of effect, checked their quantities, and verified their expiration dates. Then he must have changed his mind because, suddenly removing them from their packaging, he threw the contents of each bottle down the toilet. After emptying all his vials down there too, he flushed everything away, put on his coat, and buttoned it up to his neck.

Getting ready to go out, he checked four times that the windows were shut and that he hadn't left the water running or the gas on. Then, dawdling on the landing outside his open door, he took his key from his pocket and examined it to make sure—even though it was the only key he possessed—that it was the right one. He double-locked the door and left his building, then started walking toward the closest metro station, Colonel Fabien. On the platform for the train heading to Porte Dauphine, Pélestor followed the countdown minute by minute on the liquid crystal display screen where the arrival of the next few trains are displayed (1ST TRAIN 02 MIN, 2ND TRAIN 06 MIN) above the time (17:02).

As for Tausk, at four thirty he was heading toward the Courcelles station to take the Line 2 train in the other direction. After eating lunch, he'd enjoyed a pleasant session with Nadine Alcover, which put him in a good enough mood that he decided to go and work in the studio. He stood at the end of the platform for the train going toward Nation, in line with the front car, and in his mind revisited the greatest hits of the afternoon's session.

When the train surged out of the tunnel, Tausk recognized Hyacinth in the driver's cab, who signaled that he should join him. I don't want to butt in, Tausk said as he smiled, gesturing with his chin at the latest attractive woman to be sitting next to Hyacinth. No problem, smiled Hyacinth in return. Get out here, Geneviève, he affectionately ordered the woman. I'll see you later, eight o'clock at the Cintra, okay? Geneviève nodded, smiled at Tausk—what a smiley scene this is—and left him her place in the cabin. And so we set off toward Nation.

In the tunnels, dotted with pale fluorescent lights, Hyacinth first brought up the fuse box, which should last a few years but will eventually have to be replaced by a new model that meets current standards. Then, after Anvers station, the train went aboveground and Tausk and Hyacinth talked about the city around them, the way this area was changing and its probable future—plans for renovation, the demolition and construction of buildings, whether or not to continue providing train lines from the Gare du Nord and the Gare de l'Est, the development of the Bassin de la Villette and the Nicolas Ledoux rotunda—before they plunged underground again after Jaurès. The station after Jaurès, if you are heading eastward, is called Colonel Fabien, and that is where things went horribly wrong.

They were about to enter the station, watching as the yellowish vaulted ceiling grew clearer, as if through a zoom lens, against the black background, when they also saw a man at the end of the platform calmly descend onto the rails. The man lay down in front of the train, then turned his head to see it arrive, even attempting to look the driver in the eyes, and perhaps also the other occupant of the cabin: Tausk, recognizing Pélestor with horror, will never know if his former partner identified him before the impact. Hyacinth honked his horn for all it was worth, while punching the emergency brake so hard that he drew blood without even realizing it, and started screaming so he wouldn't hear the sound of the collision, so that his voice would fill the cabin and drown out the dreadful thud of impact.

As soon as the train came to a halt, Hyacinth followed the usual procedure for such cases, blocking the doors and making an announcement. We have just run over someone, he forced himself to declare. Would everyone please remain seated while we wait for the emergency services to arrive. As he was announcing this, he set off the alarms that would stop the next train coming in the other direction: the man under his train might not be completely dead, so better not to let him be finished off by the one coming the other way. After that, he called the dispatcher, who, surveying the traffic on the network, is the metro's equivalent of a control tower.

I've just run over a customer, stammered Hyacinth to the dispatcher. My train has stopped, so has the line next to mine, and we're waiting for the emergency services. Without any audible emotion, the dispatcher asked Hyacinth to go and check that the other line was free: Make sure none of the pieces are on the other rails, he ordered the driver. Go down and take a look, and then at least we can let the other trains pass. But Hyacinth said, No, I can't.

They had to wait a moment for a manager on call to arrive, accompanied by a driver who could take over from Hyacinth, after which the police would arrive. It was a very long moment. While Tausk remained in his seat, Hyacinth opened the door between the cab and the first carriage. He walked toward the passengers, and one of them pointed out that he had blood on his pants. Hyacinth, disoriented, said it was the blood of the man who had killed himself before realizing—when he saw the wound in his hand caused by hitting the emergency brake—that it was his own. Then the police arrived. The judiciary police officer told him: Come down with me, we're going to take a look at the body. But again Hyacinth said no, he just couldn't.

While the policeman began writing his report, Hyacinth went back into the cab and Tausk heard him talking to himself, the tears rolling down his handsome face: It's over, whispered Hyacinth, it's all over. A good hour must have passed before he called Geneviève to cancel their date at the Cintra.

18

CHRISTIAN GOT UP FIRST. Slumped over, dragging his heels, he silently left the lodging that had been set up inside the farmhouse for the two henchmen. Jean-Pierre, from his twin bed, watched him go with a frown. After that, he too got up, showered, combed his hair, shaved, then swapped his usual clothes—dusty old jeans, baggy shirt—for something that seemed to him more dressy: synthetic leather pants and a counterfeit Ralph Lauren polo shirt. Outside, he headed over to Constance's flower bed, where he picked a few zinnias and tied them up with a bulrush. He grimaced when he saw his first attempt, then started over with another bulrush.

Back in the farmhouse, he walked through the shared living room—past Christian, who remained motionless on a low stool near the fireplace—went upstairs, grimacing once again as the steps creaked, and reached the tiny landing. In one corner was a green plastic bucket covered with a floorcloth, bleached white. He threw his head back and took two deep breaths before knocking lightly three times on the door.

It opened on Constance, who had not quite finished dressing—her blouse was still unbuttoned, her belt still unbuckled—a fact that did not make Jean-Pierre's task any easier. So, speaking to the right side of the doorframe rather than to the young woman, fiddling with his bouquet without daring to hand it to her, as if it were a hat he'd just removed, he sighed: I am sorry for my colleague, madame. I don't know what got into him the other day. He feels deeply ashamed of himself. The whole incident really disturbed him, and he doesn't dare come up here to apologize in person. Don't worry, Constance reassured him, it's not a big deal. I would just like to say that I disapprove of what he did, Jean-Pierre made clear, still without managing to look the young woman in the eyes, and that I share his embarrassment. Forget it, said Constance. I understand perfectly. The isolation, the lack of women, the boredom . . . I'm sure it's not easy. Hang on while I finish getting ready.

Jean-Pierre waited on the landing, lifting up the lid of the bucket for a moment; then—when Constance emerged—they went downstairs to see Christian, who, sitting in his corner, stared at the floor, too scared to look up at the young woman, and muttered: I am really sorry, madame. I don't know what got into me. Please accept my apologies. It's nothing, Constance reassured him, let's just forget about it. No, it's not nothing, Christian insisted. I behaved like a pathetic loser. In fact, I am a pathetic loser, I know that, and believe me—but, preferring to interrupt, Jean-Pierre coughed behind him.

Anyway, said Constance, let's move on. I want to do the cooking. She looked lively and determined, suddenly keen to take things in hand in a manner—like that of a tourist guide, or a den mother, or a TV game show host—that did not seem to fit with her status as a captive. What can we make for dinner tonight? What would you like to eat? Jean-Pierre and Christian looked at each other without responding. I know a pretty good recipe for duck confit with lentils, she went on. How does that sound? Sounds very, very good to me, said Jean-Pierre, relaxing. I'm going to Bénévent to do the shopping now, said Christian eagerly. What do you need? It's simple, replied Constance: a big can of duck confit and a packet of lentils. And if you can find some raspberry vinegar, that goes perfectly with it. I'll find some, proclaimed Christian frantically, already headed toward the door.

They ate lunch on the go and, all afternoon, the three of them worked in a relaxed atmosphere to prepare the evening meal. Having unearthed a rusty candlestick in the barn, Jean-Pierre furiously cleaned it so that this dinner could be candlelit. After another expedition to Bénévent-l'Abbaye to buy a paper tablecloth, a dessert, some wine, and a can of Miror to get the candlestick really sparkling, Christian arranged a new bouquet of flowers and, at around six o'clock, Constance got started in the kitchen. Dinner went very well. They laughed a lot, drank quite a bit, told lots of stories in a soothing eurythmy that, over the following days, was constantly added to by little acts of kindness and consideration from all sides. Things were changing.

19

OFTEN PEOPLE EXASPERATE US during their lifetime and it is only when they are dead that we see the extent of our loss: that is how it was for Tausk after the suicide of his lyricist. Pélestor had not been without his faults, but not only could he create impossibly catchy words that fitted as tightly as a snake's skin to a bass line; he could also suggest orchestral or rhythmic nuances to that melody that its composer would never have imagined. He was no ordinary wordsmith.

Three fruitless solo sessions at the studio on Rue de Pali-Kao were enough for Tausk to realize the scale of his loss, and, deprived of Pélestorian inspiration, he did not think he could make any progress at all without help. He even, very quickly, had the feeling that he was only a shadow of his former self, a shadow that was rapidly fading. In fact, this feeling was so strong that he was compelled to consider, before it was too late, canceling his latest commitments, tearing up his contracts, breaking with his record label, selling his back catalogue, and forgetting the whole thing. Having considered this, he decided to do it. He should plan to speak with Hubert about it.

There was nothing very audacious about this plan, nothing very risky. Tausk is, as we have already mentioned, in a very comfortable financial position, a position that allows him to live without taking

care of anything at all—except for Nadine Alcover, who is now living in his apartment. It all happened very fast with her, and now
the two of them are practically inseparable. They talk a lot, mostly
in bed, where they are drawing up the classic plan of fleeing to the
end of the world to live happily ever after. But where to flee to? Well,
we'll see. In the meantime, they are enjoying coming up with a list
of possible world's ends. There's no rush to make a decision. So, as
I said, they are mostly inseparable except that, every day, Nadine
Alcover has to keep going to work for Hubert in Neuilly. And soon,
every day seems too much. So they decide that she won't go to work
there anymore. One morning, they prepare to call Hubert. Better to
talk on the telephone than in person; that way, he won't be able to
dust off our jackets, point out a new wrinkle, or inform us that one
of our eyebrows is too bushy. Yes, we'll call him.

In Neuilly, at that very moment, after typing the code into his
fireproof safe, Hubert comes back behind his desk and collapses
into his chair, which is swiveled toward the window overlooking the
interior courtyard. Using his index finger to lift up one of the slats
on the Venetian blinds that cover this view, Hubert watches as his last
visitors walk over to a large cardinal-red Infiniti sedan. Those visitors comprise a small, neat man (belt, laces, tie, all tightly knotted)
followed by a tall man in sports clothing who is carrying an empty
canvas bag over his shoulder. The small man—serrated hair, bowlegs,
rolling gait, frowning at his smartphone—stops and puts on a pair
of sunglasses whose mirror lenses, as he turns around for a moment,
shoot a dazzling reflection at Hubert's eyes. His tooth-filled mouth
cracks into an amphibological smile; then he signals to the tall man
to open the Infiniti's passenger door and dives inside, before the tall
one, after tossing the bag in the sedan's trunk, sits behind the wheel.
The Infiniti sets off and the office telephone rings. Hubert picks

up without taking his eyes off the vehicle. It's me, announces Tausk. Louis.

My dear Louis, how wonderful to hear from you, exclaims Hubert, exaggerating his enthusiasm, though not by much. He seems to be in a good mood and Tausk takes advantage of this by getting straight to the heart of the matter. He has made the decision to put an end to his career. Age, fatigue, money put aside . . . basically, his argument is: I can stop, so I'm stopping. He is, he says, going to retire, in a way, if you see what I mean. He wants to cancel all previously concluded contracts, agreements, and other arrangements—you're the one who has all the papers, how do we go about this? Nothing could be simpler, declares Hubert. I just saw your dossier in the safe. We'll just invent some amendments and termination clauses; I know exactly what to do. So don't worry about it, I'll take care of it all and it'll be wham, bam, thank you, ma'am. Tausk raises an eyebrow at this. All you need to do, Hubert continues, is drop by here to sign a few papers one of these days. Whenever you want. As you like. He swings back and forth in his chair as he says this. He really does appear to be in a very good mood indeed.

You seem very happy, says Tausk. What's going on? How could I not be? Hubert smiles. My clientele is evolving and I am diversifying. I am opening myself up to new perspectives, accumulating excellent commissions, and I'm using the money to buy new works. I've been enriching my collection of art from the 1910s, you remember. And indeed he is, through the open door of his office, watching a factotum on a stepladder who is at this moment hanging a recently acquired work on the wall of the waiting room: a very large nude with a very long neck by Jean-Gabriel Domergue, intended to form a pair—same epoch, same school, same style—with the Tancrède Synave in the entrance hall. I'm pleased for you, says Tausk, but there is something else I wanted to talk to you about. Hang on two seconds, says Hubert, swiveling the chair back to face the window.

A massive black Hummer H2 with jacked-up wheels and tinted windows has just entered the interior courtyard. A man who looks like an accountant gets out. With his heavy eyelids and frameless glasses, he resembles the French actor Jean Bouise. He is followed by two guys who look like loss-prevention officers: dark suits, tinted sunglasses covering the kind of eyes you wouldn't want to meet. As he walks, the supposed accountant opens a slender briefcase from which he extracts some stapled sheets of paper; behind him, each security guard carries two voluminous, apparently very heavy beige leather bags, and Hubert smiles again at their weight. Okay, go ahead, he tells Tausk, who in turn says, Hang on. Then: Here's Nadine.

Like someone tiptoeing through a minefield, Nadine Alcover loses herself in fearful circumlocutions as she attempts to express her desire to quit her job at Hubert's office, anxious as she is that her employer will take the news badly. But no, not at all: I understand completely, Nadine, the lawyer interrupts her. You have your own life to lead. Even going so far as to offer her a severance payment, he implies that replacing her will not pose any difficulties: I have someone else in mind, in fact, a blonde, quite attractive, not as pretty as you, Nadine, obviously, but she works very well, so don't worry, I'll be fine. Could you pass me back to Louis? I wanted to ask you something. Go ahead, says Tausk. Tell me, Louis, says Hubert, have you had any news about Constance? No, replies Tausk. Then they hang up without further comment. What did he want? asks Nadine Alcover. Nothing, says Tausk.

Hey, suggests Nadine Alcover, why don't I organize a dinner party to celebrate? Celebrate what? asks Tausk. Well, you, says Nadine Alcover, me. You know, us. To mark the occasion. With guests. I'll invite a friend of mine. She's a bit unusual, but you'll like her. And she's in love with an older guy too. What do you mean by that? Lou Tausk says, frowning. He touches one of his cheeks and, without re-plying, Nadine Alcover brushes her fingers against his temple, which is, let's be honest, graying. Ah yes, Tausk admits, I'll take care of it. I have plenty of time now, after all. It is ten in the morning.

At about eleven, he returns to the hairdressing salon, where the employee, wriggling excitedly at the sight of him, expresses her surprise at seeing him again so soon after his last visit. It's for my temples, says Tausk, pressing his fingers against them as if he had a headache, to color them. First time? asks Marie-Odile. First time, confirms Tausk, sitting down. I'm going to start by opening up your cuticles a little bit, explains the hairdresser as she picks up a bottle of peroxide, to help the dye get into the roots. She applies the product to his hair, first with a brush and then with a tail comb. I'm going to put you under a dryer for a little while now. Under a dryer? Tausk panics. Well, yeah, she says, it helps to even out the pre-softening. Would you like some magazines to read while you wait?

Once the lengths and tips are dry, Tausk returns to the chair and Marie-Odile picks up her brush again. Tongue sticking out sideways from her mouth as she coats each hair in turn with dye, she brings up a few obvious topics of conversation: the weather, the places they live, the vacations they're planning. Then, venturing into more inti-mate terrain: And are you married? Tausk avoids the question. We're going to pause for a little while again, decides Marie-Odile, to give the pigments time to take.

After which, standing next to her customer and contemplating his reflection, she appears satisfied and starts coating the hairs again. As for me, she confides, I have a steady boyfriend now, and believe me, that changes everything. I'm pleased for you, Tausk responds politely.

Is he good to you? Good to me? Oh, like you wouldn't believe, the hairdresser exclaims before starting to list the virtues of her steady boyfriend, his habits, his tastes, his physical appearance down to the tiniest details, among them the fact that he has a W-shaped scar on his cheek. Tausk shivers. Don't move like that, Marie-Odile orders him, or it'll go everywhere. The word *good* doesn't do him justice, she goes on. In fact, his name really suits him. Clément—it's a nice name, don't you think? Well anyway, that's him, down to a tee. And this time, Tausk jumps as a flashback runs through his mind: thirty years earlier, Avenue de Bouvines, the bank, the security guard lying in a pool of blood, the desperate getaway. Pognel, he says, through gritted teeth. The name escapes his lips before he can prevent it. Instantly he regrets it, but it's too late. She heard.

Do you know him? cries Marie-Odile. Not at all, blusters Tausk, it's just what you said vaguely reminded me of someone. You know him, of course you do, Marie-Odile exclaims delightedly, you just said his name. No, he insists, no, but she is not listening anymore, too busy marveling over the vagaries of fate, the odds against such coincidences, and the smallness of the world. Hey, she decides, I'm finishing earlier than usual this morning. I'm going to pick him up from his job. He always says he doesn't want me to meet him there, but I'm sure he'll be happy. I can't wait to see the look on his face when I tell him about this. Alas, it is too late for Tausk to say no. No. Absolutely not.

20

THE FOLLOWING AFTERNOON, as we had nothing better to do and happened to be in the area, we discreetly slipped into Lessertisseur's apartment, on the left-hand side of the third floor of a poorly maintained building on Rue du Faubourg-Saint-Denis. Closing the door silently behind us, we stood at one end of a corridor with a succession of rooms leading off to the right. From where we stood, we could make out a brightly lit kitchen, a dark bathroom, and a softly lit bedroom. Coming from the last of these, we could hear music: the volume was on low, but we instantly recognized the Boz Scaggs album *Silk Degrees*. The corridor—opaque or luminous depending on the radiance of the rooms leading off it—ended with what looked like a living room, though we could see only one corner of it from our vantage point: a tired armchair covered with a brown batik cloth, a wobbly shelf with an old-fashioned corded phone on it, a triangle of tatty carpet. Behind the armchair was a lamp with a dirty shade that gave a halo of light from an economy bulb.

So the corridor was strongly lit at the entrance to the kitchen, dark a little farther on, dimly lit outside the bedroom, and brighter at the end, next to the living room: we moved forward. The kitchen, no bigger than a closet, was stuffed full of household electrical appliances, each with a digital clock displaying a different time, none of them correct. On the ceiling, the light dispensed by a large circular fluorescent tube, designed for a room six times bigger than this one, was dully reflected from the acrylic and Formica surfaces or from grubby pans and filthy plates. Three plastic bags overflowing with trash swayed on the tile floor. We continued on our way, passing the bathroom, and, as we came level with the bedroom, we glanced in to see what was happening there.

Well, at some point, there had to be a bit of explicit sex in this story. On his bed, at the far end of that bedroom, Lessertisseur was lying on his back, mostly dressed, while Lucile was crouched between his legs, administering what is sometimes known as a blow job. And as she was proceeding in a manner—slow and deep—particularly beloved of Maurice Lessertisseur, he was happy. But just as "What Do You Want the Girl to Do?" entered its final fade-out, the cell phone on the nightstand started to ring. Lessertisseur moved slowly so he could pick up the phone without causing Lucile to interrupt her action. In fact, he encouraged her to continue, whispering, Keep going, this makes it even sexier. And then, three seconds later, covering the lower part of the phone: Stop a minute, this is serious. It's him. Lucile slid off to the side, sniffling, while Lessertisseur cleared his throat and said: I'm listening. This is dragging on too long, the voice of the silent partner announced bluntly. We have to meet, very soon. Of course, sighed Lessertisseur. Later this afternoon, for example? No, said his superior, now.

So a meeting was arranged in a bar located a ten-minute walk from Lessertisseur's home, on the corner of Rue du Faubourg-Poissonnière and Rue d'Abbeville, opposite an art nouveau corner building situated at number 14 featuring beautifully sculpted caryatids whose stirring breasts, exposed to the eyes of all, would perhaps, given how things are, be forbidden these days. In the meantime, Lessertisseur buttoned up his pants, informing Lucile that he had to leave and, as she insisted on accompanying him, he rashly said yes. And so they went there.

He immediately spotted his silent partner at the back of the bar—slender, pale, fashionably dressed—and Lessertisseur snickered inwardly at the fact that the man had thought it necessary to wear dark glasses. I'm very annoyed, the silent partner warned him as soon as he reached the table. What are you drinking? A club soda for Lessertisseur and, for Lucile, a cup of tea. The silent partner considerately asked if she would like it with milk, sugar, lemon? No, nothing, said Lucile, just au naturel. Thank you, that's kind of you. Yes, agreed the silent partner. When I am especially annoyed, I can be especially kind.

Anyway, he said, let's get to the point. This whole thing is taking way too long. We're not getting anywhere. You're not doing your job properly. Lowering his eyes at this observation, and instead of again suggesting that they drop the job in favor of something more profitable, Lessertisseur had to admit that, yes, it did seem to be stuck in a rut. Although, he went on, from another point of view, strategically it's not so bad. It might be a good idea to let the subject stew. That could produce results. It's happened before. Drumming his fingers on the table as he listened to this, the silent partner—who seemed until this point to be staring at Lessertisseur behind his dark glasses—ended up turning them (they were slowly sliding down his nose toward the cusp of his nostrils) on the fingerstall covering the bandage at the end of Lucile's little finger.

Appearing to immediately grasp what must have happened regarding the phalanx sent to Tausk, he slowly pushed his glasses back up his nose. Well, now, he articulated. What the hell kind of a trick are you trying to play on me with that story of the finger? he shouted, and Lessertisseur was forced to acknowledge that it wasn't the correct finger but, frankly, what difference did it make? The effect was bound to be the same, he argued, and this subterfuge even has the advantage of allowing us to hold more fingers in reserve, just in case. Do you take me for a fool? the silent partner barked, turning pale—which strengthened the contrast between his dark glasses and his white skin. He took a breath and then: You don't really think that's how it works, do you? he yelled quietly (technically, this is possible) as he got to his feet, knocking over the club soda and the unsweetened black tea.

We're going outside so you can give me a better explanation, he said, dropping some cash on the table before pushing and dragging Lessertisseur toward the door: an entertaining spectacle for the other customers, who, imagining a drunkards' brawl, despite the nature of the drinks that had been spilled on their table, were above all surprised that the disproportion between the two men's morphologies (Lessertisseur sturdy, the silent partner frail) did not prevent the latter from expelling the former from the premises. Seeing this, Lucile said in a panicked voice: I think I'll leave you to it, before running off and almost being hit by a car as she blindly fled across Rue de Maubeuge, then disappearing out of sight in Rue Condorcet.

With Lucile and her fingerstall now offscreen, the silent partner unceremoniously guided Lessertisseur toward the end of Rue d'Abbeville, where, at number 5, there was a large parking garage, open 24/7, which had two underground floors. The silent partner, however, did not bother going down to the lowest level before shoving Lessertisseur between two parked cars, in a space hidden from prying eyes. And there, visibly furious, he violently whispered (again, this is technically possible) that, at the risk of repeating himself, he really had the feeling that Lessertisseur took him for a fool. And, matching his words with actions, he took an object from his pocket.

At some point, too, a gun had to appear in our story: this one is an Astra Cub .25 ACP and it is a very attractive semiautomatic pocket pistol, hardly any bigger than a pack of cigarettes, manufactured in Guernica by the company Astra-Unceta y Cia S.A. and easily available through specialist dealers, or even via a simple ad on the Internet, for a sum not exceeding €200.

Intending to use this weapon purely in an intimidatory fashion, the silent partner had taken care to secure the safety, situated to the left, behind the trigger guard. Unfortunately, in his agitation, his thumb clumsily turned off said safety and, as his index finger was, at that moment, quivering on the trigger (pretty sensitive on the Astra Cub), a projectile unexpectedly shot out and pierced Lessertisseur's anatomy, close to his groin. Seeing the big man collapse, the silent partner fled in a panic toward the nearest crossroads—at Place Franz-Liszt—where, by chance, an unoccupied taxi was passing. The driver stopped, picked him up, and took him to his current residence, near the Gambetta metro station.

HE WAS A NERVOUS WRECK by the time he turned into Rue de la Chine. As soon as he opened the door, he was greeted by the smell of an onion omelet—and also by a dog, which—standing on its hind legs, panting and drooling, its forelegs resting on the silent partner's knees—guided him toward the kitchen, where a woman in a flower-patterned apron stood in front of the gas stove and refrained from smiling at him. Oh, it's you, she observed. We didn't see much of you last night. I had things to do, claimed the silent partner, removing the dog's paws from his pant legs before dusting them off. Well, I have a few things to tell you about yesterday, she told him. I had a strange kind of day. This news came as a relief to the silent partner, who, having no desire to describe his own day, was able simply to listen instead. Turning off the gas cooktop, at the risk of letting the omelet (currently being ogled by the quadruped) congeal, the woman sat down and looked at the silent partner with an expression on her face that meant that he, too, should sit down. Which he did.

They stayed like that for a moment, in the kitchen, sitting on either side of the red Formica table with its black metal tube legs, looking at each other. Well, first of all, said the woman at last, with a tense smile, guess who I saw again in the salon, yesterday? That guy. What guy? the silent partner asked, mechanically, still feeling soothed by the beginning of what seemed like a distractingly banal conversation. You know, she said, the guy who's a pop star, Lou something, I can't remember now if I've told you about him already. That was the third time he's come, and we're starting to tell each other things. I remember, said the silent partner, stiffening. So? So he said that he used to know you, back in the old days! That's pretty funny, don't you think? And when I say back in the old days, I get the feeling it was a long time ago. Yeah, that's funny, the silent partner forced himself to reply, without seeming very keen to go into further details.

At that, the woman stood up and carefully poured the omelet onto a plate, gradually increasing the angle of the frying pan until the omelet curled elegantly over itself. As for the tense, vexed silent partner, he started nervously scratching at an imaginary stain on the tabletop. As for the dog, torn between its desire for the omelet, which was urging it to stay in the kitchen, and its perception of the oppressive atmosphere, which was urging it to flee, it no longer knew what to do with itself. As for any readers who have not yet understood that the silent partner's name is Clément Pognel, we are happy to inform them of that fact now.

Marie-Odile sat down again and her expression changed. So, you see, there's something else I'd like to understand. And the tone of her voice, too, seemed to have changed. Go on, muttered Pognel. So it was that she recounted the rest of her morning, after she had dyed the temples of that guy, Lou what's his name. As she did not have any other customers, she had decided to use her spare time to go and pick Pognel up from his workplace. I know you told me that you didn't like that, she acknowledged, but I thought it would make you happy. Just a little surprise, if you like.

Following the directions that Pognel had given her regarding his journey on the metro and then the RER, she had gone to Villeneuve-Saint-Georges, where, after wandering all over the neighborhood, then asking various people for help, she had concluded it wasn't possible that Pognel worked for Titan-Guss as he had assured her, not only because that business was completely unknown in Villeneuve-Saint-Georges, but even more so because a quick Google search had allowed her to discover that the firm Titan-Guss simply did not exist. And I would really like to understand that, she said. Really, I would like you to explain it to me.

We can, and must, admit that, from the point of view of Clément Pognel, this is quite a lot to deal with in a single day. He might just about be able to cope with his meeting with Lessertisseur, and what he did to him in the parking garage on Rue d'Abbeville, as well as what he learned about Lucile's little finger . . . he might. None of that changes very much, and he could probably deal with it. But, first of all, it is highly embarrassing that Tausk should have met Marie-Odile. And then her discovery of the nonexistence of Titan-Guss leads Pognel beyond the realm of embarrassment. There is the very real feeling that he is done for. He could take some time to think, to come up with another tale to cover himself, even if only temporarily. He could—he's seen it done before—but he doesn't think about it, never even considers it, because he sees himself backed against a wall, trapped in a dark passageway, with nothing to cling to, with no way out but to rid himself of his present danger.

And so it was that Clément Pognel, without any premeditation, without really thinking about it at all, took his Astra Cub from his pocket and, not really aiming at anything in particular, simply fired at what was directly in front of him: this time, the .25 ACP projectile entering Marie-Odile Zwang's skull through her right eye, his victim died instantly, watched placidly by Biscuit, who did not even jump at the sound of the gunshot. After that, Pognel sat for a long time on his chair, staring blankly at Marie-Odile's corpse. Then he went to look for the dead woman's cell phone on the kitchen countertop, where the omelet was going cold, and dialed a number. While he waited for it to start ringing, he put a piece of omelet in his mouth and swallowed it without chewing. Biscuit began to sniff his owner's dead body, hesitating before tasting, out of curiosity, the blood that dripped from her eye socket.

Three seconds later, on Boulevard Mortier: I hope you don't mind if I answer that, General, said Paul Objat, his hand reaching into his pocket. You know perfectly well, Objat, grumbled Bourgeaud, that I don't like it when you answer your phone in my office. I know, General, Objat acknowledged, and I'm terribly sorry, but something tells me that maybe—and he pressed the green button on his phone. The general pouted, but in fact Objat was on the phone for only a very short time, not more than thirty seconds, before he pressed the red button, without having spoken a single word. So, was it worth it? Bourgeaud asked sarcastically. Barely, said Objat. There was some news, but it was nothing too serious. It's just that guy Pognel—I have the feeling he's going soft. The general shuddered. Do you think this might compromise our plans? I don't think so, Objat reassured him. He didn't say much, but I can tell he's tired, a bit stressed. He's a moody guy. He's going to take a few days off, but that doesn't make much difference to us. I think everything will be fine.

Good, condescended Bourgeaud. So where exactly are we at the moment, in terms of the operation? Well, said Objat, I would say we're ready. This first phase of the treatment should be coming to an end. I believe we can move on to phase two. Although there is also some news from Creuse. Do you remember, General, about Stockholm and Lima? Well, I fear that's where we are. What on earth are you talking about? the general frowned.

22

EVERYONE REMEMBERS HOW in August 1973, in the Swedish capital, Jan-Erik Olsson, having just escaped prison, held up a branch of the Kreditbanken, took four hostages, and coerced the police into allowing his fellow prisoner Clark Olofsson to join him in the bank. It was difficult to liberate their captives because they were essentially sympathetic to Olsson and Olofsson and didn't want to leave them. Not only did they refuse to testify against them at the trial; they even defended them and—once the verdict had been delivered, and Jan-Erik and Clark were back behind bars—went to visit them regularly. This is what has become known as Stockholm syndrome. It is a classic psychological response, but it is not the only one.

Fewer people remember how, twenty-three years later, in the Peruvian capital, a heavily armed guerrilla commando invaded the Japanese embassy and used the staff members as human shields. Pretty soon, however, developing an affection for their hostages, charmed as they were by their good manners and polite objections, the revolutionaries freed the majority of them. Then, sympathy blossoming into true friendship, the guerrillas who were supposed to liquidate the last hostages in the event of a police intervention admitted that they were incapable of going through with it. This phenomenon became known as Lima syndrome.

A combination of these two syndromes—a coexistence, even a fusion, of the two clinically opposed scenarios—could be designated Creuse syndrome, because, after the evening of the lentil confit, a reciprocal feeling began to grow between Constance and her guards. It reached unprecedented levels of empathy when Jean-Pierre and Christian—not having seen Victor or Lessertisseur for some time—started worrying about what fate those men might have in store for Constance when they did eventually return. Fearing that this event would fracture the new harmony between them and Constance, they decided to steal her away somewhere. In other words, they were going to protect their captive from their own bosses.

Considering various retreats, searching for the most discreet they could find, Jean-Pierre and Christian absented themselves more and more often on scouting missions. Naturally this meant that Constance was left alone, that she was free to flee, but a tacit agreement seemed to exclude this possibility: in fact, it never even entered Constance's head. She actually found there were plenty of things to do here—looking after the garden, helping with the cooking or housecleaning, playing dice or card games, a quick game of badminton with Christian while Jean-Pierre cooked spaghetti, continuing her perusal of the Quillet encyclopedia (she was currently on volume *L–O*).

At last, Jean-Pierre and Christian thought they had found the perfect spot. In the middle of the night, they put Constance in the back of the gray Renault. They did not do this briskly or roughly as they had during her previous transfer; on the contrary, they treated her with the utmost consideration. They had to drive a dozen miles or so, the landscape invisible in the absolute darkness, before parking the car by the side of a minor road. Getting out of the car and quietly closing the doors, they crossed what appeared to be a field, finding their way with the aid of flashlights. They reached a building and opened a narrow door into an empty, circular, windowless room, only a few feet across but very tall: it turned out to be a vertical tube with a metal ladder rising through it. They climbed this ladder together, Jean-Pierre going first, lighting up the darkness ahead of him with his flashlight, Constance following, and Christian below her, shining his flashlight beam anywhere but up so he wouldn't see her legs.

At the top of this tube was a tiny space, a sort of glass-walled cockpit with a control panel (whose function Constance did not grasp) that filled most of the room. Jean-Pierre and Christian had done their best to turn this space into an efficiency apartment: a folding bed, a tiny storage unit containing a few belongings, a shelf where volumes *P–R* and *S–Z* of the Quillet—not yet read by Constance—were arranged. Well, Jean-Pierre admitted, I know it's not very spacious, but at least you'll have plenty of light. And I've heard that in Japan there are capsule hotels with even less space.

Before leaving her, that night, he pointed out to Constance that her only difficulty would be bathroom-related activities. As far as drinking water was concerned, he had brought up two big bottles, but when it came to her ablutions she would have to go back down the ladder. Christian's fixed it so that, when the water arrives, you will be able to use this faucet—protected by a screen made of reeds—behind which, if you will forgive this detail, we've set up a composting toilet. Unfortunately there's no hot water, but the weather's still warm enough for that to be okay. And at least here, no one will bother you. We'll drop by every day to bring you some food. We'll never be far away. And, if you ever have a problem, he concluded—contravening the hostage taker's most basic protocol—here's a cell phone so you can get in touch with us. The charger is here. And the power outlet's over there.

The two men left so she could go to sleep, and the next day, through the floor-to-ceiling windows, Constance was able to enjoy an uninterrupted 180-degree view of a landscape whose geographic location she still knew nothing (and cared even less) about. At regular intervals, the countryside was briefly blacked out by what looked like gigantic clock hands, until she finally realized that they were the blades of a huge propeller and that she was living at the top of one of those wind turbines that you often see as you are driving down a highway. Most people are not aware that, in addition to their function in transforming wind into energy, the latest models are also (in a rudimentary fashion, admittedly) residential.

Jean-Pierre and Christian went back to the farm, apparently doing some kind of work there during the day and at night abandoning all idea of staying there. As there was no hotel in Châtelus-le-Marcheix, they took two rooms at the Campanile in Bénévent-l'Abbaye, knowing that they were abusing their employers and well aware of the consequences of this, but it was Constance's fate that mattered most to them now. They drove to the wind turbine every day. Jean-Pierre took charge of carrying up her food, a battery-powered radio, an old illustrated Larousse dictionary, and an old *Encyclopedia Universalis* that he'd ordered on Amazon but which he had to bring back down because there wasn't enough space for it in the room. Christian, meanwhile, preferred to wait in the car so as not to disturb the young woman's privacy, and also to avoid the risk that he would once again fall victim to his urges.

A few days later, Victor called them to inform them that the plan had changed, that they were going to free Constance, and that they ought to get ready. See you in a couple of weeks, then. Jean-Pierre and Christian appeared evasive and dilatory, acting as if nothing had changed, while Constance, still reasonably comfortable in spite of this precarious new location, was starting to get used to life in the wind turbine. She spent most of her time lying on the folding bed and reading, with the radio tuned permanently to a music station. Sometimes she would tape pictures cut out of the dictionary to the windows, while gazing out at the landscape and noting how it changed as summer grew to a close. Days passed. More days passed.

Only once did she examine the large control panel that occupied an entire wall of the room. Constance inspected it, hoping (though not really believing) that she might understand something about the electrical system. She quickly gave up this hope but, as a game, tried pressing a button just to see what would happen. As far as she could tell, nothing did. Without her noticing it, however, the blades of the turbine very gradually slowed down, stopped for a moment, and then began rotating in the opposite direction. Constance, unaware that the propeller was now turning clockwise, went back to her bed to lie down and opened her encyclopedia: letter *P*, for *perfidy.*

23

TWO WEEKS, VICTOR HAD SAID. So, okay, let's be patient. But in the meantime, why don't we quickly deal with the Pognel storyline.

Despite getting rid of Marie-Odile because there was a risk she might figure out too many details about his life, Clément Pognel did not leave her apartment on Rue de la Chine, continuing to live there for a while afterward. First, though, in the hours immediately following his act, he had to get busy. Before rigor mortis could set in, he had to drag the hairdresser's corpse—heavier than you'd imagine—into a storeroom, where he folded it over so it would take up the least amount of space possible, before wrapping it in a bedspread, which he held in place with clothespins. Having accomplished this, under the intrigued gaze of Biscuit, Pognel gave the kitchen a brief cleanup, deciding that he would wash the dishes more carefully later on. Then he took Biscuit downstairs to piss, a task he carried out regularly over the next few days, using each of these little trips to acquire various acids and solvents, bottle by bottle, buying each one in a different supermarket or drugstore.

Because after a while, this body had to be made to disappear for reasons that we can easily imagine and that quickly made themselves known. After accumulating enough chemicals, which he arrayed close to the bathtub, Pognel carried out his task in accordance with tried and tested techniques, learned from professionals during his stay in prison, which there is really no point in describing here. In doing this, he took particular care not to damage the bathtub. After this long, laborious operation, he painstakingly cleaned the apartment, room by room, object by object, wiping all fingerprints and wearing rubber gloves whenever he had to touch anything. Biscuit observed all of this passively, probably aware that it was a good idea to watch its step: given what Pognel had done to its mistress, the dog was well-advised not to intervene for fear of receiving the same treatment itself.

So, to begin with, Biscuit limited itself to appearing unconcerned while concealing its nervousness around Pognel. The murderer, however, knowing that the animal was incapable of testifying against him, started feeling a certain affection for it. In an attempt to win it over, he began feeding it better, replacing its ordinary dog biscuits with a more expensive brand (86 percent poultry meat enriched with salmon oil for a good supply of omega-3 and omega-6), a tactic that, naturally opportunistic and driven primarily by its appetites, Biscuit was incapable of resisting. Attentively taking care of the animal—brushing it, delousing it, and washing it regularly—Pognel figured he could also wash its brain, if only by giving it a new name more to his taste, a more manly, serious name, before training it in new (and no less serious) exercises for which the beagle as a breed is well suited: guarding, attacking, hunting, fighting. The lavishing of all this attention had the desired effect—because, sadly, dogs are sometimes just as ungrateful and forgetful as people—and, pretty quickly, Pognel and the animal became as thick as thieves, even if it took Biscuit a while to get used to (and instantly react to) its new name: Faust.

But all of that will be developed later because, as a precaution, we are not going to outstay our welcome at Rue de la Chine. So, after ridding the apartment of all traces of his presence, Pognel left, slamming the door behind him, with Faust on a leash. But that was his big mistake. Because, even if Marie-Odile had no family, her colleagues at the hairdressing salon would eventually worry about her prolonged absence; they would call her phone, they would ring her doorbell, and, getting no reply and seeing the mailbox overflowing, they would decide to inform the police, who, forcing open her apartment, would initially find nothing at all. But they would not give up that easily, and, despite Pognel's meticulous cleaning job and cunning mind, the forensics team ended up finding a DNA trace—on the handle of the door that he banged shut when he was leaving. Well, you can't think of everything . . .

So Clément Pognel disappeared, accompanied by Faust. Although we were boasting not so long ago about being better informed than everyone else, in this case we are forced to admit that, at this moment in time, we don't know where he's gone. But let's trust our informers to keep us in the loop: they've been alerted, so we should hear something soon. In the meantime, as Pognel was—given his past—well-known to the police department, the DNA trace enabled him to be quickly identified. Very soon, the case came to the attention of Objat, who immediately organized a meeting with the general: I'll expect you in an hour, said Bourgeaud—and three-quarters of an hour later, fondling a Panter Silhouette as Objat entered his office, he inquired: So what's going on?

The man I found to play the role of the silent partner, Objat reminded him, well, he's gone berserk. First he shot a guy who was working for him. For us, you mean? the general asked with a frown. Of course, Objat reassured him, like all the others, but that wasn't enough for him. I managed to locate him at a woman's apartment and, well, quite simply, he killed her. Was she one of ours too? the general asked. No, said Objat, she was nothing to do with it. Well, that's something, Bourgeaud sighed, taking a Bic lighter from his pocket, but still, it's very unfortunate. And this man, do you know him well? I always took care, Objat said, to keep my distance. I only communicate with him from a distance. The general played with the wheel of the lighter, then changed his mind, put it back in his pocket, and put the Panter back in its box.

Well, those are the risks, he observed. As a general rule, this is probably a good thing. A few less links in the chain . . . it simplifies the picture. All the same, it's very distressing. But anyway, we still need to recuperate the girl—do you think she's ripe now? After three months of treatment, mused Objat, I would say she could be operational. We'll have to see. Indeed, indeed, nodded the general. Do your best. Take your time. These things mustn't be rushed. See the process through and keep me informed. At your command, declared Objat.

24

AS FAR AS LOU TAUSK and Nadine Alcover were concerned, nothing much had happened recently, except that they had become slightly less enthusiastic about the idea of going off to the end of the world. The thing was, when they thought about this world with its wars (active or dormant), its entrenched divisions (ethnic, political, religious, tribal, racial, clannish), its conflicts over nuclear testing, its systematic bleeding of natural resources, its terrorism and its tourism and its identical stores everywhere you go, well, they decided they could talk about it later because, after all, they were happy together and things were not too bad here at home, so let's just fuck. However, the idea of that dinner, suggested by Nadine Alcover, had not been dropped, so she tried to call Lucile to invite her.

But Lucile, for the moment, is not in a position to speak to anyone because she is, once again, in her slow, deep way, taking care of Maurice Lessertisseur as he lies on his hospital bed, arms covered in bandages and perfusions. Lucile is attentive, methodical, devoted: no sooner has the wounded man suggested it than she immediately gets her head down. This should reassure us on many levels about this man's state: beyond his current genital contentment, Lessertisseur has clearly not been badly wounded enough to rule out such treatment. Moreover, there are flowers to brighten up his nightstand, the window overlooks a park, and the fact that he has an individual room in a private clinic in west Paris suggests he must have very good health insurance. Lessertisseur is happy. He is thinking about nothing. And he has no desire to hear anything, for the moment, about his mission or his bosses.

Talking of which, Paul Objat is on his way to Creuse. The current experiment on Constance has, in his view, gone on long enough that he can, with the general's approval, recuperate the young woman. So he is driving to the farm in an unmarked car, taking minor roads rather than highways since he is not in a rush; in fact, taking slightly longer to get there, he thinks, will be to his advantage. The trip from Paris to Châtelus-le-Marcheix, if you take these smaller roads, is a pretty and more or less vertical ride through France of roughly 250 miles. Some of the landscapes you pass through aren't bad—I mean, they're not always wonderful either, but sometimes they're really not bad at all. After leaving the barracks quite early, Objat even allowed himself a detour about two-thirds of the way through his journey to eat lunch in a Michelin-starred restaurant he spotted in the *Red Guide*.

Around five o'clock, after crossing the border between Indre and Creuse without incident, as the autumn sun went down in the west, Objat took the small, winding forest road that, in a bend to the left just before Châtelus-le-Marcheix, splits off into a byroad that heads to the farm. He followed this path—asphalted, then rocky, with its fair share of ruts and potholes—until it led him to the building, in front of which not one single vehicle was parked. Objat raised an eyebrow. After getting out of his car, he walked to the door—unlocked—and, entering, found out just how things stood now.

Because not only was the farm apparently unoccupied, but it had been completely renovated: repainted, refurbished, relieved of all its former contents. The old furniture had been replaced by some basic new models, probably purchased in discount stores like But or Super U rather than Ikea. The table was new, and so were the chairs. There was even a plastic ring where the label had been held hanging from the metal bars of one of those chairs. The kitchenette had also been renovated, in a simple but practical way: three induction hobs in place of the camping stove, a microwave, a mini-refrigerator (empty). In front of the old fireplace was an energy-efficient electric radiator on wheels. There were no longer any decorations on the walls, which still gave off a strong paint smell. Upstairs, Objat found a similar scene: nothing remained of the old bedroom occupied by Constance, which was now fitted out with the same kind of cheap, minimalist furniture as before, but all of it brand-new: polypropylene closet and nightstand, single bed with synthetic bedding folded on top of it.

Objat shook his head, a thin smile playing on his face as he went downstairs. Out in the yard, despite his self-control, he could not help staring wide-eyed: they had not confined themselves to transforming the interior of the farm but had worked on its surroundings too, notably—the zenith of the metamorphosis—even the big lime tree was no longer there. It had vanished. Or rather, what had gone was the peaceful, scented shade offered by its branches and leaves. The tree itself was still there, in the same place, but in another form: cut up into regular-length logs and assembled in a rectangular parallelepiped (13 by 8.2 by 4 feet), it now offered its interstitial shade only to insects, lizards, rodents, and other little creatures—and, even then, not all the time, mostly just early in the morning and late in the evening when the sun was low in the sky. Which was, at that moment, increasingly the case.

Night would soon fall. Paul Objat took a travel bag containing a few belongings from the trunk of the car. He preferred to stay here rather than look for a hotel in the area. True, they (Jean-Pierre and Christian, presumably—who else?) had made the place neutral and impersonal but, all in all, it was now more comfortable than it had been before. He'd bought two sandwiches during the trip, and he sat down to eat them now. He heard the sound of his own chewing and smelled the aroma of paint. He regretted the absence of a radio. He went upstairs to make the bed.

The next morning, and over the days that followed, Objat began roaming the surrounding area with the aid of a 1/25,000 map. Something told him that Constance—vanished without trace from the farm—could not be far away, so he systematically explored the perimeter, road by road, field by field, for almost a week, crossing off each place one after another, without result. Until the moment when these investigations seemed futile, until he was close to giving up— and wondering how he would explain things to General Bourgeaud.

Until the moment when, driving for the tenth time along a minor road whose every derivation he had already inspected, he went past a large meadow with, in the distance, a field of wind turbines that his peripheral vision had already registered, their blades turning peace- fully. But this time, something struck him as wrong. It was only a vague intuition, but he suddenly slammed on the brakes, put the car in reverse, and came to a halt again in the middle of the road, level with those aerogenerators, which he observed more attentively under the bright late-fall sun. It took him a little while to notice that the propeller of one of those turbines was turning in the opposite direc- tion to all the others, but when he did, he smiled.

After he'd parked his car by the roadside and cut the engine, his smile grew wider as he noted that a wavy line ran across the yel- lowing grass between this shoulder and the wind turbine, probably created by numerous comings and goings. He got out of the car and followed this path, rummaging around in his pockets until he took out a thin metal rod, always useful in his line of work. At the bottom of the wind turbine, the rod allowed him to quickly pick the lock of the door. He went inside and climbed the ladder. At the top was a trapdoor, which Objat lifted without difficulty. Poking his head through the gap, he discovered a very small room filled with light, its rudimentary furnishings including a sort of Lilliputian bed on which—while listening to "Y'en a des Biens" by Didier Super on the radio—Constance was rereading the article on *slaughter* in her encyclopedia.

Oh, Victor, she exclaimed, at the sight of his head emerging from the floor. I haven't seen you in a while. Where've you been?

25

THREE DAYS LATER, at the café in Limoges train station, Jean-Pierre and Christian sit side by side, in silence, under the icy glare of Paul Objat. Jean-Pierre lowers his head, using his right thumbnail to push back the little bits of skin that cover the lunula of his left thumbnail, while Christian squirms on the bench, staring into space. Well, I'm not going to congratulate you, Objat has just said to them.

Three days before this, returning from grocery shopping in Bénévent-l'Abbaye, Jean-Pierre had gone up the ladder to deliver the food to Constance and found the room empty. As the young woman had shown no desire to escape—on the contrary, he thought, she had seemed perfectly at ease up here in her cockpit—he had deduced that Objat must have come here and taken her away. Aware of their breach of duty and less fearful of Lessertisseur's reaction (since he was in no fit state to punish anyone) than Objat's (since he was generally stricter), he and Christian had decided to take off, to blend in with the crowd and flee their employers, first in their car and then by train.

But having recaptured Constance, Objat then turned his attention to finding his henchmen too. And as he is even better than us at that, he soon located them and trapped them at the station in Limoges.

There, on platform number 4, they were waiting for the intercity train to Paris-Austerlitz, planning to go from there to Hazebrouck, where they would be able to lie low, get some fresh air, and think about the future while staying with Christian's brother-in-law. Sadly for them, Objat arrived on the platform six minutes before the intercity train. He herded them toward the station café, where he admonished them and they sat in silence, looking pathetic. Ordering another sandwich, he asked them if they wanted anything and they assured him that they weren't hungry anymore. No, thank you, Victor, said Jean-Pierre, thank you very much. We had a *croque-monsieur* earlier.

Professional misconduct, Objat emphasized. Serious professional misconduct. Exemplary punishment, he added, without going into details. They apologized again. They had become used to this exercise since Christian's fiasco with Constance. You have to understand, muttered Jean-Pierre, she was a nice girl; we ended up growing fond of her. We didn't really know what you wanted to do with her, pleaded Christian, and we started worrying about her. It seemed safer to take her out of harm's way.

Well, Objat admitted, it wasn't too serious, luckily for you. And in a way, unwittingly, what you did might not turn out so bad. But we are about to enter the second phase of this operation. That means new techniques to learn, new methods. If you want us to continue working together, you're going to need some training. I'm going to send you an address in a few days, and you will go there. Okay, Victor, agreed Jean-Pierre, we'll do whatever you want. Good, said Objat, paying for his sandwich. But where are we going? asked Christian in a frightened voice. And what about our train tickets—can we exchange them? How do we get reimbursed? Wait until you hear from me, said Objat, getting to his feet.

After retaking possession of Constance the other day, he had driven her back to Paris without explaining anything whatsoever to her and dropped her outside the building near the Trocadéro where she had her pied-à-terre, leaving her on the sidewalk with her handbag. It wasn't a warm day: winter was approaching. Shivering and suddenly alone, Constance felt disoriented. All in all, as intended, she did not understand anything, particularly regarding the behavior of Objat—Victor was his code name, apparently, though she still had difficulty not calling him by that name. What, she wondered as she stood in the elevator, had been the point of kidnapping her and keeping her all that time, only to liberate her without warning, without conditions, with only a muttered line about seeing each other again sometime, and abandoning her outside her apartment building?

And her apartment struck her as hostile, anonymous and—even after she turned the heating up as high as it would go—freezing cold. Constance, unsure what to do with her body or her thoughts, wandered from room to room without any idea of what she wanted to do, as happens sometimes when you return from a long trip with the vague feeling that you have lots of things to take care of, tidy away, bring up to date, and then it turns out that, in fact, you don't. You have no desire to unpack your suitcase, and it doesn't even cross your mind to pick up the months of mail piled up in the concierge's office. For lack of anything better to do, you take a long shower, but it doesn't relax you or bring you as much pleasure as you'd hoped. Then you do your hair, your makeup, you choose some clothes and get dressed, but this has the same effect: neutral, as if you didn't care about anything, as if your life had glaciated, as if a glass wall separated you from the rest of the world. Now this feeling—this feeling that you don't care about anything at all—is exactly what Paul Objat and General Bourgeaud had intended, planned, and developed. You are ripe.

You did try, after forcing yourself, to call Tausk, if only to inform him that you were back. But Louis, happy in his new life with Nadine Alcover, had barely even sounded polite when he assured you that he was pleased to hear it. And your finger? he asked. What about my finger? you said. And the money? he insisted. What money? you asked. Well, said Tausk, never mind, let's forget it. There was no mention of divorce and, all in all, that brief interview was more a relief than a source of distress. Having hung up the phone, you felt no wish to use it again, to contact friends or old flames who might offer you some distraction. No, your last smile—your only smile in quite some time—was when you remembered Jean-Pierre and Christian. And then you felt hungry.

But that's enough now. Stop imagining that you're Constance, who, consequently, went out to buy something to eat. Even in the convenience store, things didn't go well: the cart kept veering to the left; despite wandering all around the store, she barely filled the bottom of it; and, between the air-conditioned meat and dairy aisles, Constance felt sure she'd caught a cold again. Whereas, up in her wind turbine, the rigors of the Creuse fall had never affected her at all.

Coming out of the store, she made herself walk down the street. She read the property ads, as she always used to, but mechanically now, without any real interest. She couldn't summon any interest either in the announcements she saw in store windows—the meat we sell is fresh and well-sourced; we also supply clothes for plus-size women; incredible sale on mirrors—and Constance's body was shaken with a sort of spasm as she walked, eventually stopping in front of (though still at some distance from) an animal lovers' protest by the doors of an Air France agency. There were only about a dozen women, but they were ranting and raving very loudly about the air transportation of laboratory animals. Constance did not attempt to talk to any of the protesters, but—while she had never been particularly moved by the fate of such animals, however sad and unpleasant it might be—this incident must have started some kind of engine inside her. Because she suddenly started crying. She went home and it didn't stop: Constance started crying all the time.

All the time. She sobbed ceaselessly—for the smallest of reasons, sometimes for no reason at all—which was in fact not entirely disagreeable. Whether they were tears of pain, emotion, joy, or grief, shedding them did her good. In the end, did it really matter what they were about? Tears bring so much relief. Pouring from our eyes, they soothe our whole body. And by the way, this phenomenon applies to more or less everything that the body expels: from the moment when something liquid, solid, or gaseous escapes the organism—so probably about ten different modes of evacuation that we will abstain from listing in detail—it is, each time, a specific pleasure, from the sublime to the ridiculous. No matter what anyone says, it is— albeit to varying degrees—always a good feeling. The only possible exceptions to this rule are sweating—and even there, in a sauna or hammam, it's not always so bad—and, of course, bleeding, which is frankly debatable.

And so, in the days that followed, Constance did not stop crying. While listening to music—so she turned off the music. While watching ads on TV—so she turned off the TV. Once, she turned on the radio: Today, we welcome Gérard Delplanque, whose movie, *The Uncertainties and Doubts of Nitchika, the Spy in Love*, is released on Wednesday. Gérard Delplanque, hello, and let me begin by saying:

that title sounds a little like—how can I put this?—a provocation. So that will be my first question: homage or parody? Your question is meaningless, Gérard Delplanque replied angrily. Neither, obviously. It is, above all, an action movie. And at that moment the doorbell rang.

Constance turned off the radio and went to open the door. And there, once more, was Paul Objat. Ah, Victor, Constance said again. But Objat noticed that she did not pronounce these words in the same lighthearted tone she had used the other day in the wind turbine. Her modulation was now lackluster, absent, clearly lacrimal, and Objat thought: Perfect. I came to find you, he said, but don't worry. I just wanted to introduce you to someone.

They left in his car and joined the outer loop at the Porte de Passy, turning off at the Porte des Lilas, from where it was only a one-minute drive to 141 Boulevard Mortier. After Objat showed his badge at the gate, they entered the barracks courtyard and parked in a reserved space. From there, they went through a door, crossed an entrance hall, and, after another flash of the badge, climbed a staircase, went along a corridor, knocked at an anonymous door, and opened it without awaiting a response.

Sitting behind his desk, General Bourgeaud was immersed in a recalcitrant dossier, cursing between his teeth as he discreetly underlined passages with the tip of his Panter Small. He did not seem to have noticed their presence, and it might have gone on forever like this had not Objat loudly cleared his throat, causing the general to look up at his visitors. This is the person, General, said Objat. Without speaking a word to her or even nodding at her, the general slowly looked Constance up and down, with a brief detour via his cigarillo. This was not the first time Constance had been inspected this way, but it was the first time, she thought, that it had been done without either medical or libidinal motivations. Then, turning to Objat, the general said: You were right, I think she'll do nicely.

I beg your pardon, interrupted Constance, but what are you talking about? Well, it's very simple, the general replied. You're going to destabilize North Korea.

III

26

YOU'RE MAKING FUN OF ME, Constance supposed. Not in the least, Bourgeaud reassured her. Then you must be completely nuts, she diagnosed. Not completely, he replied, pointing to a map of the Korean peninsula pinned to a wall of the office. Let me explain.

Although everyone knows or thinks they know what North Korea is, I would remind you that it is a dynastic and practically theocratic tyranny, with the last three generations of leaders having elevated themselves to divine status. Surveillance is omnipresent there; nobody trusts anybody; they denounce one another as naturally as they breathe—because they would be denounced for not denouncing— all while desperately seeking, often in vain, something to eat.

Note that on this point—food—there is a chasm between the capital and the rest of the country. While some people in Pyongyang run on sturgeon and *grands crus classés*, life is not quite so pleasant in the countryside or in other towns. There's been famine after famine, and the best they can hope to eat is about ten ounces of corn per day. The average height is now as low as five feet. But it's not a good idea to complain. In fact, it's much better for them if they don't say anything at all. The slightest word or gesture that might be interpreted as critical of the regime will land you in a camp where, between twenty hours of hard labor and two highly imaginative torture sessions per day, you would be happy to catch a rat or a snake and eat it raw, and genuinely thrilled if you could discreetly cook it, even if the penalty for such behavior would be further torture prior to your public execution, whether that is by firing squad, hanging, or stoning, a choice that would depend on the mood of the camp's director. But of course you know all this, said the general, catching his breath after this very long sentence.

You also know, he went on, that this country is always ready to fight. Its leaders' speeches are relentlessly bellicose, all the more so as the nation is technically at war with South Korea, and the army consists of two million active soldiers or reservists, a considerable stock of planes, tanks, warships (even if this arsenal is often obsolete), enough plutonium to build several atomic bombs, and vast reserves of chemical and biological weapons. They also make some excellent missiles—the No-Dong-1 and the Taepodong-2—which they sell at high prices to various global hot spots (Syria, Libya, Iraq, Iran, Yemen, and Pakistan), as the arms trade represents one of the regime's largest sources of revenue.

Among the specialties of said regime, Bourgeaud then mentioned a few airplane hijackings and various kidnappings, the sale of military equipment and experts to African countries, and a warm welcome for foreign terrorists, whom they immediately betray by selling them to their enemies. So, basically, they have everything they need to make lots of cash. Mass production of various drugs—including the best methamphetamine in the world—the trafficking of anything that can be trafficked, the counterfeiting of foreign currencies (fake dollars and fake yen in particular), the billion-dollar swindling of international insurance firms, and that's without even mentioning cyberattacks and the hacking of bank details and other information all over the world.

If you're interested, the general added, pointing the end of his Panter at the map, the largest concentration camps are situated here, here, and here, although obviously I am only talking about the most severe camps. And why are you telling me about this shitty country? Constance asked. I'm getting to that, said the general.

Mentalities change gradually, don't they? Very slowly, but there are clues. For the past few years, the population, which used to know nothing about the outside world, has begun to learn more: they secretly listen to foreign radio stations, they receive DVDs and USB keys from the South. It's very discreet, but it is happening, even if the punishment for such crimes is torture or execution. The same is true for any escape attempts, which generally go through China, Mongolia, or Southeast Asia—Thailand or Laos. There are a few pretty good people-smuggling networks. Constance tried to cut him off by saying I actually know quite a bit about this, I've read newspaper articles about it. I'm nearly done, said the general. I'm getting to the point.

So, let me sum up. When Kim Jong-un, the new Supreme Leader— son of the Dear Leader Kim Jong-il and grandson of the Eternal Leader Kim Il-sung—came to power, he was for a time encircled by seven historic leaders of the country, among them his uncle, the regime's number two. But it didn't take him long to get rid of this group. The uncle was publicly arrested and then executed. A bit like *Hamlet*, if you see what I mean? Silence from Constance.

Hamlet, Objat, the general said, you know about that at least, don't you? Ah no, replied Objat without turning away from the window, I'm sorry, I don't know that work either. Well, anyway, Bourgeaud snapped unhappily, the uncle's liquidation was followed by that of the head of state security and some high-ranking army leaders. Minister, vice marshal, chief of general staff . . . I don't remember their names but they were all demoted, fired, probably killed. At the same time, quite a few ambassadors close to that clique were brought back to Pyongyang and sent to concentration camps or physically eliminated. Do you follow?

Silence from Constance. Well, repeated Bourgeaud, this purge in the highest echelons of the state naturally led to a more general clear-out of others associated with the former regime: about ten thousand apparatchiks who must have met the same fate. This presumes a completely new team to replace them, all of them under the Supreme Leader's heel. And, among these recent promotions, there is one that interests us. He's a new adviser. The Supreme Leader consults him on various points, particularly in the nuclear field. A young man, quite discreet, brought up in Switzerland like his boss. He seems pretty open-minded to us, and we think he's someone we might be able to talk with. We need to develop a connection with him, the general concluded. He's the target. And this is where you come in.

Why me? asked Constance. Bourgeaud paused deliberately for a moment, pretending to look for something inside a drawer and then another one. Paul Objat, at the back of the office, was staring through the window at the barracks courtyard. For some time now, a light rain had begun to fall in that courtyard, the quiet, sighing hiss it made forming a harmony with the purr of a printer in the office next door.

You're the ideal subject, the general replied at last. Perhaps you don't know this, but you are an idol for the North Korean leadership. I beg your pardon? said Constance. Ah yes, he sighed, that is an essential element. Let me remind you that you were the original singer of "너무 해." Could you repeat that, please? asked Constance, alarmed. It's the Korean version of "Excessif," Bourgeaud explained. You know, that little ditty you sang quite a few years ago. Well, believe it or not, that song is still very popular over there. They adapted it to their language, but that is no longer enough for them. Apparently the original version—that's to say, *your* version—is played constantly at Workers' Party banquets. Even the Supreme Leader has a crush on you. We know that for a fact.

You're kidding, said Constance. Not at all, insisted the general. That is how you will enter the country. You'll be welcomed as a star. But don't worry—you won't be alone. We'll have two professional contacts to watch over you. The first objective, then, is that adviser. We'll tell you how to contact him—although you'll see that it will happen of its own accord—and after that, you will receive instructions. And what's his name, this guy? Constance asked. Gang Un-ok, the general articulated clearly. Pretty easy to remember, don't you think? We have researched his background in great detail and you are just his type, apparently. That could be helpful in your work. That's disgusting, Constance objected. It is, above all, the general pronounced gravely as he stood up, in the interests of the international community. But I must leave you now. I believe we will see each other again soon. Shall I accompany you? offered Objat.

27

IT WAS ALSO IN SWITZERLAND, though in a very different kind of camp, that the two aforementioned professional contacts were sweating blood, after an intensive accelerated course to bring them up to the title of personal protection agent.

Nothing predisposed them to such training. Neither of them, particularly Christian, had done any physical exercise in a long time. When they arrived, they were chilled by the welcoming speech of the chief instructor. You are here, he told them, to acquire technical, psychological, physical, tactical, and conceptual intelligence in personal protection. That seemed quite a lot, to them.

An imposing stature is no gauge of effectiveness, the instructor then went on, which was reassuring to Christian. However, he said, the personal protection agent must be educated, cultivated, polyglot, versatile, observant and perceptive, capable of adapting to the society he's in, aware of the current laws applicable to his field, psychologically stable, discreet, unassuming, athletic, healthy in body and mind. The two men were thoroughly daunted by now. Jean-Pierre bit his lip and they didn't dare look at each other.

They were immediately put to work in order to acclimatize to paramilitary life. Their mornings began early with a six-mile group run: to start with, Christian would often collapse with exhaustion and the instructor would not let the others help him up, making him get his breath back and stand up on his own before resuming his run with a limp. The rest of the day was devoted to theoretical and practical training: the observation and scouting of locations; the searching and securing of a site; martial arts and self-defense; weapons handling; the extraction of a VIP in difficulty; the neutralization of a civilian; exercises in holding someone on the ground; procedures to follow after an attack with a gun, a knife, or any other object; first aid and emergency rescue in a hostile environment; and use of a bulletproof Kevlar folding briefcase. All of this was very tiring. They went to bed early, too weak to speak, and fell asleep quickly.

When the training ended, it was less difficult to get used to the black suit, the black tie (or, according to circumstances, the black bow tie), and the black glasses, or to having a wire earpiece wedged behind their ear. It was trickier to learn how to shave their heads, so Jean-Pierre and Christian began by shaving each other's before moving on to performing the operation unilaterally. It burns, groaned Christian while massaging his head. It irritates my scalp. You wouldn't have any lotion or anything, would you?

The day before their departure, after they had—not without indulgence or kindness (and perhaps also an eagerness to be rid of them)—been judged competent to protect someone, they were given one night off to relax and open a bottle in their room, each of them sitting on a twin bed, above which, respectively, Jean-Pierre had pinned a Bazaine reproduction and Christian two photographs of naked women. Well, we did it, said Christian while pouring as little water as possible into his Pastis 51, we made it through. I'd never have believed I was capable of that, admitted Jean-Pierre, twisting the ice tray to push the cubes out. But I reckon it did me good. Physically, it got me back in shape again. Makes a change from Creuse, doesn't it?

They drank to their stay in Creuse, remembering the good times. The girl, though, said Christian, I mean, say what you like, but she was *hot*. That's a fact, Jean-Pierre agreed, loosening the knot of his tie. I had a soft spot for her too, but what can you do? That's not our world. I wonder what happened to her, Christian said dreamily. If I understood things correctly, analyzed Jean-Pierre, we should be seeing her again pretty soon. And her idiot husband, Christian wondered, you think he ended up paying?

The idiot is at this moment sprawled on his barrel-dyed leather couch, in front of his BeoVision Bang & Olufsen, a glass of Laphroaig Cask Strength Red Stripe in one hand, his other containing a Logitech Harmony Touch remote control, with which he zaps through several hundred channels, each one flashing up on-screen for no more than a few seconds. In the kitchen, behind the bar, Nadine Alcover is loading the dishwasher. She and the idiot ate dinner together just now, without finding much to say to each other: I made a mess of this roast, Nadine Alcover said between two silences. Not at all, it was very nice, Tausk replied after a moment of silence, all the while checking his texts on his smartphone. And that is how things stand now: calm, very calm.

Once she has started the dishwasher, Nadine Alcover goes up to her bedroom and calls Lucile, who answers right away. They exchange some small talk before quickly moving on to the subject of their love lives. How's it going, Nadine Alcover asks, with your old man? He's recovered from his accident, replies Lucile, but sometimes . . . I don't know . . . I have the feeling that, sexually, there's only one thing he's interested in. As if that's all I'm good for. There are days when I wonder. I think I see what you mean, says Nadine Alcover. It's not exactly like that with Louis. But I do think sometimes, him or someone else, you know? I think I see what you mean, echoes Lucile. So are you still coming tomorrow night? Nadine Alcover asks her.

And the next day, Lucile and Lessertisseur do indeed turn up at Lou Tausk's apartment for dinner. This is the first time and they are embarrassed, Lessertisseur in particular. But then again, Tausk knows nothing about his role in the kidnapping of Constance, and neither does Nadine Alcover. And Lucile's an idiot, so she won't cause any problems. Little by little, Maurice Lessertisseur relaxes. Anyway, that whole thing is over now: the actors have dispersed; Constance has gone home. Lessertisseur accepts a drink and a chair, and by the time he's finished his second drink his scruples have dissolved. So let's turn the page. And go through to the dining room. And soon, sitting at the table, the page does turn. The page seems to turn effortlessly, in fact, as soon as they begin conversing, animatedly, on various subjects.

Here, we had planned to transcribe that conversation in detail. As it warmed up and developed, we had even planned to go into greater depth on the subjects mentioned: political, social, cultural, and soon even intimate events. We were just about to do that when the double gong on the front door rings in a descending major third. Are you expecting someone? Lucile asks. I don't think so, says Nadine Alcover, surprised. Go see who it is, suggests Tausk.

Less than a minute later, followed by a perplexed Nadine Alcover, we open the door to Clément Pognel, a skinny dog at his heels, one hand raised, containing his Astra Cub pistol, and suddenly the page seems to have more difficulty turning. Yes, it's really struggling. It's resolutely stuck, in fact. The page wouldn't turn if you put a gun to its head. The joke's over, declares Pognel.

28

BUT THE EVENING did not last long. And the next morning, Lou Tausk got up early, letting Nadine Alcover sleep in, so he could go to the studio on Rue de Pali-Kao, where he limited himself to reading the newspaper and glancing at his mail, tidying away four papers on his desk, moving two objects—a stapler and an ashtray—and then immediately putting them back where they were before. Around one o'clock, with the air having grown milder and the sun tempting a breakaway, he went out to eat lunch at the Pensive Mandarin. He sat alone on the terrace, warmed by infrared lamps and protected from the wind by a translucent tarpaulin.

Let's observe him as he sits in front of a bowl of *bún bò*, remembering the previous night's events. He did not really understand Clément Pognel's intervention, as—to sum up—his former partner in crime stayed no more than fifteen minutes, quickly pocketing the Astra Cub before accepting a drink and caressing his dog, looking around at the people and the place, not saying much at all except a brief, cold line addressed to Tausk to the effect that he was glad to see he was doing well. Tausk did have time to notice how Pognel had changed in the last thirty years, however. And he really had changed in quite a lot of ways. Not only did he walk with a limp now, but Tausk had been surprised by his insolence when he took a seat between Lucile and Nadine Alcover, brushing against them and staring at them disdainfully—he had not been like that back in the day—and, even more so, when he rudely grabbed a piece of rind from Lucile's plate and dropped it on the carpet for his dog, which devoured it, growling and slobbering with satisfaction. Take it easy, Faust. Pognel had smiled then, and Tausk had not liked that mutt of his at all. He did not understand the reasons for this brief intrusion, nor for that sudden departure, as if Pognel had come only to verify something. Nor did he understand why Lucile and Maurice had looked so embarrassed before they, too, left in a hurry.

Looking up for a moment from the terrace of the Mandarin, Tausk sees a Boeing with the usual vapor trails behind it, the water condensed by the minus four degrees Fahrenheit temperature up there, forming a white thread of ice crystals that blooms in an irregular triangular halo, an artificial cloud that soon turns fluffy and, already blurred by the translucent tarpaulin, fades before lightening and falling to pieces. Returning his attention to his *bún bò*, Tausk quickly forgets that Air China B777-300ER, headed to Beijing, boarded, one hour before this, by Constance and her bodyguards, who are sitting in different parts of the plane: the guards in economy class, she in the luxurious Forbidden Pavilion class, where she has just been served her second glass of Armand de Brignac with a dish of raw caviar while Jean-Pierre and Christian, many rows behind, were given only a defrosted club sandwich in a blister pack and a lukewarm Tsingtao.

The flight lasted eleven hours: Constance slept pretty well, Jean-Pierre and Christian hardly at all. Broken in three on their seats, they watched the beginnings of a few movies, yawning, tried a couple of video games, and fruitlessly begged for another beer before the 777 started its descent—cabin crew, doors to manual and cross-check—to the international airport, where all three of them were transferred to a transit lounge.

The visa formalities had already been dealt with by General Bourgeaud's department, but they still had to fill out quite a few forms: following the instructions they'd been given in Paris, Jean-Pierre and Christian wrote "tour operator" in the box for occupation, and Constance "singer." They then flew to Pyongyang on board a single-class Yunshuji Y-7 twin-engine turboprop, designed to land and take off in a rural setting and belonging to the national fleet of Air Koryo. Even though this airline figures in flashing red capital letters on the blacklist of companies at risk, and despite the dilapidation of the airplane itself—wobbly seats with missing armrests, tables not properly attached to seatbacks, frayed seat belts—they reached their destination without too much in the way of turbulence, air pockets, or other problems.

First, they saw two surprisingly long runways, above which, before landing, the plane seemed to circle endlessly, as if to let the passengers admire their immensity. After landing, they had to stay in their seats for a while, the roar of the engines slowly dying like at the end of a washing machine's spin cycle. The international airport of Sunan was merely a modest, low, old-fashioned building. The only new (or perhaps old but meticulously maintained) ornaments inside it were tall, full-length portraits of the forebears (father and grandfather) of the incumbent dictator. About five hundred yards away, perhaps in anticipation of a massive rise in air traffic, stood another, much bigger building, made of glass and steel. This building was surrounded by fields that looked as if they had not been sown extensively. Standing in those fields, arms hanging uselessly, dressed in gray, brown, or beige anoraks and quilted parkas, were a few farmers who, for lack of anything better to do, were watching the planes land and take off.

In the airport's opaque lobby, soldiers stood guard and a few Chinese businessmen waited in cerulean-blue plastic chairs below display screens that in airports all over the world usually blink with hundreds of arrivals and departures but which here showed only three destinations: Vladivostok, Kuala Lumpur (twice a week), and Beijing. Some elegant locals, who'd gotten off the airplane at the same time as Constance, and who must have been pretty close to the regime to have been allowed to leave the country in the first place, pushed carts full of Western alcohol, designer clothes, and flat-screen TVs toward the exits. She had attempted, during the flight, to address a few words in English to one of these North Koreans, who was sitting next to her, but—whether through ignorance or suspicion—he had responded only with a silent quarter smile. Going through customs was much simpler than she'd imagined, with the formalities reduced to a bare minimum: a glance at her passport, automatically confiscated; another at the brand of her telephone, also seized; and a receipt certifying that all this would be returned to her upon departure.

At the end of the lobby, a soldier made a right-angle bow in front of Constance before introducing himself: Major Bakh Kang-dae or something like that. A star on his cap, a badge depicting the father and grandfather, a shoulder harness buckled over an extremely well-ironed uniform. He wished to welcome her to the country, a huge honor, etcetera, and to announce that they were now going to take her to her residence. Constance followed him to a Pyeonghwa Junma limousine, a copy of South Korea's SsangYong Chairman, which is in turn merely a clone of the Mercedes E. As Jean-Pierre and Christian attempted to follow this movement, they were courteously intercepted by two civilians who were waiting just behind

Major Bakh: a man and a woman, smiling, relaxed, who introduced themselves—Yun Sam-yong, Im Chin-sun—as a (male) guide and (female) translator who were here to take care of them and, first of all, accompany them to their hotel. Sorry, said Jean-Pierre, offended, but we're traveling with madame. But Im and Yun did not seem to hear him and, no less smiley but more determined, guided the two men to a less luxurious vehicle, the Pyeonghwa Premio. They got inside.

The Hotel Yanggakdo, said Im, a very good hotel, you'll see, you'll be fine there. And her smile grew wider as the car picked up speed. She gave them the usual instructions, all in the form of interdictions— talking politics, leaving the hotel unaccompanied, talking politics, going out at night, and talking politics—while they moved through a formless countryside, then an indistinct suburb, before finally entering Pyongyang.

And in the capital, all seemed peaceful, normal, new. Peaceful were the cyclists, the groups of people waiting at bus stations, the pedestrians walking along or crossing the broad tree-lined avenues, their wide sidewalks lined with little lawns where, here and there, a man or a woman was crouching, apparently searching in the grass for some indeterminate purpose, perhaps cleaning or harvesting. Normal was the traffic: well, there wasn't a great deal of it, but it wasn't suspiciously sparse either—more cars than you might expect, all of them recently manufactured, as well as trams, vans, buses, some of these considerably older, with exhaust pipes that sometimes emitted thick dark farts of smoke. New were the numerous tall, pale buildings; there were also some less-new buildings in pastel colors: pink, ocher, yellow, mauve. It was normal, too, that everything should be new, as the U.S. Air Force had destroyed the city with millions of liters of napalm and millions of tons of incendiary bombs and earthquake bombs in the winter of 1950, which is not really that long ago. Right now, it was definitely lacking in exoticism; the atmosphere was calm and the sky cloudless.

The Yanggakdo, an upmarket hotel, had been built on an island of the Taedong River, in the center of the capital, a location that simplified the prohibition on going out after nightfall. Fifty stories high (though only the top six appeared to be in use), it comprised one thousand rooms. Among the buttons on its six elevators—the wait for which was often long and uncertain—there was no number 5, even though it was clear from outside that a fifth floor existed. Other than that, the empty corridors were vast and the chambermaids quite pretty.

Jean-Pierre and Christian were given two neighboring rooms on the forty-fifth floor. They were spacious and poorly lit—none of the bulbs being more than twelve watts—which did not help to distinguish the style of furniture (midway between Lévitan and Brezhnev). The quite pretty receptionist told them right away that there would be (relatively) hot water for a brief while around six thirty p.m., and then again tomorrow, around six thirty a.m. The windows in these rooms overlooked the river, separated from the base of the hotel by narrow bands of sloping gardens and a construction site.

After leaving their bags in the rooms, they went downstairs and looked around. The hotel had several restaurants, albeit only one that was open: a vast, cube-shaped, empty dining room where they absorbed two or three indistinct bits of meat that they did not try to identify, soaked in a puddle of oil: it wasn't great, obviously, but nor was it any worse than they'd feared. Near a bar decorated with aquariums containing turtles and suckerfish, a tailor was offering to make—in five minutes, and for next to nothing—tracksuits and safari jackets in the style of Kim Jong-il and dark jackets à la Sun

Yat-sen. They knocked back a Taedonggang beer at the bar before taking a quick look at the few game rooms—a bowling alley, pool and Ping-Pong tables lit by dim fluorescent tubes—then, before nightfall, they went back to their rooms, where, in the absence of television sets, they again looked out of the window: on the sloping gardens, a swarm of men and women seemed to be weeding the grass, unless their objective was botanical or nutritious.

They had also been warned that the electricity would be cut at ten p.m., a fact that did not prevent the men on the construction site opposite the hotel from working late into the night, the rumble reaching them even on the forty-fifth floor. Its sound was joined by that of martial music and propaganda slogans disseminated by a number of vans equipped with loudspeakers, which blared their message until midnight.

29

AS FOR CONSTANCE, the residence where Major Bakh was supposed to take her looked very different. Located in Munsu-dong, one of the more salubrious districts in the capital, and surrounded by beautifully maintained grounds, this opulent villa was no different from all the opulent European or American villas inhabited here and there, in very rich countries, by very rich people in their very own private ghettos. Protected from prying eyes by a wall of weeping willows, its architecture showed not the slightest Asian influence—no pagoda roof, no stone lions or varnished tiles or what have you—and the crunch of the Junma's white tires on the equally white gravel, when the limousine braked outside the porch, surmounted by a majestic awning, was the same as everywhere else in the world, from Palm Beach to Monaco.

They were stopped several times before entering this domain, situated in an occupied zone cut off from the rest of the city by barriers, barbed-wire fences, and three successive filter blockades, reinforced by sandbags and guarded by impassive soldiers in sentry boxes. Bowing perpendicularly at the approach of the limousine, these sentries opened the barriers as soon as Major Bakh, lowering his window, flashed them a badge between two gloved fingers.

The major, sitting next to Constance on the backseat, remained silent throughout the journey. Then, in front of the porch, after the chauffeur had cut the engine, he told her: You're going to get some rest here. It's a winter residence belonging to Comrade Gang Un-ok. And Constance, recalling this name mentioned by the general, realized that she was close to her goal. A servant rushed over to open the car door for her, another grabbed her bags, and then a third, after the ascension of three wide waxed ceramic steps, threw open the villa's double-leaf door. In the marble entrance hall, illuminated by immense windows and with two symmetrical staircases rising from its center, stood a squadron of staff in impeccable uniforms. Arranged in a perfect line, they first bowed in unanimous reverence, then one after another: they were democratic people's versions of stewards, butlers, chambermaids, linen maids, cooks, gardeners, factotums, and other footmen. They all seemed happy with their lives and well fed, and all displayed the same delighted smile. The major entrusted Constance to the steward, articulating three laconic syllables before bowing in turn to the young woman and disappearing. Left alone with the staff, she listened as the smooth snore of the limousine faded slowly to silence.

After Constance had been led to her room by the steward, followed by a footman carrying her suitcase, he asked her if there was anything she required, offering tea or other refreshments. She politely declined and then she was alone, and she felt the same impression again: the villa was, like the villas of rich people in our own lands, luxuriously decorated and impersonally furnished, and above all there was nothing to indicate that she was in Asia, except for two antiques—a celadon duckling on the chest of drawers and a Joseon-era seal on a pedestal near the window. To the right of the seal there was a massive Samsung television, which Constance turned on without much hope. To her surprise, there was a multitude of channels available: Chinese, Japanese, Australian, even CNN, BBC World, and TV5 Monde, although the latter three were supposed to personify the image and the voice of evil.

But she didn't linger there. She went downstairs and walked around the grounds, apparently alone but imagining—probably correctly—that she was being watched, closely or from a distance, by a dozen pairs of eyes. Said grounds, sheltered from all other eyes by the willows that lined them, featured a variety of trees within its borders: cedars, thujas, aspens, larches, and birches, with bushes and flower beds of hibiscus, azaleas, and hyacinths, with precious hybrid cultivars of gerberas, but most of all, everywhere you looked, there was an amazing proliferation of bright red tuberous begonias and mauve orchids. When she had completed her tour, Constance went back to her room.

A few hours later, Major Bakh appeared at her door with a slim bouquet of other flowers that he held out, wrapped in a square of international cellophane. Oh. Constance smiled. Is that for me? That's kind of you, she added as she began to unwrap the flowers, already looking around for a vase, but the major reached out to stop her. Well, you see, he said, looking embarrassed, it's for you but not exactly. First we have something to do. They got back in the Junma.

Driving through certain areas of the capital, she was surprised to see young people playing basketball on pretty nice courts, children slaloming down the sidewalk on Rollerblades or skateboards, young or less-young women dressed just as well as they would be in Seoul, their outfits just as fashionable as in any Western megacity. It was interesting, and she wondered if the whole thing had been staged for her benefit. Of course, there was no way of posing this question to Major Bakh, who broke the silence to speak two words to the chauffeur as the limousine climbed up to the Mansu hill, in the high part of the city.

From pretty far off, as they came out of a bend, Constance caught sight of two monumental statues: seventy feet high, standing side by side, the former leaders, father and son, were reproduced in gilt bronze. Draped in a long coat, the generalissimo Kim Il-sung, notably qualified as the Sun of the Nation, Hero of the Workers, Professor of All Humanity, and Eternal Leader, reached out his right arm toward the radiant future, the magnificent past, the way to follow, or all three at the same time, unless he was hailing a taxi. To his left, dressed in an open anorak, one hand leaning on his hip, Marshal Kim Jong-il, supreme commander of the People's Army and general secretary of the Workers' Party, who also responded to the names Genius of the Revolution, Perfect Brain, Polar Star, and Dear Leader, smiled proudly at the result of all this hailing.

At the feet of these two giants, held back by armed guards, a crowd waited patiently before being allowed to advance in orderly lines to lay bouquets or floral arrangements before bowing—again, at right angles—before those exceptional beings. You do have your flowers, don't you? the major asked anxiously. We're not going there, are we? Constance asked anxiously in return. I have no choice, said the major; this is the custom. Please notice, he proudly indicated, accompanying her to the next line of respect-payers, that the statues of our leaders have been improved recently by the alteration of a few small details. The Eternal Leader smiles at us now, and we have put his glasses on so that he can see us better. As for the Dear Leader, he used to wear a midlength jacket, but that was not right at all. We replaced it with this anorak, which was more in line with his habits. It's much better, don't you think? Constance did not think it a good idea to disagree as she moved forward and bent double with all the others. After putting her little bouquet on top of the large pile that already lay there, she took three steps back.

The people around her were not as well dressed as those in the areas they had driven though before. While some of the women wore a vaguely traditional outfit—short jacket and baggy pants—the majority of them wore the same type of clothes as the men: fur-lined coats or jackets made from Vinalon, a synthetic fiber invented here two years after nylon, and which—rigid, shiny, uncomfortable, and with a tendency to shrink—has no advantage over its Western rival except that it is fabricated from limestone and anthracite, both of which are to be found in abundance in North Korea. When Constance expressed her surprise to the major that all the men had almost exactly the same haircut, he replied that they were obligated to keep their hair at a length of two inches—two and a half for men over fifty years old who were beginning to go bald—and to cut it every two weeks, because, as everyone knows, long hair steals energy from the brain.

After that ceremony, they went back in the limousine to the villa, with the major identifying himself once again at each checkpoint. When they had passed all those barriers and were inside the protection of the weeping willows, Constance saw another long and very official-looking car, parked empty outside the building. Ah, exclaimed Major Bakh, opening the car door for Constance, I think Comrade Gang has arrived. As they were walking through the grounds to the villa, she decided it would be a good idea to toss the major a compliment about the floral arrangements. And these begonias, she said, pointing to the beds of red and purple flowers, and all these orchids, it's all very nicely done. Yes, but I believe you are wrong about the names, replied the major stiffly. The mauve flowers are kimilsungias and the red ones are kimjongilias. As for the others, I'm not too sure. My training was mostly military, you see.

In the lobby, he went off in the direction of what looked like offices on the first floor while two minions escorted Constance upstairs to her room. Nothing had changed inside, except that this time, as in the most upscale Western hotels, posed on a coffee table was a new bouquet of flowers—kimilsungias, apparently—a basket of blueberries from, according to the label, Mount Paektu, legendary spot and official birthplace of the Supreme Leader, and an envelope with her name on it, containing an invitation for the next day, though with no mention of the time or the address. Now there was nothing to do but wait. An hour of CNN, for the want of anything better, until there was a knock on the door and Gang Un-ok appeared.

Without wishing to offend anyone, Gang Un-ok was unusually handsome for a Korean, with regular features, a face that was more oval-shaped than round, soulful eyes, lascivious lips, and all that jazz. Even his haircut, slightly mussed up, was different from the national norm. It was not that Gang's countrymen, glimpsed by Constance through the limousine's tinted windows, were ugly, but she had not spotted anyone particularly attractive either. Because of the country's aforementioned nutritional deficiencies, they had become short and frail, whereas the dignitary Gang was tall and athletic, highlighting his nicely designed civilian suit, so that even the obligatory badge representing the Leader's ancestors seemed somehow more discreet on his torso than on others'. So, to sum up, he really wasn't bad at all and—why not just say it?—Constance immediately felt something—yes, something—when she first laid eyes on him.

And Gang, too, presumably, as it must have been pretty special for him to meet the original singer of "너무 해," so much so that it must have taken quite a bit of self-control not to ask for an autograph right away. That could wait. In the meantime, after he had invited her to dinner, they left in his long, official-looking vehicle. As they traveled through the city, he pointed out to Constance the most noteworthy monuments, as Major Bakh had already done, but in a more elegant, detached, and amusing way, embellishing his descriptions with delicately crafted anecdotes. Because Gang Un-ok, thanks to his bilingual education in Switzerland, spoke French perfectly. Which certainly suits us, as it spares us the need for interpreters: cumbersome secondary characters, not to mention potentially embarrassing witnesses, which we wouldn't know what to do with afterward.

After reaching Ghangguang Avenue, the car parked outside a very large luxury hotel reserved for officials, delegations, diplomats, and foreign businessmen. First they had a good time in one of the hotel's bars, knocking back two or three dry martinis to warm things up— and, let's be honest, Gang was probably hoping to get Constance, already disoriented from the jet lag, a little tipsy—before going up to the restaurant on the top floor, which—to add to Constance's burgeoning dizziness—was revolving. There, they enjoyed a panoramic view of the capital, the only city in North Korea to benefit from nocturnal illumination or, more generally, from electricity, the rest of the country being plunged in darkness. So much so that, at night, when viewed from space stations, the country is invisible, a dark absence between China and South Korea, meaning that a cosmonaut with a poor grounding in geography might have taken it for a wide shipping lane connecting the Yellow Sea to the Sea of Japan.

Far from the provinces where people were starving in the dark, they sat in subdued lighting, with easy-listening music playing quietly in the background, and ate a delicate meal composed of seaweed leaves with soybeans followed by a dish of freshwater turtle and a rooster stuffed with chestnuts, jujube fruit, and ginger root, washed down with some excellent imported French wines, with a digestif of 65 percent rose-flavored wheat alcohol, by which point, according to Gang's calculations, he should have her pretty much where he wanted her.

And so, as is often the case in such an ambience, things moved quickly and—not to beat about the bush—in room 9104 of that establishment, the dignitary Gang Un-ok did not have much difficulty having his way with Constance: married name Coste, maiden name Thoraval, but above all, from the point of view of the starfucker that the dignitary had at that moment become, briefly famous back in the good old days under the stage name of So Thalasso.

30

THAT'S IT, EXCLAIMED THE GENERAL, contact has been established. You mean . . . ? Objat asked. I mean, explained the general, rubbing a Panter Vanilla against his ear, that Gang screwed the girl less than twenty-four hours ago and that that is a good start. How do you know that? Objat inquired. That's not complicated, said Bourgeaud, puffing up his chest. The Americans have listening stations in Mongolia: they can surveil anything they want in the region. I get along well with them. We exchange tips. It's much better with them than it is with the Chinese, for example. There's also MI6, who have a very small branch over there, but the English never find much—the Americans are better. He was looking at his cigarillo ambivalently now. Objat abstained from comment, remaining where he stood, near the window: from there, at that moment, he could see a torrential downpour transforming the barracks courtyard into a lake.

Anyway, we're off to a good start, the general reiterated, but what worries me a little bit is your two men. I know they went through the training, but their report was not very positive. Apparently—he grimaced as he leafed through this report—they are very willing but not very talented. Mediocre performance. Lack of attention. Not much presence of mind. No initiative. Pretty clueless, basically. You wouldn't have anyone else, would you, just in case? Someone more radical, if you know what I mean, more battle hardened. I might have an idea, said Objat after some thought.

And at that very moment: I have an idea, Lucile announced. What if we invited Nadine and Louis one night soon? They invited us, didn't they? Certainly not, grumbled Lessertisseur. Their place is really chic and ours is shabby. It'd be humiliating. What do you take me for? And what if that madman turns up with his gun and his dog like he did the other day?

Still, at that very same moment (a notably thought-heavy moment, it has to be said), that madman and the potential problems he posed were the subject of Lou Tausk's preoccupations. Like Objat, he was staring out as it rained cats and dogs on Rue Claude-Pouillet. He thought about putting the radio on, then remembered it wasn't working; then he thought about asking Nadine Alcover what she thought, then remembered that she had gone out, as she was doing more and more often these days. The idea of consulting someone else must have stuck with him because he headed toward the telephone, picked it up while grabbing a Pall Mall from the desk, lit it, and hesitated for a moment before dialing Hubert's number.

The voice of a new assistant asked him to kindly wait a moment; then, as often happened, Hubert first answered coldly before relaxing and, unable to resist his urge to make personal remarks, remarked: Your voice sounds strange, you know. Did you catch a cold or something? Well, not surprising with this weather. You could try gargling agrimony. I often take that before pleading—it's very effective. And there's also homeopathy, which isn't bad either. I'll think about it, promised Tausk, but could I drop by to see you? Of course, sighed Hubert, drop by, by all means.

In a raincoat, under an umbrella, Tausk walked to the Villiers metro station. Taking another Pall Mall from his pocket, he closed his hand around it like a shell to protect it from the rain, then noticed as he rummaged in his other pocket that he had forgotten his lighter. At the entrance to the metro, a beggar begged him for a cigarette, and, distractedly, instead of giving him one, Tausk asked him if he had a light. Now, that just isn't done. It is simply one of those things that you do not do. What terrible manners! And yet, the beggar searched his pockets for a long time while Tausk waited impatiently. He even made a joke: Yeah, too many pockets in winter, not enough in summer. When the poor homeless person finally handed him a lighter, he lit his cigarette, returned the lighter without thanks, took two or three drags as he went down the steps, then, remembering that smoking is prohibited in the metro, threw the soaked Pall Mall onto the ground, where the beggar dived on it.

In Neuilly, Hubert's new assistant, who once again asked him to kindly wait, could not hold a candle to Nadine Alcover in a physical sense—a face that sloped like a steep staircase, with a large platinum bun to act as a counterweight—and Tausk, just to say something, complimented her on its color. You think? she quivered, revealing long ivory teeth as she smiled. That's nice of you, because I'm a brunette, naturally, you see, and then I decided to dye it blond. Good idea: it suits you, Tausk said encouragingly. You're not going to seduce this one too, surely? Hubert exclaimed tactlessly, coming out of his office. Follow me. What can I do for you?

Half an hour later, Tausk emerged from Hubert's office without having made much progress: Don't worry about it, let him make the next move, the lawyer had once again advised him. On his way out, he waved good-bye to the new assistant, who was sitting opposite a man with a closed face and a closed briefcase on his knees, flanked by a not-very-affable-looking bodyguard. Outside, the rain was still pouring down, so he ran to a taxi rank and—as he was not the only one looking for a ride in weather like this—took his place in the line that meandered between metal barriers arranged in the shape of a paper clip. When his turn came to get in a taxi, a tired-looking Dacia, Tausk gave his address to the driver, who was silent for a moment. We should go through town, the driver suggested, because the beltline looks pretty busy, and Tausk did not notice that he abstained from starting the meter. Then the driver's eyes, staring at him in the rearview mirror, reminded him of someone else's eyes. But whose? He couldn't remember. Those eyes were like a pale shadow of someone else's, the same but faded, like an old fax that we rediscover after all these years, the way we often forget the original document in the photocopier. It took Tausk a great deal of effort, pixel by pixel, to recall those eyes.

While he was doing this, the windshield wipers kept squeaking under the percussive precipitation and it was only as they came near the Porte des Ternes that Tausk finally thought he had recognized the driver. Is that you, Hyacinth? he asked softly. Yes, replied Hyacinth in a muted voice, sounding unsurprised and not turning around, it's me. I got a new job, you see. Had to give up the old one. Silence. Which Tausk didn't dare break. It killed me, that incident, Hyacinth went on as he entered Boulevard Péreire. After that guy committed suicide, I just couldn't drive a train anymore. Never again. Another silence. Which Tausk continued to respect.

I did try, Hyacinth said, somewhere near Place du Maréchal-Juin, but I wasn't sleeping anymore; I couldn't stop thinking about it. I avoided closing my eyes, so I wouldn't have to see that again. If I took a shower, though, for example, and I had to close my eyes so I wouldn't get water in them, it would start right away, the movie in my head. I'd see the look on that guy's face as he waited for my train to roll over him. I was in shock, you know. I stopped work for a week, and then I tried to do it again, but no, I could never get back in the cab. I couldn't drive a train anymore, so I decided to try driving a taxi. At least that way, I'm still in the person-transporting business. The license costs a fortune, but never mind. And what about you . . . how are things? My goodness, was all Tausk could think to say. A third silence. Which Hyacinth broke.

You don't need anything repaired these days? he asked. No little jobs that need doing in your apartment? I can always drop by like I used to, if you want. I've got some free time on Tuesday. It might do me good, a change of air. My goodness, repeated Tausk, uh, let me see. Oh yeah, I think there's a little problem with my stereo. Could you take a look at the radio, CD player, all that? Of course, said Hyacinth. High fidelity is absolutely my thing. But I think we're here now. Thank you, Tausk said. How much do I owe you? Forget it, replied Hyacinth. Take my card instead.

And not at all at the same moment, because now we are going back to the start of this chapter: Yes, declared Objat, I think my idea is developing. I'll leave you now, General. Let me see what I can do. Do, do, encouraged the senior officer, proudly tearing apart his cigarillo. Objat left the office, walked along a corridor, opened the door of an empty office, picked up the telephone, and dialed a number. It rang two or three times before it was answered. Hello? said Objat. I'm listening, replied Pognel as he caressed Faust.

31

WHILE JEAN-PIERRE AND CHRISTIAN might well have shown a lack of initiative, as the general suspected based on the training report, they did have a reasonable excuse, because their room for maneuver was slim. Trapped in their hotel, reduced to the status of mere tourists, they had not been allowed to perform the task that they had, in principle, been hired to do: guarding Constance's body. Their constant suggestions, requests, and innuendos on this topic resulted only in more delaying tactics from their guides.

They only ever left the Yanggakdo with those guides in close attendance. Yun Sam-yong and Im Chin-sun had completely different personalities. The former was austere and reserved and spent his time napping and taking notes as the car moved through the capital, whose sights were praised in a stream of robotic compliments by the latter, their smiling and determined interpreter. It seemed that the principal role of the former was to surveil the latter—although it was probably the other way around. While displaying an excessive mutual friendliness, the two guides spent as much time watching each other as they did their guests, vigilant above all that they did not have the slightest contact with any passersby.

So, a tourist trip. After having to bow, like Constance and

everyone else, before the giant statues, they were taken to rhapsodize over every possible monument. Kim Il-sung Square, the Kim Il-sung Arch of Triumph, and the Kim Il-sung Mausoleum, to start with. Then the Grand People's Study House, the Schoolchildren's Palace, the Victorious War Museum, not forgetting a quick visit to the USS *Pueblo*—the American spy boat captured in January 1968 and now moored on the right bank of the Taedong River—before ending the morning at the Embroidery Institute, where Im Chin-sun encouraged Jean-Pierre and Christian to buy a few overpriced souvenirs—in euros, dollars, whatever they preferred—for their wives. We don't have wives, they said, starting to feel tired.

In the afternoon, they were taken to the metro to admire its monumental architecture, its fiddly details, its bronze and marble, its chandeliers and colonnades, its multicolored portraits of the leaders, and its vast murals. The rolling stock was mostly Chinese-made, although they did glimpse—despite the best attempts of Yun to screen its furtive passage—an old train of East German origin, still covered with pre-1989 graffiti, unrenovated, unstandardized. Their metro journey, however, was limited to the last two stops on Line 1, between Puhung and Yonggwang: Jean-Pierre and Christian made this trip in the company of their guides, of course, along with a handful of natives, supposedly just random fellow travelers but too well dressed, perhaps, to be anything other than extras. Those two stations, presumably the most attractive on the network, were the only ones shown to the visitors, opening the door to the hypothesis that there were in fact no other stations, or maybe that this was a parallel network for government use only, inspired by the secret lines on the Moscow metro.

To end the day on a high note, they were taken to see the Juche Tower, symbol of the *juche* ideology, the North Korean version of communism, which is based less on orthodox, rational Marxism-Leninism and more on principles of political independence, economic self-sufficiency, and military autonomy. The tower was five hundred feet tall, and from its peak, which you could reach by means of a rapid, optional elevator—payable in dollars or euros—you commanded a panoramic view of the capital. After that, they were taken back to the hotel, with Im and Yun promising other climbs (notably the mountains of Paektu, Songak, and Kumgang) and wonders in the coming days.

Jean-Pierre and Christian felt saturated, exhausted, and especially frustrated not to have been able to decipher the slogans that they saw everywhere on banners, posters, and gigantic billboards. These slogans, invariably ending with an exclamation point, were presumably exhortations to the masses to praise their leaders, celebrate the party's actions, vilify those imperialist American bastards—as well as the faggot puppets installed in power in the South by said imperialist bastards—and blindly follow the essential principles of *juche*, among many other excellent pieces of advice.

Christian, in particular, could barely summon the strength to remain upright by the end of the day, and Jean-Pierre had to force him to go downstairs to eat dinner in the hotel restaurant. There, they found themselves with plates full of the local delicacy, noodles in sweet potato starch, floating in a cold beef broth. After two beers, they didn't even feel like going outside to get some air, which was in any case forbidden. Back in their rooms, it seemed all the easier just to try to sleep, given that the power always went off at ten p.m. Jean-Pierre managed this without difficulty but was woken by Christian banging on his door one hour later, complaining of gastric discomfort: You wouldn't have any MiraLax or something like that, would you? I think I've gotten rid of the noodles, but it's the broth . . .

The power did not go out at the residence where Constance was staying. On the contrary, even the garden was lit up. Gang Un-ok had been busy all day and in the early part of the evening with high-level meetings, so she had spent her time walking in town accompanied by her own guides, two women who were much funnier and more likable than Im and Yun. Once again, the people she passed in the streets did not look particularly unhappy, because Pyongyang enjoyed a privileged status. It was separated from the rest of the country by numerous checkpoints, and its inhabitants had been handpicked for their loyalty to the dynastic regime.

At nightfall, she ate dinner alone in her room—a light meal of pea mousse with pomelo zest—then turned on the TV and channel-surfed until she found TV5 Monde: Tonight I welcome Pierre Michon, whose appearances are, as we all know, very rare, and I would like to thank you sincerely, Pierre Michon, for accepting my invitation. You're welcome, smiled Michon. And first of all, Pierre Michon, a question that seems to me central to your work: the style, by which I mean that singular manner that is your own, does that provoke the content or is it the consequence of that content? I don't know if I'm making myself clear. Absolutely, absolutely, answered Michon after a long silence, but it's perhaps a little more complicated than that. It's not that binary, you see. He was about to say more when the bedroom door opened without warning and Gang Un-ok appeared. Constance pressed the power button on the TV remote control.

First, Gang threw himself on her, which took up quite a bit of our time. Then, when they'd both gotten their breath back, he suggested they go to a few nightclubs. They did this, and Constance observed that in the chic areas of Pyongyang the nightclubs were in every way similar to nightclubs all over the world. Large, shiny, brand-new European cars, some of them convertibles, were parked outside the entrance of the first club. Inside, a mostly young crowd of people filled the vast space, dancing, talking very loud, fooling around, singing karaoke in front of giant screens, buying drinks for the pretty hostesses, spending their foreign money without counting, and chugging drinks. On this last point, Gang refused to be outdone, and Constance watched as he became more and more talkative. Sometimes I feel like I can't bear those meetings anymore, he shouted so she could hear him over the din, and she began to listen carefully: as General Bourgeaud had envisaged, internationally important confidences seemed about to be shared any minute now.

Back at the villa in the early morning, after watching the apparatchik bump into the walls of the corridor as they walked to their room, Constance thought she could make the most of his inebriation while they undressed: So what was that meeting about? Sitting on the edge of the bed, taking his shoes off without undoing the laces, using the toe section of his right to push the heel section of his left, Gang said: Just a routine Workers' Party Central Military Committee meeting. I have to go to one every month, and they're exhausting. Were there many of you? Constance asked, with a yawn. Let me think, said Gang, pulling his socks off so they ended up inside out. Well, there was the director of the People's Army General Political Bureau, the army chief of staff, the head of the defense office, the head of the air force, the minister of state security, the financial director of the Workers' Party . . . and who else? Oh yeah, three party assistant directors. And me. So, you see, quite a few people. What about your president? suggested Constance as she unhooked her bra. Of course, smiled Gang, struggling with his shirt buttons, Kim was there. For meetings of that level, he always comes. But what do you talk about, in that kind of thing? Constance asked casually. Why? He had stopped smiling. Are you interested? Not really, laughed Constance, leaping on top of him, I just wanted to hear your voice.

Now it is five in the morning. The sun is rising over Pyongyang. The recently installed nocturnal illuminations have all gone out except for the eternal red flame at the top of the Juche Tower. They fucked, then they grew drowsy and fell asleep. Gang Un-ok soon started snoring quietly, and before long Constance was doing the same.

Jean-Pierre, too, was asleep when there was a loud knock at his door: Christian stood in the corridor, looking pale and holding his hand to his abdomen, dressed in a striped pajama jacket that Jean-Pierre noticed had the buttons in the wrong holes. Jesus, do you know what time it is? he protested. Shut up, Christian shouted, this is an emergency. You wouldn't have any Imodium or something like that, would you? I really don't feel good at all. Ah, it's nothing, Jean-Pierre diagnosed. All you have, my boy, is a classic case of Pyongyang tummy. I'm not your boy, Christian yelled. Now show me what drugs you have. Immediately.

32

THAT SOUNDS FINE, Pognel says, but on one condition. I want to be able to impose my own conditions.

No conditions, Objat replies. You won't be imposing anything at all.

They are sitting on a bench, two feet apart. They are speaking in low voices, barely moving their lips and not looking at each other at all, as is customary during spy meetings. The few people who stroll past cannot imagine that they are deep in discussion, as they don't appear to know each other at all; they look like two strangers who happen to be sitting on the same bench by chance or because they're tired or idle, or because they want to observe three swans splashing around on the surface of the lake—which is, in fact, not a lake but an artificial pond with an equally artificial island at its center, in the shape of a half-melted sugarloaf, crowned with a peripteral rotunda inspired by the Temple of Vesta in Tivoli. Even Faust, busy watching the pigeons around the bench (and wondering if their latest physical-chemical status renders them still edible), seems unconcerned by these two men, as if, obeying their instructions, he did not know them either.

Late morning, midweek, steel-gray sky, forty-three degrees Fahrenheit: the park is practically deserted. Even if it is the richest park in Paris in terms of varieties of flora, they all look artificial and everything here is fake: the lake, the island, its rocks, and its grotto decorated with reinforced cement stalactites. To the right of Pognel and Objat, we can see the traces of a ghostly bandstand. To their left, a bridge composed of a single semicircular arch vaults over the lake. In the background, toward the northeast, we can hazily make out the tall buildings that line the Canal de l'Ourcq.

Of course I can impose them, my conditions, says Pognel. You've got nothing over me. I did my time in prison, I paid for my crimes, and I don't owe anybody anything. Oh really, says Objat, and what about the hairdresser? Icy silence from Pognel: the temperature suddenly plunges by three degrees. There's overwhelming evidence against you where the hairdresser is concerned, continues Objat. Your DNA on the door . . . Even someone like me, who has no experience in such matters, I might have thought to wipe the door handle. And that thing with the bathtub . . . Frankly, a first-year forensics student would have seen that in an instant.

The sweat freezes on Pognel's forehead as he stammeringly attempts to whisper the word *careful*. Forget it, Objat advises him. Where murder is concerned, you're just an amateur, but I do acknowledge that you have your qualities. You did okay with the girl's kidnapping; you did what I asked. That's why I wanted to see you. I have another proposal for you. Pognel shrinks backward. Objat calms him: Still the same girl, don't worry. Nothing complicated. And you have no choice anyway. For now, I'm blocking the hairdresser investigation, but I could set it in motion again like that [finger snap]. So, anyway, I'm sorry to put it like this, but I think I have you by the balls. All right, mutters Pognel, go ahead.

It's simple, Objat reassures him. For the hairdresser, I'll hush it up.

The investigation will be suspended and you'll have nothing to fear. For you, we're just talking about a brief trip and some instructions to follow. But where is it, this brief trip? Pognel asks. Far away, says Objat. I'll tell you more later. Okay, but just one more thing, says Pognel uneasily as he gets to his feet. Could I take my dog with me? As you like, shrugs Objat, but I wash my hands of all responsibility. I'll take him, come what may, Pognel stiffens. I'll take him wherever I go because I love him.

I think we've covered everything for now, concludes Objat, lifting the collar of his coat. Meet me next week for instructions. Same day, same place, same time. Okay, repeats Pognel, before whistling for Faust and zipping up his jacket. In the meantime, I'm going to take him for a walk, seeing as we're in the park already. I have to make him run, you see, a little bit every day. Objat watches him limp away, then starts walking back to the Mortier barracks, which—if you go up Rue de Crimée and Rue de Belleville—is only three or four stations from Parc des Buttes-Chaumont.

And not much farther from Couronnes station, from where Tausk emerges at that moment to head over to his studio. He's been going there more and more frequently recently. He even sleeps there sometimes and is a regular at the Pensive Mandarin again. Yes, I'm afraid things are not going well with Nadine Alcover. When Tausk goes home to his apartment on Rue Claude-Pouillet, either she's gone out for a walk or she's there but barely says a word except on the telephone; she can sometimes lock herself up with the telephone for hours before going out for a walk again. In the end, Tausk starts wondering if maybe she's having an affair or something.

In fact, it is precisely that subject which she is discussing at the moment with Lucile on the phone: I've known him for two months, yeah, replies Nadine Alcover. No, he's older than the other one, but he's still great. Very attentive, very well dressed, very discreet. What about money? Lucile asks. Lots, summarizes Nadine Alcover. Seems to have lots, anyway. Married? asks Lucile, alarmed. I don't think so, Nadine Alcover reassures her, I see him more as a widower. What does he do? wonders Lucile. I'm not sure about that, admits Nadine Alcover, he never really talks about it. Maybe retired. Sometimes I think he's like an old soldier, but not at all the rough, brutal type. He's more the elite type—you know, Saint-Cyr, Cadre Noir, that type of thing. Where did you meet him? asks Lucile. In a museum, Nadine Alcover remembers. One afternoon, I think it was the Jacquemart-André Museum. We were both standing in front of a Caillebotte painting. You know who that is, Caillebotte? Not a clue, admits Lucile. Doesn't matter, shrugs Nadine Alcover. So anyway, we talked about the painting, we talked about Caillebotte and lots of other things and then he invited me to have some tea with him, and there you go. I see, Lucile nods. Sorry, will you hang on for a second?

As the bedroom door has just been opened by Lessertisseur, holding a shopping basket, Lucile turns away and covers the mouthpiece of the old, dusty Alcatel phone with her hand. Listen, Maurice, can't you see that I'm busy? Lessertisseur gestures questioningly at the shopping basket. I was thinking of broccoli, he says in a low voice, but what would go with it? I don't know, Lucile says exasperatedly, just get a couple of escalopes. With broccoli, good, good, I'll see you later. Sorry again, Nadine, she breathes, it was just Maurice, going out to buy groceries.

So how are things with him? asks Nadine Alcover. Still the same, more or less, says Lucile, but he gets on my nerves sometimes. He's not a bad guy, Maurice, you know, but I have the feeling I don't love him as much as I did before. And as I told you before, sexually, he just has one thing on his mind and that, sometimes, frankly . . .

They're so egotistical. I know, agrees Nadine Alcover. Wait a second, I've got another call, let me just get rid of them.

Nadine Alcover touches her Samsung Galaxy Trend: Yes, Georges, no, not at all, on the contrary, I'm delighted to hear from you. Excellent, seven o'clock, as we said. I don't know, wherever you like. Place du Palais-Bourbon? You mean the large café at the end of Rue de Bourgogne? Perfect, it's just next to Philippe's place. Oh, no, not at all! He's my hairdresser. I'll be there. See you later, Georges. Excuse me, Lucile, that was him, the other one. The new one, I mean.

33

CONSTANCE'S FIRST FOUR DAYS in the villa were more or less identical, similar to the way that her days in Creuse had blurred into one. Indeed, there were several elements in common, and there was nothing in particular that made her feel she might be in Asia rather than anywhere else in the world.

She spent most of her mornings reading in the villa's grounds, again on a sun lounger, and with even better service than before. She was provided with a few French books or books translated into French, a disparate mix from who knew where, chosen by who knew who, ranging from the *Treatise on Style* to the *Treatise on Passions of the Soul*, from Pearl Buck to Pierre Daninos, via *Let Us Now Praise Famous Men*, *The Life of Bees*, and an old paperback edition of *Forever Amber* by Kathleen Winsor.

In the afternoons, her guides took her on tours of the city, always in the same wealthy areas where there were luxury stores for the elite, who drove around in Range Rover Sport V8s or Mercedes Coupes. A parallel economy was beginning to flourish in Pyongyang, with boutiques open to an elegant clientele of women with dyed or wavy hair instead of the standard bun, dressed in Versace or Ferragamo instead of the traditional *hanbok*. In an undertone, one of the guides explained to Constance that this commercial strategy perhaps had something to do with the Leader's wife, whose elegance and beauty were widely praised, although she was not merely a decorative object but a woman of influence too, so much so that since their marriage this capitalist liberalization had begun to bloom.

While waiting for the return of Gang Un-ok, Constance spent her early evenings watching foreign television, seeing him again only at night, when her real work as a pillow-talk informer began. She diligently collected all the data the Korean apparatchik let slip about the highest echelons of the regime. As these highest echelons had learned about the presence in Pyongyang of the singer of "Excessif," Constance and Gang were invited, on her fifth day, to a party on one of the Kim family's private yachts, anchored at sea off Wonsan on the country's eastern coast. They went there after lunch: ninety miles by limousine on a deserted and arrow-straight, almost autistically single-minded highway with no interchanges or access roads or any kind of rest areas at all: they reached the quay in an hour. The yacht was like a floating amusement park, with swimming pools, water-skiing and windsurfing equipment, multiple bars and bands on every floor, fifteen incredibly luxurious suites, gold-plated plumbing, and precious woods everywhere. They spent the afternoon at the pool on the boat's top floor.

In the evening, before the banquet, the Supreme Leader himself appeared to the sound of the song "Footsteps" by Ri Jong-o, instantly provoking a unanimous low bow. Solid and paunchy, his large, chubby, oval-shaped head in proportion with his large oval torso—a duck egg atop an ostrich egg with no neck to join them—he moved forward obstinately, awkwardly, compensating for his lack of height (like his Dear Leader father) with thick heelpieces, holding his arms out wide to keep his balance. Constance quickly learned that he was cultivating his resemblance to his Eternal Leader grandfather, reproducing the same gestures, the same gait, wearing the same suits, his hair styled in the same way: temples shaved, the back puffed up, the middle parted. It was even rumored (though there were so many rumors) that this resemblance had been accentuated by no less than six surgical operations.

He had come with his wife, an ex-cheerleader for the national athletics team, an ex–pop star well known for her hits "I Adore Pyongyang" and "We Are the Troops of the Party." With her doll-like, fresh-faced appearance, she looked very sweet, though the spinach and bottle-green outfit she wore was less flattering. The Supreme Leader was also accompanied by his younger sister, recently promoted to the head of the department in charge of directing and organizing the Central Committee after previously leading the Workers' Party's mephitic Department 54, tasked with collecting foreign currency by any means necessary. With her diaphanous skin and oblong figure, dressed in a dark suit, the sister wasn't bad-looking either, and Constance remembered seeing her on propaganda posters, astride a white Turkoman stallion with blue eyes—considered by some to be the most beautiful horse in the world—the Kim family always keen to show off its horse-riding prowess, intended to identify it, consciously or subconsciously, in the mind of the people as a dynasty of centaurs.

Chain-smoking cigarettes, his glass of scotch refilled ad libitum, the Supreme Leader kept eating slices of Emmental from the dishes that were passed around. He apparently discovered this cheese during his years of study in Switzerland and now found it irresistible, though he was unhappy enough with its local fabrication to have sent some Korean cheese makers to Besançon in order to finish their training at the National School of the Dairy Industry. He smiled most of the time, the only alternative to this smile being a blank expression that somehow seemed to exude a combination of mistrust, envy, anger, menace, and sulkiness, as if his emotions were completely binary, with no shades of gray in between. He greeted Constance with an extended-play version of his smile number 1 before flashing Gang his expression number 2 and asking for a word in private. After that, the Supreme Leader went back to Constance and beamed an even wider version of number 1 at her as if he were casually seducing her, and his wife shot Constance a brief look in which various possible fates could be deciphered, from a strict labor camp to death by machine gun.

In honor of Constance, the band was silenced and the original version of "Excessif" was played over the sound system. This was greeted with copious applause, before the Korean version—"너무 해"—was played, and its blushing, trembling singer introduced. The trembling may have resulted from the prospect of being sent to the Supreme Leader's personal labor camp when the evening was over, as all artists were automatically regarded as potential dissidents, along with their family and friends, in accordance with the widely applied principle of guilt by kinship and association.

After aperitifs, they sat down for the banquet, whose menu was beyond not only the imagination but also the digestive capacities of the guests. Conch and royal shark's fin soup, mushrooms sautéed with quenelles of salmon, crawfish stew, fire-grilled whiting, horse mackerel and tuna, roast kid, Uzbek and Iranian caviar, Danish pork, and, best of all, special beef, exclusively for the use of the nomenklatura, reared on ultrasecret livestock farms run by communities of reclusive farmers on land protected by deep ditches and lined by trees, in the Hwanghaenam-do Province.

The next morning, as they were lying in bed after getting back to the villa late after the party on the yacht, Constance ingenuously commented: It wasn't bad, that party, was it? There are days when I can't stand this anymore, confessed Gang, feeding the hopes of General Bourgeaud. I'm sorry if this is indiscreet, whispered Constance, nuzzling close to him, but what did he ask you yesterday, your boss, when he took you aside? He's getting crazier and crazier, said Gang. He wants me to get my hair cut like him now. So you're going to get your hair cut off? Constance asked. Better my hair than my head, Gang decided, not without discernment.

34

FOR THE PAST TWO WEEKS, Nadine Alcover has not spent much time at the apartment in Rue Claude-Pouillet. In the evenings, Lou Tausk will sometimes see her, coming home late after he's eaten dinner alone and going to bed in the back bedroom. But during the day, he is left in peace. Now, for example, it's late morning and Lou Tausk is at a loose end. Sometimes when we have nothing to do, we tidy up, and so it was that, as Tausk was tidying up his papers, he found a few from Pélestor, which made him think of Hyacinth. So he called Hyacinth, who had dropped by a few days before to provide Tausk with a technical report on his stereo, a diagnosis so thorough that Tausk went out and bought another one. Hyacinth is waiting in his taxi at a rank near Botzaris when he receives the call: Are you free for lunch? I know a pretty good Chinese place, not too far from where you are. Sounds good, says Hyacinth, I'm not too busy at the moment. Not many customers these days, on account of the financial crisis.

So they met outside the Pensive Mandarin, went inside, and were guided to Tausk's usual table near the aquarium, whose inhabitants Hyacinth observed. They did not look back at him. In fact, they seemed to avoid or even flee his gaze, having spotted him as a former expert in halieutics, because when he was young Hyacinth used to take his dugout canoe—made from iroko wood and propelled by a combination of sail and paddle—out to sea beyond Sassandra's mangroves. There, he would fish for local varieties such as the polygamous pearly razor fish (whose harem, at a loss when the male is hooked, chooses the largest female, who then devotes herself to changing sex), the dream fish (care required as it feeds on hallucinogenic seaweed), the completely inedible Atlantic stargazer, the combative pagrus, and the blind beaux-yeux.

We are deep in these reflections when Tausk's cell phone vibrates in his pocket: Hubert, announces Hubert. Hubert rarely calls Tausk, but he decides to complain: You only ever get in touch with me when you need me for something. You'd rather call your friends. Maybe you think it's cheaper because they live closer to you. I don't have many friends, admits Tausk. Me neither, acknowledges Hubert. Well, that makes things simpler. Why don't you come and see me? Sure, says Tausk, but I don't have much to tell you. Ah, but I have plenty to tell you, unfortunately, says Hubert.

After lunch, Hyacinth was happy to take Tausk to Neuilly. They didn't talk much in the car, except for a few comparisons about food from around the world. I like Chinese food, says Hyacinth, of course. They do it well. But if you've ever eaten food from my homeland—*alloco* or agouti or *soso*—well, it's something else. Don't you miss it sometimes, the Ivory Coast? Tausk asks him. Of course I miss it, exclaims Hyacinth. Every day. Maybe it was a bad idea to come to France. And they arrived in Neuilly.

When we go through the front door of Hubert's residence, we see the new assistant's shimmering blond bun to our left, like an extra lamp; to our right, we see two men sitting in chairs. We have already seen one of them before—the one who looks like Jean Bouise and who has let his mustache grow since the other day in order to increase this resemblance. He is playing with a calculator beneath the magnetic lid of his open briefcase while the other one, whom we have never seen, consults his Patek Philippe, then gestures nervously with his chin toward the assistant. Who asks him to please be patient, because Maître Coste is very busy. As Tausk goes into Hubert's office before them, the Patek wearer calls out coldly: What about him? We were here first. He's family, says the assistant. It's different.

As expected, Hubert remarks to Tausk that the flap of his jacket pocket is tucked in. Now, as far as pocket flaps are concerned, you have a choice of two possibilities: either you tuck them in, or you leave them out. But whichever option you go for, you have to do the same for both. And yet Hubert seems distracted as he says this, as if he no longer really believes it, as if his heart's not in it. I'm involved in something shady, he admits as he paces around his office, and I'm worried about a certain number of problems. I'm dealing with some increasingly questionable people. I wanted to talk to you about this to get your opinion, but I don't have much time—they're here. Can I call you back tonight?

Tausk, leaving the office to the questionable people, hangs about for a while near the assistant with the bun. She's actually not bad-looking: imagining her when she's not wearing glasses, or even when she's not wearing anything at all, he asks: Is Hubert in trouble? The girl frowns in the direction of the two empty chairs. I can't talk about it, she says. Of course, Tausk agrees, I understand completely. But there are lots of other things we could talk about. Maybe we could go out one evening? I'll give you my card, replies the assistant, scrawling ten figures on the back. This is my cell number. You never know. That's true, thinks Tausk. I'm Charlotte, she says. And I'm Louis, he says. On his way out of Hubert's house, passing a gray BMW with a gorilla inside, he examines the card: Charlotte Guglielmi. Good.

When he got back to Rue Claude-Pouillet, he sensed something had changed. It was hard to put his finger on what it was exactly, but he felt quite sure. Something in the air had changed, unless it was something in the cupboards. A quick search of the cupboards revealed the fact that all of Nadine Alcover's possessions had disappeared. All that remained of her was a note, inside an envelope, placed on the coffee table.

35

DURING THOSE SAME TWO WEEKS, Constance extended her knowledge of the city. As she was bored of the sightseeing, her two guides took her to see the movie studios (sets of a spectral Chinese or European or Japanese city, depending on the screenplay for the film that was being shot), to spend the afternoon at the circus (a small circle filled with gym apparatus on which, pretty often, the acrobats fell flat on their faces), to go on a roller coaster at the local amusement park (rusty armrests and handles), or to visit an ostrich farm (ostriches were very useful animals: their flesh was savored by the party bigwigs, and their feathers and skin were sold for high prices to foreign hatters and tanners).

They also organized a few trips outside the capital for her: standard tourist excursions, to begin with, sometimes verdant, sometimes not, but always narrowly circumscribed. Then when she asked to see the provinces, she was told that all towns and cities beyond the capital were off-limits despite Gang Un-ok's status and his various passes. They stuck to the highways, from which they saw a countryside that was bare, open, uniform, the earth apparently arid and mutilated, as if it had been turned in vain, as if it were exhausted, as if even the trees found it hard to grow here—and most of them were sawed down by the locals anyway, to feed their stoves.

No derivation from the schedule was allowed to visit the villages they saw in the background, and whenever a secondary road took them past one of these villages, they always looked exactly the same: swept by two or three women pointed out to Constance as volunteers, with other volunteers digging in the grass on the roadside; men carrying bags, alone or in small groups, a man herding six goats, another pushing his bicycle. Sometimes an oxcart would go past, or a truck carrying some soldiers standing crammed together on its flatbed. Once, when they were blocked by a broken-down bus, Constance had time to count the eleven soldiers who pushed it out of the way. Maybe they weren't all soldiers necessarily, but they were all wearing similar types of uniforms, often mismatched, in shades of brown, gray-beige, and dark green. Or perhaps this was just the local fashion? In the end, Constance stopped going on these excursions.

When Gang Un-ok managed to get a day or two off work, they would go to vacation resorts for oligarchs, which—less luxurious than the Leader's yacht—resembled the palaces of Saddam Hussein as discovered after his fall: successions of large, empty rooms, with monumental gold-fringed couches and coffee tables made of glass and convoluted wrought-iron patterns, of a kind that you can find on Rue du Faubourg-Saint-Antoine in Paris (notably at numbers 2 to 12). The walls were decorated with historical and revolutionary tapestries, which sometimes hung side by side, incongruously, with French paintings from the 1950s, Yves Brayer or Bernard Buffet, once an Utrillo. They went out in the garden to get some air; then they spent most of their time in the basement, in swimming pools or projection rooms, smelling respectively (and very strongly) of chlorine and cresol.

While Gang's schedule was slightly more flexible now, he admitted to Constance one night that it was part of a reduction—at first barely perceptible—in his responsibilities. His place in the hierarchy seemed to have taken a few blows: sensitive to the tiniest details, with a knowledge of political codes—the obliqueness of a look, a slipped precedence, an extra half smile—he was able to interpret all this, and the news was not good. Having had his hair cut (though perhaps not quite short enough) on the advice of the Leader, he feared he had fallen into disgrace, and soon he was no longer even invited to some Saturday meetings. When this happened, he and Constance went away for the weekend.

On their way back from one of these weekends, Gang's limousine passed near the airport where Clément Pognel had, at that moment, just landed. Bourgeaud's services had fabricated a role for him as an agri-food adviser, and his visa was accepted without comment. In order not to risk any interference between agents, they had booked him into the Potonggang, another tourist hotel, far away from the Yanggakdo, where Jean-Pierre and Christian were beginning to feel downhearted, even though their hotel was much nicer than Pognel's. Because the Potonggang, considerably less expensive than the Yanggakdo, did have a few inconveniences: little hot water most of the time, no water at all at night, frequent power cuts (hence the blocked elevators), an ice-cold bedroom, with the window and balcony sealed shut, disturbing nocturnal noises when Pognel was trying to fall asleep on his granite bed, which was even less comfortable than his tourist-class plane seat.

The presence of Faust did not pose any problems. The inevitable guides, waiting for Pognel at the airport, even seemed amused by the dog, playing fearfully with him, though they did not go as far as feeding him. Unfortunately, two days after his arrival, Pognel would observe upon waking that Faust had vanished, probably abducted during the night by the guides, even if they immediately pretended to do everything they could to make sure he was found. These supposed searches were in vain, however, and there can be little doubt about the poor animal's fate. While Faust had certainly been taken, first of all, for comestible reasons—because, when well prepared, dog is extremely tasty—it was also, of course, his fur that was targeted, as dogs are almost as versatile in their uses as ostriches. That beagle's pelt, not big enough to line a coat, would probably be used in the confection of a hat or a muff that would be the delight of some neoliberal Pyongyang lady.

And so a few days later, Pognel, in mourning for his pet, was in a very bad mood when he contacted Constance in accordance with the modus operandi indicated by Objat: in the toilet of the Hotel Koryo, with the two of them escaping the attentions of their guides for a few minutes. Given this context, their meeting was brief. And unbalanced: Pognel, having organized her kidnapping, knew exactly who Constance was, whereas she knew nothing about him at all. Well, Pognel asked, where do things stand with this guy? I think he's starting to ripen, Constance replied, as in the days when people spoke of her in these terms. Things don't seem to be going well for him, and I can see that he's afraid. Perfect, said Pognel. I'll await instructions and keep you informed. Let's get back to the others now, before they start having doubts.

And when she returned to the villa, Gang did indeed seem distraught. He had just been moved from the National Defense Committee to a subsection on economic exchange with Syria. He had also been stripped of his functions as an adviser, which did not bode well at all since he had not been informed of this man-to-man, but through cold circumlocutions. But there was even worse news: while Gang's status before now had allowed him to travel to China as part of various cooperation programs, those authorizations had now been removed, making him seriously worried. Why, Constance asked, did you want to go there?

It's not that, but it all happens quickly once it starts like that, answered Gang, becoming ensnared in demonstrative pronouns. He then went on: Well, the best thing would obviously have been to take advantage of an official visit. Now, if they won't let me leave anymore, I don't know how I'll manage it. Don't worry, Constance reassured him, we'll find a solution. How could you solve this? Gang snapped. You don't know anything about the system. You have no idea what they're capable of being capable of.

Constance again noted that, despite his mastery of the French language, the really quite simple syntax of this last sentence had put the dignitary in difficulty. I don't know yet, she smiled, pulling him toward their king-size bed. We'll have to see.

36

SO THINGS ARE PROGRESSING, the general says, rubbing his hands together. The Americans are going to be happy. If all goes to plan, Gang should be in Seoul a few weeks from now. Except they suspect something, points out Objat, looking through the window, where the rain has stopped. If they won't let him leave anymore, that could be a bit annoying.

He'll just have to manage, supposes Bourgeaud. There's no question of going through the demilitarized zone, of course. The best thing would be to travel via China. Even if they've increased security, the border is still pretty porous. But he'd better not hang around. The South Korean consulates in Beijing are carefully monitored by Kim's regime. To avoid problems, they sometimes turn people back and hand them over to the Chinese police, who take great pleasure in sending them back to North Korea.

This could be tricky, remarks Objat, turning to the general. Not necessarily, replies Bourgeaud, standing up. He'll have to get out of China as quickly as possible, and for that we have two solutions. The general heads over to a map of the region pinned to the wall and, without recourse to any sort of cigarillo, punctuates the following words with his finger.

To the north, you have Mongolia and to the south, you have Laos. The Mongolian network isn't bad. The South Korean diplomats in Ulaanbaatar are generally quite welcoming. It would mean a long trip, obviously—you have to cross the entire Gobi desert— but it's the nearest border. And, of course, there are trains, people can be bought. Gang must have put quite a bit of money aside for palm-greasing purposes. There's also a whole gang of Protestant pastors in the area who kindly devote themselves to helping defectors. They could be useful.

As for Laos, the general continues, the good thing is that it's very easy to get into Thailand, and from there, you're in the clear. The less good thing is that it's complicated, Laos. No train lines. Nothing but buses and planes, and there's no question of taking either of those. You have to walk, while avoiding roads for safety reasons. And that means putting up with the jungle, moving forward only at night, with the snakes, the wild animals, the leeches, the risk of being picked up by a patrol who'll send you back to Pyongyang without a second's thought. Apparently it's exhausting. Personally, I would recommend the Mongolian option.

What about Vietnam? suggests Objat. Don't even think about it, the general interrupts him, you can't count on Hanoi. They'll send him back home in a flash. So, we're definitely not out of the woods yet, observes Objat. Listen, the general says irritably, there are plenty of people who've managed to get away without any money or connections or anything. I assume Gang has maintained contacts in various places. He has everything he needs to get through this. If you say so, shrugs Objat. If necessary, he offers, I could go over there and give him a helping hand. I'm not too busy at the moment. If you like, but don't be gone too long, objects Bourgeaud. I have another project for you.

This is a medium-term project whose broad outlines he goes on to sketch: It will be different, in Africa, but the system should be more or less similar. We'll have to use an amateur, like the young woman you found me for Pyongyang. An innocent, if you like, who understands nothing about our activities. In terms of recruitment and training and so on, it should be simpler than it was with her. No need to purge him before the mission like you did with the girl. Just keep him under pressure. After two seconds of thought, Objat announces once again: I may have an idea for that. He salutes the general and goes to his own office.

There, in accordance with methods known only to him—and which, lacking familiarity with such techniques, we don't really understand anyway—Paul Objat first gets in touch with Clément Pognel. He gives him a few instructions regarding the affair they're dealing with now, but the call does not end there: he also asks for some information about another, much older affair, insisting on certain details. And then, even though it's not raining, Objat takes his raincoat, goes downstairs, walks through the barracks courtyard, shows his badge at the exit yet again, comes to a halt on Boulevard Mortier, and hails a taxi. Inside, he sits in silence for a moment until the driver—no, it's not Hyacinth—turns around and asks: Where to, sir? Objat replies: Parc Monceau.

And it is in Parc Monceau that Tausk has arranged to meet Hubert's new assistant. As it is very close to where he lives, the choice of this location constitutes the first part of a plan. For the same reason, Charlotte is wearing perfume and a plunging neckline and she has loosened her bun, which, in its usual tightly knotted work position, has the unfortunate side effect of accentuating her face's flaws: this more relaxed version of the bun—aka a loose bun—falling over her neck a little bit and allowing a few locks to escape, produces a much

more appealing effect. Her dark roots are also more visible beneath
the blond, and Tausk finds this pretty exciting, so he sets out to
seduce Hubert's assistant without any qualms whatsoever. She talks
about Hubert, whose latest clients, she suspects, are involved in some
dubious business. They are not the first clients to entrust Hubert
with shady cases, and consequently Charlotte is worried for her employer and, naturally, for her own employment prospects.

While conversing, they walk along the paths in the park, where,
strategically placed, Objat observes their comings and goings. And
no, we don't really understand either, despite our omniscience, how
he could have come to find out about this meeting, which does, it has
to be said, seem to be going pretty well. Charlotte has a tendency to
become enthusiastic about practically everything she sees in the park.
Though not very interested in the statues of the artists, she goes into
raptures over the languid, pensive, lascivious women who accompany
them: Gounod's mistress, one of Maupassant's whores, Musset's fan
club, Chopin's girlfriend.

Seeing her reaction to these poses and shifting into a higher se-
duction gear, Tausk ventures, at the risk of heavy-handedness (and
alliterative overkill): They're not nearly as nice as you, just to see
what effect it produces. As she reacts with a glimmer in her eye and
a provocative half smile, Tausk concludes that far from being limited
to the artists' groupies, Charlotte's enthusiasm will bloom even more
rapturously in his bed. The plan is shaping up nicely.

So, having walked around the park and courted the girl for a sufficient length of time, Tausk suggests they go to his place—I live just
over there—for a drink: this is phase two of the plan. Oh, she exclaims in apparent alarm, not on the first date! A phrase that suggests
a second date, which is positive, but that also involves the postpone-
ment and complication of the plan. Without agreeing on a date for

their next date, they part, Tausk careful not to kiss her on the cheek, as in such scenarios he has found that gazing deeply into the other's eyes is generally more effective. When she has left, Tausk goes back to his apartment.

There, he paces around for a while, turns the television on, and then immediately turns it off again. Opens a magazine, a window, the refrigerator, and closes each one in turn. Checks his fingernails again and goes for a piss. Sees himself in a mirror. And just then, the doorbell rings: has Charlotte changed her mind?

Nope. It's a man, in fact, quite good-looking (better-looking than Tausk in any case, which annoys him right away), and about forty years old (hence younger than Tausk, which also annoys him). The man looks at him in silence, half smiling, wearing the sort of kind, affectionate, understanding expression that nonetheless augurs the worst, again like Billy Bob Thornton in some of his roles. Monsieur Louis Coste? the man asks. Yes, replies Tausk suspiciously and also irritably, as he never likes being named in that way: it is generally tax inspectors, police officers, or similar pains in the ass who address him by his full, correct name. That's me, he says, but I don't think I know you. I know you, though, says the man. Can I talk to you for a minute?

Tausk hesitates briefly, and then, ever naïve, it crosses his mind that this man could also be an admirer of his work or even—why not dream?—a producer or an agent keen to help him make his comeback. It could even be a journalist. You never know. Come in, then, he says, pointing the man toward the living room. Please take a seat, he adds, sitting down himself. Thank you, but I'd prefer to stand, the man replies. This won't take very long.

With him ensconced in his chair and the man standing, looming over him in a low-angle shot that disconcertingly tilts the balance of power away from him, Lou Tausk regrets having sat down too quickly. I'm listening, he says. It's a simple matter and I'll be brief, the man tells him. Do you remember a bank on Avenue de Bouvines, near the Nation metro, quite a few years ago? Ring any bells? If not, I could remind you of certain details that might interest you. Oh God, Tausk sighs. Exactly, acknowledges Paul Objat.

37

A TORRENTIAL FLOOD of mud poured under the bridges of the Tae-dong River, then Constance left the movie theater before the end of a very popular film entitled *Sea of Blood*, which tells the story of the Japanese massacres of the North Korean people when the Koreans were under their protectorate. She stood up discreetly and headed noiselessly toward the exit under the disapproving gaze of the other viewers and her guides, who were determined to watch the movie until its conclusion. So it was that the driver, waiting outside the theater, took her back to the villa alone, leaving her there earlier than scheduled and, contrary to usual protocol, driving off immediately afterward. Constance saw an ambulance parked near the villa. Also contrary to usual protocol, however, she did not see a single servant in the entrance hall, though she did spot, lined up at the foot of the stairs, a dozen jerry cans smelling strongly of gasoline. Then, going upstairs and opening the door of her bedroom, she came upon an unexpected scene.

There were five intruders. Two men in white coats and three in black overalls surrounded Gang Un-ok, who lay naked on the floor, tied up with translucent plastic straps, gagged with sticky tape, his eyes flickering from face to face. The men in white were crouched down next to him. One of them tore off the sticky tape and opened Gang's jaws, sliding a red funnel into his mouth, a demijohn of opaque green liquid to hand. The other was taking a large amount of equipment from a bag, but—one of the black overalls grabbing Constance from behind and immobilizing her, and another placing a hood over her head—she did not have time to examine this equipment in any detail.

The procedure in progress was what is known as the plastering of anti-party elements, a technique developed under the reign of the current leader's father. This treatment is reserved in particular for diplomats stationed abroad who are convicted or merely suspected of ideological deviation by state security agents, who monitor all embassy employees. In such cases, the diplomat must be repatriated urgently, and the following method is used. After being given a massive dose of a soporific, the suspect is stripped and his body wrapped in gauze before being covered up to the neck in fast-drying plaster, immobilizing him in the blink of an eye, then swathed in rubber bands. With a house fire claimed—or started—to justify this intervention, the diplomat's body is then put on a stretcher, shoved into an ambulance, and evacuated by specially chartered plane to his homeland, where, rest assured, a specialized treatment center is waiting to welcome the wounded man. Such centers really do exist, and such treatment really is very specialized.

The equipment glimpsed by Constance and unwrapped by the second white coat consisted of bags of fine plaster, rolls of gauze, and rubber bands, along with all the appropriate tools, plus a bucket of water. The jerry cans she saw in the entrance hall presumably being intended to set fire to the villa, the procedure was all set to be carried out as planned. Admittedly, it was not necessarily essential, within North Korea itself, to go to such trouble over Gang, but perhaps the procedure was followed simply because it always gives such pleasure to the security agency's leaders and agents.

Things followed their course, quickly and efficiently. Once Gang was wrapped in gauze, the plastering began: beginning with his feet, the white coats covered him up to his shoulders. While one of the black overalls continued immobilizing the hooded Constance, the others, hands behind their backs, watched calmly as the operation unfolded. One of them, having already prepared the stretcher, whistled "Footsteps," not inappropriately. So everything was going well, from the intruders' point of view, when the door burst open and two European-looking men charged at the three black overalls. Trained in tae kwon do, the Koreans put up a fierce resistance.

We know that tae kwon do, a martial art native to Korea, consists in delivering violent blows to one's opponent with the aid of all one's limbs. The upper limbs, of course—fist, side of the hand, fingertips, elbow, forearm—but most of all (and this is what distinguishes tae kwon do from wing chun or bando, for example) the lower limbs. The knee is used to some degree, but the foot in all its aspects— side, tip, ball, heel, bridge—is the main weapon, being utilized to perform all imaginable variants of kick: direct, lateral, scissor, circular, downward . . . and that's without even mentioning the acrobatic flying kicks popularized by Bruce Lee and his imitators.

What is less well-known is that, while the impact of classic tae kwon do, when the contact is part of the sport, can touch the opponent's face, legs, solar plexus, or ribs without risk of injury, there is also a variant known as black tae kwon do, which is much more dangerous. Reserved for a fighting elite (to which the men in black overalls belonged), this practice is based on the supposition that any kick must be delivered with the intention to kill. The technique, then, is to target certain crucial areas such as the throat or the temple or—most sensitive of all—the genital triangle.

But anyway . . . When it came to this martial art, the Europeans, to general surprise—or at least to ours, as Constance, still being hooded, was unable to enjoy the spectacle—proved themselves technically excellent, overpowering the black overalls while ignoring their raucous insults: in no time at all, the three Koreans were defeated. As for the men in white coats, they had very little combat training and offered only minimal resistance before also being thoroughly neutralized.

When that was done, the Europeans removed the hood from Constance's head. Initially dazzled and frightened by the scene's soundtrack, she covered her eyes with her hands. Then, peeking through her fingers, she recognized the two Europeans. Having recently met him in the restroom of the Hotel Koryo, she immediately identified Pognel (whom, incidentally, we wouldn't have thought capable of such pugilistic brio), but it took her a few seconds longer to place Objat, whom she had not seen since his return to Creuse, and who had obviously decided to intervene personally in this operation, as he'd suggested to the general in the previous chapter. Oh, Victor, she said, appearing surprisingly unsurprised given the overall context.

After that, they left as quickly as they could while carrying the stretcher downstairs and slid said stretcher into the back of the ambulance, which was still parked in the same spot, the driver having been permanently subdued with a simple, well-aimed forearm smash followed by a pinch of the carotid artery. And before leaving, to make things look less suspicious—and delay the doubtless imminent intervention of the army—they set fire to the villa using the contents of the jerry cans.

As the building blazed, they climbed into the ambulance, and Pognel—who, despite the incomplete city maps, had managed to scout the area—got behind the wheel. In the back of the vehicle, Objat, aided by Constance, removed the plaster from the unconscious apparatchik, not without difficulty even if the cast was not yet hard enough to require the use of a hammer. Then Objat, having thought of everything, took a hypodermic syringe and a vial of an analeptic drug from his pocket and injected said drug into Gang's bloodstream. The Korean's body jumped as if he'd been electrocuted, but his consciousness seemed to come back only gradually.

In the meantime, the ambulance crossed the city, its official appearance allowing it to avoid being intercepted by the military checkpoints posted at street corners. It came to a halt at the end of a short dead-end road in a quiet neighborhood. Apparently it was expected: barely had it stopped before a garage door opened. Though it was impossible to distinguish anyone inside it, the two-car garage already contained a government-style sedan, decorated with official stickers and pennants. The ambulance went inside and the garage door promptly closed behind it. They got out, carefully covered the vehicle with a tarpaulin, and—Objat and Pognel supporting the still-wobbly Gang—headed toward the back of the garage. There, a curtain concealed a narrow entrance to a narrow staircase. Still no one around. They climbed the stairs. At the top, a door opened and the face of a man named Pak Dong-bok appeared.

We are not going to bother describing Pak Dong-bok: he will play only a minor role and we have more important things to do. Living in a cramped one-bedroom apartment in the Kangan District, he had been pointed out to Objat as an opponent of the regime: an extremely discreet opponent, as you might imagine, above suspicion but somehow detected by Bourgeaud's networks. He worked as a cook in the Ministry of Electronics, where his specialized knowledge made him irreplaceable: he was the only man in the country, and probably in the world, who knew how to prepare sea cucumber. Pak was rightly fearful for his life, so it was only after long negotiations, the opening of a generous Swiss bank account, and the promise of being rapidly exfiltrated that the networks convinced him to let his apartment be used as a hideout, if only for a few hours, and to supply an official-looking vehicle. Which might seem a little implausible in a country with such strict surveillance, but what can I do? That's just how things happened.

Pak offered them beer and they all refused, so he served them tea with four portions of sea cucumber before withdrawing to let them speak in private. The main topic of their conversation was, of course, how best to get out of there. It has to be the Chinese border, said Objat, there's no other way. And we should go our separate ways, of course. This prospect made Constance shudder. Well, I'll keep the young woman with me, of course. And Constance stopped shuddering.

That won't even be possible now, said Gang discouragingly. There'll be twice as much surveillance because of me. And even in the most discreet areas, it's become practically impossible with the ribbons of justice. The what? asked Objat. It's a new thing, Gang explained: keen to stop the demographic hemorrhage, the Supreme Leader came up with the idea of installing bands of extremely strong paper, eighty feet high and soaked with ultrastrong glue capable of immobilizing a buffalo, never mind a defector. Once caught, the defector dies of hunger while the border patrol guards all laugh at him.

In that case, said Paul Objat, I don't know how we're going to manage. Pognel put his head in his hands. Constance, with only a vague grasp on the situation, seemed less preoccupied, reassured as she was by the promise that she would be accompanied by Objat. Some time passed, which they filled by nibbling the sea cucumbers. Which were absolutely disgusting. The atmosphere grew gloomy. The only thing we can try, Gang said finally, is to go through the DMZ.

You're crazy, Objat objected. Don't even think about it.

38

NO, REALLY, GANG INSISTED, I'm sure that there's a crossing point in the DMZ. Not many of us know about it, obviously, but it does exist.

The acronym DMZ, for those who've forgotten, stands for the demilitarized zone that separates North Korea from South Korea, constituting a sort of buffer between the two countries. Straddling the thirty-eighth parallel, it is a vast strip of land, roughly 160 miles long and two and a half miles wide, covering a surface area of about four hundred square miles—the size of a large French département.

So, it's demilitarized, this zone, but it is also surveilled by nearly two million soldiers—more than a million in the North, 650,000 in the South, assisted by 37,000 Americans—and it is the most sensitive and dangerous DMZ in the world; some say, even in the history of the world. One thing everyone can agree on is that it is completely impassable. Compared to the Korean DMZ, the Berlin Wall was about as watertight as a colander.

Not only is it lined on the north side with thick barbed and electric wire, and on the south side with a concrete wall between sixteen and twenty-six feet high, but the two borders are systematically punctuated by lines of military posts, with heavily armed brigades ceaselessly patrolling between them. And, not content with being stuffed full of bunkers, watchtowers, and artillery batteries, the DMZ is also carpeted with a million mines.

In such conditions, it being obviously impossible to tend the forests in this area, they have grown exceptionally dense and are home to a rare flora that has disappeared from the rest of the peninsula. And the same is true for the fauna: free of all human presence, the DMZ has, in the space of sixty years, accidentally become a nature reserve—the same fate as, among others and for other reasons, the site of Chernobyl and the Montebello archipelago. In other words, a sanctuary where species that can hardly be found anywhere else on the planet are able to reproduce in peace, including the black bear, the spotted deer, the wild angora goat, the Chinese panther, and the Amur leopard.

Of course, despite a number of upsetting incidents, these animals did not immediately become aware of the omnipresent mines and their deplorable effects, but, over time, they learned to skirt around them. Thousands of migratory birds (herons and white cranes, mostly), naturally less bothered by this problem, spent many happy days there in the branches of the trees during winter. So, yes, to sum up, one unforeseen consequence of the final repercussions of the Cold War was that the Korean demilitarized zone was transformed into an animal paradise. Its rich fauna even led international animal rights' organizations, never short of good ideas, to demand that the DMZ be registered as a UNESCO World Heritage Protected Area.

All of this is anecdotal, of course, and does not alter the fact that the DMZ is a site of great, unrelenting tension between the armies of the North and the South, in a state of red alert since the 1953 armistice, with the two countries still officially at war. They watch each other ceaselessly, never actually fighting but on the lookout for the slightest movement or unforeseen gesture—a soldier scratching his ear, for example, or tying his laces—which might, misinterpreted, provoke a flurry of well-aimed gunfire.

Before braving this dangerous zone, Constance and the three men spent the night at Pak Dong-bok's apartment, all four of them in the same room: she took the narrow couch, while the others tried to sleep on the floor. Not that they had much time: up very early the next morning, they climbed into the official vehicle provided for them by their host and drove along the capital's wide, empty, tree-lined avenues to the dead-straight highway that led to the DMZ. Nine miles before this, there was a discreet bypass, barely visible but blocked by an electronic gate, with a strongly dissuasive sign standing next to it. The sedan turned into this path at a signal from Gang, who produced a chip card that had been sewn into his clothes, and the gate opened. They followed this path—asphalted to start with, before becoming a dirt track—as it wound its way through the open countryside. At another order from Gang, the vehicle stopped as soon as the border walls began to appear in the distance. I think it's over there, he indicated. That's the only place where the timetable for patrols is fairly slack. We'll wait here until night.

And so they patiently waited. It was a long wait. They didn't speak much, only in whispers, and Paul Objat did not speak at all. When night at last fell—abruptly, as it always does in these latitudes—it was six forty-five p.m., local time.

At the same moment in Paris—in other words, before lunch, local time—General Bourgeaud had summoned Lou Tausk. Thinking it would be premature to meet him in his office, he arranged to meet him in a bar with a clientele that was mostly unemployed and immigrant (the two not being mutually exclusive) on the corner of Rue Saint-Blaise and Boulevard Davout, about a six-minute walk from the barracks. He got there early, giving himself time to choose a discreetly located table. There, he sat down and—to kill the time—flicked through an old copy of *Madame Figaro* that was hanging around hopelessly on the next table.

When Tausk arrived at the bar, he had no idea of the general's name or appearance. But the general, knowing everything about Tausk, waved at him with his left hand while his right hand pointed out a chair on the other side of the table. It's aperitif time, he said by way of greeting. What would you like? I don't know, Tausk hesitated, maybe a dry white wine? Bourgeaud waved to a waiter, who came over unhurriedly. Two dry white wines, he ordered. What dry whites do you have? When the waiter offered them only Muscadet, he grimaced: Are you sure you don't have anything else? Chablis, Sancerre, Chardonnay, something like that? The waiter did not even bother replying to this, so the general sighed: Very well, then, two Muscadets.

While he waited for the drinks to arrive, Bourgeaud leaned toward Tausk: I think you know why I wanted to see you. Tausk guardedly shook his head, so the general said: My colleague didn't say anything? Same lateral movement from Tausk's head. So the general claimed to be the director of a company specializing in the transfer of technology from France overseas, particularly in the field of fossil fuels and on the African continent. Carefully avoiding the use of the words *industrial espionage*, the general explained that his company needed someone to—how to put this?—inspect certain existing installations. That it was currently recruiting staff. That it had identified Tausk as a good fit for this task. You have the right profile, as they say. I don't have a profile at all, answered Tausk, and I don't understand a word you're saying to me. Exactly, said Bourgeaud, becoming animated, that's why you interest us.

Then, after a brief silence while the Muscadets were delivered to the table: I don't think you have any choice, in any case. At least, that's what my colleague told me. That was my understanding too, Tausk replied with a grimace. In fact, he even explained to me that he had me by the balls. Really? the general recoiled. I'm very surprised. That's not at all the kind of vocabulary he uses. But, well, if you say so.

Anyway, let's get back to the task at hand. You must go to Africa, as a matter of urgency. My God, sighed Tausk, what next? And where exactly in Africa? I mean, it's a big place, Africa. The general leaned forward: Zimbabwe. You know where that is? Well, I know the name, replied Tausk evasively. Everyone knows the name, acknowledged the general. It's true that President Mugabe is rather special but, apart from that, it's actually a very pretty country. It's verdant, airy, full of nature reserves and waterfalls, good weather, just really a very nice place. It's also full of diamonds. All right, Tausk shrugged with one shoulder, if I don't have a choice in the matter. One thing, though: do I have to go there on my own? As this seemed self-evident to the general, Tausk asked if there was any chance he might be able to take a friend with him. He's looking for a job and a change of environment, but he's a very good guy, I can vouch for him completely. Absolutely not, Bourgeaud stiffened instantly. This is a confidential operation.

When Tausk added, incidentally and without any particular hope, that this friend of his was African, the general relaxed just as instantly as he had stiffened, then squinted as if in deep thought. Well, obviously, that changes matters, he articulated while searching for his wallet. Let me think about this. We might be able to use him, if he looks the part. Leave it, please, I insist. I'll take care of that.

39

BUT WHEN NIGHT did finally fall: No, Gang whispered, we're going to wait a little longer. As the patrols theoretically became more spaced-out after midnight, it was worth postponing any action until a more comfortable timeframe.

A little longer, however, turned out to mean nearly five interminable hours in conditions of increasing cold and hunger, not to mention increasing fear. And comfortable was not the most appropriate word for their situation either, each of them sitting or lying down, unable even to kill the time by chatting. Instead, they thought about themselves and then about the situation and then about themselves again. Their only distraction was to gaze at the stars, which had come out at dusk in a remarkably pure sky. Because, while North Korea's level of development at least means the country does not pollute the atmosphere too much, the nationwide curfew also precludes the phenomenon of light pollution, which, in the West, turns the heavens into a gray murk. Gang walked off for a while, then came back with a large branch torn from a tree, which he began transforming, with his bare hands, into a stick. Constance stood next to him as he whittled his branch, but there was not even the slightest hint of intimacy between them, not a brush of skin or a whisper or a look.

Silence. Objat and Pognel were silent too, but then they'd never had much to say to each other.

As for the patrols, it was just possible to make out their presence in the distance, every twenty minutes. There were probably just half a dozen men, all in helmets with transceivers and night-vision goggles attached, dressed in camouflage, machine guns with infrared laser pointers strapped diagonally across their chests, marching past the barbed-wire fence in the same silence, disturbed occasionally by a barked monosyllabic order from the mouth of a squadron leader. And, just as Gang had forecast, the frequency of the patrols gradually diminished: by midnight, they were appearing only every hour. We can go now, he said softly. We'll only have fifty minutes.

They went. Bent double, they moved forward while taking care not to snap twigs beneath their feet, still without a word, though Gang did hold Constance's hand now. When they came to the foot of the fence, it seemed to sparkle with the superhuman, supernatural electric current that ran through it, so powerful that they could distinctly hear it vibrate. So it was with infinite care that Gang used his stick as a lever to lift up the base of the fence, micron by micron, until he had cleared enough space for them to crawl through—proving that, when faced with the highest technological marvels, nothing beats the simplest, most rustic methods—then, trapping the stick between the ground and the barbed wire to hold this gap in place, he signaled to the others to get ready.

Each of them in turn crawled, not without a great deal of fear, through this gap. When they had all gone through, hardly daring to believe it, they stood in the DMZ and Gang ordered them: No one move now. One false move and . . . boom! From here on out, there are mines everywhere. So what are we going to do? asked Pognel anxiously. We can't risk it out here without visibility, Gang replied, we wouldn't make it thirty feet. We have to wait again. Of course, said Pognel. And so they had to wait for what remained of the night to pass, cursing the sun, which seemed to take forever to rise. The hardest thing was that they had to remain standing while they waited, crouching down on their heels when standing became unbearable, although very quickly that squatting position grew even more unendurable.

When day finally deigned to break, Gang unstitched another part of his jacket and extracted a document from it. This was a map of the DMZ with all the explosive spots marked in red. Gang carefully unfolded it, examined it, then cast a circular glance around him before signaling to the others that they could start walking. So they did.

Although walking really wasn't the right word. It was more a question of slowly venturing one foot in front of the other, sometimes with the heel of the front foot touching the tip of the back foot, and often having to retrace their footsteps on the orders of Gang, who consulted his map every five seconds. But at that pace, at least, they did have plenty of time to look at the landscape. As far as trees were concerned, while it was true they grew gigantically tall, there was a distinct lack of exoticism here since the forests in this part of the world are essentially alpine: too easy to identify, predominantly pines and larches, birches and oaks, and in that regard, it was a little disappointing. True, they could also see, here and there, avalanches of splendid and probably very rare flowers, but due to lack of botanical training, they could not name any of them.

In terms of fauna, things were better. They could distinguish flocks of chilled-out birds high up in the trees, especially in the treetops. Instinctively unconcerned by anything that happened on the ground, they hung out, relaxed, sometimes in pairs, sometimes in groups of influence, sometimes in entire communities, while chirping blithely to one another. As the four escapees advanced over the ground, they came across animals that are, under normal circumstances, dangerous for humans—a white royal tiger, two panthers—but which, just as preoccupied as said humans in avoiding the mines (even if they were, by now, old hands at this exercise), had better things to do than attacking them. Or, indeed, running away from them, since—humans being unknown in the DMZ—these felines had no idea about the two-legged species' cynegetic and carnivorous proclivities. And so they simply ignored them. The humans also spotted patches of land that looked heavily trampled, where dense clouds of butterflies proliferated. In other circumstances, anyone encountering these multicolored, fluttering swarms—so thick that they blurred the landscape beyond them, their wingbeats creating a velvety, crumpled, shivery kind of music—would have stopped to marvel at them. But they didn't have time. Particularly since it was possible to deduce from their presence that, beyond the rare beasts already mentioned, there must also be elephants hanging around somewhere nearby, for reasons explained in Chapter 13.

It would be time-consuming and tedious to describe in detail the fugitives' journey south, a journey that was itself extremely time-consuming and tedious. As Gang moved forward, scouting the ground, too busy to pay any attention to Constance, she clung to Objat's arm, taking comfort in the physical contact. Even though he had, up to now, from Creuse to Korea, led her into experiences that can only be qualified as questionable, she could not imagine that he was solely responsible for these projects. Had she imagined that, she would probably not have accepted his arm—even in circumstances like these. Anyway, Pognel's limp obviously did not accelerate the process. But still, after about ten hours of this, they did finally perceive, not too far away, the concrete wall that ran along the southern border of the DMZ. We're almost there, Gang warned them. They slowly approached it.

Looking up from the base of this new barrier to its summit twenty-three feet above induced a sort of inverted vertigo. And, while it somehow had been possible to crawl under the fence that lined the northern border, it was difficult to imagine climbing over such a wall here in the South. Gang, though, seemed unfazed by this prospect, and headed over to a cluster of beech trees that concealed a double bend.

This was a sort of niche in the bulwark, designed so that—by dint of an optical illusion—it remained invisible until you stood directly next to it. Going through this chicane, they found themselves facing a thick, solid, thoroughly discouraging gate. Apparently possessing a bottomless well of resources, however, Gang loosened another hem in his jacket and removed another magnetic card, and, to our surprise, the gate began to slide along its rail, albeit with exasperating slowness. They could hardly believe their eyes, but the path was clear: they were in the South, with its abundant and varied food supply, its congested and polluted highways and flyovers, its penthouses with swimming pools and air-conditioning, its plastic surgeons and its whorehouses, its rivers of neon flashing day and night everywhere you looked, its two-figure economic growth.

But then the purr of an engine—powerful albeit muffled—arose behind them. They turned around to see a Chinese Zubr hovercraft speeding toward them in a straight line, unconcerned by mines since, buoyed up on its cushions of air, it could skim over the ground in total safety. No sooner had it come to a halt near them than two new men in black overalls, both looking rather nervous, jumped off the vehicle. One was equipped with a copy of a Dillon assault rifle with built-in grenade launcher, capable of propelling three thousand

4.45-caliber projectiles per minute, while the other had a simple but very large ax. That's really annoying, Gang had time to mutter. We almost made it.

These were his last words because, in the blink of an eye, the man with the ax took his head clean off, validating his premonition a little while earlier, back when he was still peaceably enjoying Constance's company. While his head rolled on the ground, face frozen in an exaggerated pout, the man with the assault rifle paused for a moment while smiling at Pognel before determining his fate with two volleys of gunfire. The first volley drilled a series of perforations into the former convict's waist, and the second completed the work, removing the threads of flesh between these perforations so that Clément Pognel fell to the ground in two neat halves, where they lay side by side.

Making the most of that pause, Objat grabbed Constance's hand and ran toward the open gate. Just in time—a 40 mm grenade exploded behind them, but, sheltered by the chicane, they were protected from its effects. Two seconds later, they were seized very firmly and without any words of welcome by three South Korean soldiers, technically under the orders of an American major, who led them directly, and still without a word, to a debriefing room.

From that moment on, we lose all trace of them.

40

SEVERAL MONTHS WILL PASS. Still ignorant of the failure of Gang Un-ok's attempted defection, General Bourgeaud will settle to his task in a cheerful frame of mind. He will still have plenty of time to develop the Zimbabwe operation, as his contacts there will require a delay before marking out the terrain.

With regard to certain logistical points, however, he will miss the presence of Paul Objat: still no news on that front. He doesn't know any more about him than we do; in fact, we are better informed than him, having seen Objat disappear with Constance. And, while the general could not care less about Constance—a mere subsidiary piece of bait in his eyes, no less interchangeable than a nut or bolt in an engine—we do not feel the same way at all. We miss Constance every bit as much as we miss Objat, but when it comes to their fate, we are reduced to conjecture. Did that simultaneous vanishing give rise to love or antipathy? If love, was it lasting or not, a definitive passion or a one-night fiasco? If antipathy, can we believe that after the debriefing they went their separate ways, each of them swearing never to cross paths with the other again? Or might we think that, on the contrary, they roam the world together, leading an ardent, tumultuous life? We might think that. That or something else.

Amid this uncertainty, let us rely on proven facts. Several events will occur during this time. Tausk, first, having informed Hyacinth of the Zimbabwean job offer made by General Bourgeaud, will suggest that his friend accompany him. Hyacinth, glimpsing the possibility of his life being transformed, will most enthusiastically agree. They will meet several times to speak about the project—at the Pensive Mandarin and elsewhere—and, consequently, their friendship will grow stronger again.

On the other hand, after several walks in different parks and museums and other preliminary chores, Tausk will end up screwing the platinum-bunned assistant who, over time, will prove a very good way of killing time. Charlotte will even reveal herself to be an insatiable, if somewhat exhausting partner, to the point that Tausk, by now firm friends with Hyacinth again, will invite him to form a threesome, if only so he can take a break now and again. This proposal will produce an enigmatic "Why not?" smile on Hyacinth's face and provoke an eager response from the assistant, warmly supportive of this plan.

Several vigorous sessions will then take place, after each of which Charlotte, on her last legs, will go to sleep while Tausk and Hyacinth move through to the living room, warming a glass of Rum Nation Barbados rum in their left hands, smoke curling from a huge Partagás Torpedo held in their right, each of them ensconced in a comfortable armchair, chatting quietly and daydreaming about their future in southern Africa. So, how far is it from Ivory Coast exactly, Zimbabwe? Hang on a minute, Lou Tausk will say, searching for his MacBook, let me find out. Ah yes, here it is. Okay, well, basically, it's about three thousand miles from Abidjan to Harare. Oh, I see, Hyacinth will shrug, frowning. Not exactly next door, then.

When Hyacinth has gone home, Tausk will go his bedroom and rejoin the sleeping Charlotte before she in turn goes home: having had his fingers burned by Nadine Alcover, Tausk will refrain from allowing the bun to move in with him. Not only is her conversation fairly boring, limited at best to harping on about her memories of a business trip to Chile—you've got geysers, you've got penguins, you've got lots of things like that—but Tausk will also be wary of the idea of her sponging off him. A wariness that will grow even stronger when she loses her job at Hubert's office: only to be expected—he was bound to pay the price for the bad company he was keeping. First suspected and then convicted of embezzlement, he will also be found guilty of receiving stolen goods, extortion, money laundering, and being an accessory to forgery. Promptly expelled from the Paris bar, he will go into compulsory liquidation, forcing him to shut down his business and fire his staff: Charlotte, in other words.

More bad news: General Bourgeaud will eventually find out about the failure of Operation Gang Un-ok, a project for which he was solely responsible. When his superiors are informed of this failure, soon afterwards, he will be summoned to a closed committee meeting. Here, the general will be made to understand that his bosses are very unhappy with his initiative, the success of which he had been counting on to improve his standing with them. Instead of which, the general will be dismissed, removed from his position, sent into retirement—and you're lucky that we're not demoting you. When he will attempt to protest, to justify his plan, they will scornfully reply that, even aside from its disastrous denouement, the plan he organized without informing his superiors—a serious error on an internal level—was also inopportune, even counterproductive: a much more serious error on an international level. When Bourgeaud rebels by asking why, they will tell him to be quiet. He wants explanations? Well, he's going to get them.

It is in the interests of a number of major world powers, notably those (China, Russia, Japan, the United States, South Korea) that participate in the six-party talks with the Kim regime, to maintain North Korea in its current form. Their rants about human rights are just lip service, as in reality each has excellent economic, strategic, or geopolitical reasons for wishing the preservation of such a useful state. But, the general will cut in, red-faced, haven't you seen what goes on over there? Again, he will be told to keep quiet while they explain to him that such a state, albeit based on some regrettable practices, is convenient for everyone, contributing as it does, whatever its methods, to perpetuating the global equilibrium, which is, believe us, extremely fragile, they will remind the general, before informing him that he may leave. So Bourgeaud will go back to the barracks to organize or destroy his papers and take one last look at his empty desk, having first made arrangements to cancel the Zimbabwe expedition.

Which, obviously, deprives us of a sequence that we would happily have shot aboard a Boeing: either on location or in a studio, depending on our budget. As a smokescreen, Tausk and Hyacinth would have traveled to Africa separately: the general imagined Hyacinth in business class, disguised as an African businessman, cream suit and tie with chocolate-colored shirt, black sunglasses, and a briefcase handcuffed to his wrist, downing whiskey after whiskey, while Tausk, disguised as nothing in economy class, would have stared at the plastic cup of Coke Zero posed on the narrow little folding table. Yes, that could have been a pretty nice little scene. Even if there was a strong risk that it would be cut during the editing process. Well, anyway, let's move on.

General Bourgeaud (full name: Georges Bourgeaud du Lieul de Thû) will retire to his family manor in Poitou, where he will settle down to a life of smoking and disenchantment with his young new wife, Nadine Bourgeaud du Lieul de Thû. Who, as soon as the wedding—carried out in the manor's private chapel—is completed, will phone Lucile from her spacious third-floor bedroom to give her all the details of her happiness. So, anyway, how are you? I'm okay, Lucile will reply, it's Maurice who's not in great shape.

And for good reason. Unemployed, and gradually being abandoned by Lucile, Lessertisseur is a bit of a sorry sight right now. The wound he received on Rue d'Abbeville has reopened and is very painful. Shut up in his apartment on Rue du Faubourg-Saint-Denis, unshaven, pale-faced and sticky-eyed, Maurice Lessertisseur will let himself go. Not only that, but he's completely broke and, consequently, the absence of any foundation (an expensive product) on his forehead means that his New Guinea birthmark is visible once more. He has nothing to do but go over the past (recent or remote), particularly—and nostalgically—those happy days spent in Creuse. Scenes from his time there keep flashing into his mind: the hostage's appealing physical appearance, Victor's visits, the warmth of the evenings, aperitifs under the lime tree in the company of Jean-Pierre and Christian: the tall, shy, not very bright but very likable one, and the rounder, more lively, also pretty likable and also not especially bright one. Paused friendships. What has become of them?

Well, as concerns Jean-Pierre and Christian, the news is not particularly good either. We left Christian, if you remember, suffering from food poisoning—an ailment that can usually be successfully treated with a simple medication in a matter of a few days. In his case, however, it is dragging on. Christian complained a great deal to begin with; he no longer complains but has started saying crazy things all the time. We have to call Victor, he repeats in a feeble voice. Only Victor can get me out of this. You're talking nonsense, observes

Jean-Pierre; you're delirious. Besides, we have no way of getting hold of Victor, as you know perfectly well. He's vanished off the face of the earth.

The situation is such that they never leave their room anymore. There are no more guided walks or organized visits in the capital. There is no way of obtaining a medical repatriation or any form of diplomatic aid, as France has no embassy in North Korea. Jean-Pierre, who is struggling to see a way out of this situation, will not in any case have time to find one. Because very soon after the death of Gang, whose complicity with Western agents will be established without difficulty, the authorities will quickly inventory all the foreigners residing in Pyongyang and even more quickly establish a connection to the two occupants of the Yanggakdo, where, fifteen minutes later, three civilians led by a soldier in a gigantic olive-green helmet will bypass the reception desk and go up to the room where Christian is raving continually like a madman, watched over by Jean-Pierre, who has given up trying to get a word in edgeways.

They will be arrested, imprisoned, and then put on trial for several charges: attempted subversion of the DPRK, espionage, antigovernment propaganda, and illegal entry into the country, which will be enough to condemn them in no time to the death penalty. As they will be advised to confess, they will confess, enabling their sentence to be commuted to forced labor for life, which is essentially the same thing, only slower. They will spend six trying months in Labor Camp 22, escaping imminent death thanks to a diplomatic intervention by the French government, their liberation being provided in return for a large sum of money under the official cover of food aid. And so, six months later, they will get off the airplane in Villacoublay, weakened by severe weight loss and covered in scars and bruises. In addition to this, Christian will have lost two fingers from his right hand, while Jean-Pierre will be blind in one eye.

But that's enough of the future: we have to cut from this scene because another, more urgent one has just arrived. After an equally long absence, Constance Coste and Paul Objat have also just returned to France. We will, of course, provide you with more details of this story, as and when they reach us, in the next chapter.

LET US PROCEED in an orderly fashion.

As far as we have been able to reconstruct events, Constance and Paul Objat were taken in hand by the South Korean security services as soon as they escaped from the DMZ and subjected to in-depth interrogation. An oppressive and repetitive procedure which took place in offices close to the zone: subdued lighting and microphones everywhere; cameras on tripods equipped with invisible lenses; the steady hum of air-conditioning; two-way mirrors with plainclothes agents taking notes behind them. Three weeks of individual interviews to start with, during which each of them had to give their own version of events, completely cut off from the other.

Well versed in such practices, having been part of a debriefing team when he was younger, Objat supplied his interviewers with the story he supposed they wanted, while Constance, though not well versed in anything, did the same. Transferred to Seoul, they were interrogated simultaneously to bring their versions together. Everything tallied and seemed to fit perfectly, except for the one minor detail that the young woman kept calling Paul Objat by the name Victor. But the agents of the 대한민국 국가정보원 (National

Intelligence Service) overlooked this discordance, attributing it to fatigue and stress.

After taking into consideration their completed mission, the low probability of them causing trouble, and their compatible psychological profiles, the authorities moved them into the same apartment, occupying the entire top floor of a pleasant building. The place was spacious enough to allow them to remain alone or to be together, as they preferred. To begin with, they each stayed in their own room, enjoying the peaceful terrace view of tree-lined paths in Dosan Park. Verandas, solarium, swimming pool: while the apartment had every luxury imaginable, allowing its guests to relax and abandon themselves to comfort, it was also riddled with undetectable, omnipresent cameras and microphones because, while their interrogation results seemed fine, well . . . you never know.

During their first days in Seoul, Constance and Paul Objat did not exactly avoid each other, but they might as well have. Constance slept a great deal, while Objat, keen to be left in peace, spent his time scrambling his access codes and deactivating all his passwords in order to remain beyond the reach of Bourgeaud—whose disgrace he did not yet know about—and, more generally, of anyone on Boulevard Mortier. So they didn't see much of each other, and they didn't speak much either. They would hang about near the hot tub without ever looking up at each other, their sun loungers at a distance, their eyes concealed behind sunglasses. Objat silently leafed through the international press while Constance mutely deciphered the indications on a Japanese total sunblock. This silence was, as it happens, perfectly understandable: they had no desire to mention recent events, to comment on certain facts, to clear up any points that remained obscure, as they had done enough of that during the debriefing.

When this silence became oppressive, they attempted to lighten it by exchanging newspapers for sunblock, making remarks about the viewpoints of one or the effects of the other. Tacitly, to begin with, before risking a few words, then whole sentences, initially limited to subject-verb-complement, then becoming increasingly decorated with circumstantial subordinate prepositions: the birth of a conversation, even if Objat found it hard to get through to her that his name was Paul, not Victor. And yet Paul is a very simple name. Pretty easy to remember, you'd think.

This state of play could not last, of course. One evening, they naturally wound up in bed, to the satisfaction of both Constance and Victor. Sorry, I mean Paul. When they went through the DMZ together, she had liked it when he offered her his arm. And, going farther back, during her stay in Creuse, when he came to see her at the farm. In fact, even farther back, if you can recall their first meeting in Trocadéro—nearly a year ago now—you will remember that she was not immune to his charms even then. So, the birth of a love affair, too. A love that might, given that we are in the thirty-eighth parallel north, be qualified almost as tropical, if you can ignore the odd jet missile. A love that featured as part of our hypotheses regarding the future the other day: so let's congratulate ourselves on our intuitions.

The weeks that followed were perfect, as beginnings often are. But unlike many other lovers, Constance and Paul did not fall into the usual traps, did not make the classic chimerical plans made by couples in the first flush of love. There was no question of them fleeing their past lives, running off to the ends of the earth to live there together forever, as is customary. No, they simply enjoyed these moments. True, they did spend some time, in those first evenings, sitting on the terrace together hand in hand (some things truly are obligatory), watching the sun set gloriously over the Seoul skyline. But then they started spending less and less time watching the sun. Then, after a while, they decided that Seoul, though very nice, was something they could do without. And, without telling anyone, they went home.

THERE THEY ARE. They're living together on Rue de Bretagne in a pretty nice apartment whose main advantage is that it's on a direct bus route—number 98—to the barracks. Yes, Paul Objat has resumed his duties on Boulevard Mortier, though he had to give an explanation to a committee about his collaboration with the deposed general before they would allow him to get his old job back. But all went well, and he's now working under new management who provide him with less interesting tasks. Not that he seems to care. His salary has been reduced as a consequence, but he seems blithely unconcerned about that too. He doesn't say much either, for that matter. Not that he's ever been chatty, exactly, but he now speaks markedly less than before.

On Friday evening, though, he goes back to the apartment and tells Constance about his day, because he knows this is what couples do when they see each other in the evenings: they tell each other about their day. Constance, who listened to him very attentively to begin with—because, at first sight, counterespionage appears very interesting—now only half listens. Because, when it comes down to it, counterespionage is a lot less interesting than you'd think. As for her own day, Constance does not say anything about it, primarily because she didn't do anything except hang around in the neighbor-hood, do some window-shopping in clothes stores, and microwave three frozen meals for dinner. Then they go to bed early, Paul quickly falling asleep and Constance lying on her back for a while, eyes wide open.

Saturday morning: looks like a nice day. Bright sun, cloudless sky, fairly warm. Constance, having woken early, goes out for a walk. After a brief hesitation, she sets off southward down Rue du Tem-ple, toward the Seine. When she reaches Rue de Rivoli, she heads west. Her gait is more assured now, and her objective appears to take shape as she crosses the Jardin des Tuileries, where the buds quiver impatiently on branches and stalks, like runners braced in their start-ing blocks. Blackbirds, crows, and gulls, flying upriver, squawk or shriek in the trees, and soon children are squawking too, their Baby-Style and Maclaren strollers pushed forward rapidly, clouds of dust mingling around the large pond.

Coming out of the gardens, Constance avoids Place de la Con-corde, walks up the Champs-Élysées to the traffic circle, turns left onto Avenue Montaigne (glancing at the windows of the overpriced clothing stores), and joins Avenue du Président Wilson (glancing at nothing). She looks like she knows where she's going. Yes, she does know. She's headed straight for Trocadéro. So this was not really a walk in the classical, looping sense, but a curved line following closely to the course of the river.

In the storefront window of the real estate agent on Rue Greuze, everything has changed: places for sale, places to rent . . . a whole bunch of properties that she has never seen before. And hers: still there, still without a photograph, but yellowed by a year of sunlight now. She goes inside, and the agent, Philippe Dieulangard, smiles at her sudden reappearance. After all this time, he rejoices. I was beginning to worry. Constance smiles back at him without replying. I had several inquiries regarding your apartment, but you were absent so I didn't call them back. You did the right thing, Constance said approvingly, because I want to take it back. I'll go and get your keys right away, says Dieulangard, rushing off.

Emerging from the agency, Constance walks around the square for a while, delaying the moment when she will go home. Distractedly she deciphers the golden phrases of Paul Valéry, engraved on the Palais de Chaillot. Hesitates outside the gates of the Passy Cemetery. And finally goes in, walks around, comes out again, stops, and sees a man walk past. Distinguishing features: not bad at all, nice shoulders and strong jawline, carrying a briefcase. He is busy deciphering the names on the plaques at the street corners. As she looks at him for a moment too long, the man smiles at her, walks over, asks her if she might tell him where Rue Pétrarque is, and Constance says: Of course.

ABOUT THE AUTHOR

Jean Echenoz won France's prestigious Prix Goncourt for *I'm Gone* (The New Press). He is the winner of numerous literary prizes, among them the Prix Médicis and the European Literature Jeopardy Prize. He lives in Paris.

ABOUT THE TRANSLATOR

Sam Taylor is an acclaimed translator and novelist who lives in Texas. His translations include *A Meal in Winter* by Hubert Mingarelli (The New Press), *The Arab of the Future* by Riad Sattouf, and the award-winning *HHbH* by Laurent Binet.